Book of Death

A Novel

By

S. Evan Townsend

World Castle Publishing

S. Evan Townsend

World Castle Publishing
Pensacola, Florida

Copyright © S. Evan Townsend 2012
ISBN: 9781938961267
First Edition World Castle Publishing September 15, 2012
http://www.worldcastlepublishing.com

Licensing Notes

Cover: Select-O-Grafix, LLC
Editor: Maxine Bringenberg

Dedication

Dedicated to my father, whose following of his dreams allowed me to follow mine. And dedicated to my mother, who introduced me to the magic of books.

S. Evan Townsend

Acknowledgements:

I'd like to thank the following people for their invaluable assistance in making this novel a reality. Dr. Ileana Johnson Paugh whose book *Echoes of Communism* and her willingness to patiently answer my numerous emailed questions about her life in Romania helped me make this novel as accurate as possible. Any errors about Romania's culture, history, or geography are mine alone. I'd like to thank my wife, Lynn, and my friend Sare for proofreading and helpful advice and criticisms. And I can't fail to thank my editor, Maxine H. Bringenberg, for applying the final polish to make this novel shine. Thank you all!

Prologue

**Wallachia, Eastern Europe,
September 12, 1476**

The two horse riders stopped as they came around a bend in the narrow canyon. The sun was still low on this chill autumn morning, leaving the canyon floor in shadow. On a hill dominating the gorge on the far side was Poenari Castle. The canyon was too narrow to farm and also too narrow for an attacking army to mount much force. That was probably part of the reason the castle was here in the Carpathian Mountains that separate Transylvania from Wallachia.

Brunhild sat on her steed, one of the proud beasts the Valkyrie bred for their needs. Mist was rising from its white coat in the morning chill. They had ridden hard through the night. She patted the horse on its long, strong neck: a gesture of thanks and tenderness. The horse had carried her far for this meeting: down the Scandinavian Peninsula, flying across the Skagerrak as an eagle would, and bearing her down Jutland into Germania and The Holy Roman Empire. Despite living in the wilds of northern Scandinavia, this "holy empire" struck her as wholly barbaric. A woman travelling alone often encountered those who would take advantage, until they learned of her power. Most of those encounters were fatal for the attackers. Adept ones did not like to leave survivors to spread talk about them.

The other horse, the color of charcoal, was also misting in the biting morning air. It snorted impatiently with a burst of fog from its nostrils as its rider looked to the castle.

"What grotesque trees surround Poenari?" he asked with wonder. He was speaking the ancient language as the only common tongue between them. His journey had been even farther, riding a ship from Iceland to Britannia, then another ship to Gallia. From there by horse or paid carriage or on foot across the European continent to the Wallachian village of Pitesti, where he bought his horse and saddle. As they planned to arrive during the day, they needed to look like ordinary travelers: Ingólfur had to use a local steed and saddle, but Brunhild's horse could move on the ground as easily as in the sky.

They had communicated by farseeing to ensure their arrivals were closely timed.

"I do not know, Ingólfur," Brunhild breathed, looking where her Icelandic companion peered. There would normally be no trees around a castle to deprive attackers cover and concealment. But there was something surrounding the keep, small distorted shapes, too short to be trees (an Icelander probably wouldn't know this) yet too tall to be bushes.

"Let us proceed with our business," Brunhild said strongly, to cover her own growing fear.

"I would still rather we had a sword or two to accompany us," Ingólfur growled, still looking at whatever it was surrounding the red stone walls of the castle.

"Vlad has an entire army at his command. Two swords or a hundred swords will not change matters."

Ingólfur grumbled. Brunhild wondered briefly if he were the right adept one for this mission. His long blond hair had a slight curl to it and nearly reached his saddle. He was of slight build, and the eyes that gazed at the far castle were sky blue. But he was the leader of the Icelandic Guild and that spoke to his power. Both he and Brunhild stood out in this country. Her hair was almost as long as Ingólfur's and also a golden color, but more the color of sunshine, where his was cold, almost white. Her blue eyes were darker than the Icelander's. Brunhild hadn't seen a blonde head or blue eyes since Prague.

At the Great Conclave, where this trip had been planned, it had been debated whether to have an adept one from the Iroquois League or the Tawantinsuyu Empire accompany Brunhild to reinforce the seriousness with which the guilds held this matter. But the distance to travel was deemed to be too great and would delay this trip unacceptably.

"Do my eyes deceive me?" Ingólfur cried, and Brunhild looked at him sharply. She could tell he was using farseeing to make the sights of the castle seem as close as if it were in front of them. "A forest of the bodies of men," he breathed as if he couldn't believe it. "And I see women, too," he added.

Brunhild nodded gravely. So the rumors were true about Vlad III Dracul. She did not wish to look upon impaled persons any sooner than needed.

"We need to be going," she said simply. "We must reach Poenari Castle soon. Vlad is still there, I feel him. But war beckons, and he will not resist long its cruel and bloody siren."

She gave her horse a gentle touch with her heels near its hindquarters and the beast, large even for a horse, bounded forward, its hooves pounding the dirt lane with a deep resonating beat.

Ingólfur was not as skilled a rider but he followed Brunhild as best he could. His horse was the best they could find in Pitesti, yet it looked the plow nag next to the Valkyrie's mount.

Reaching the rise that led up to the castle, she could see now the victims of Vlad's cruelty. Impaling was an acceptable form of execution among lesser ones, but Vlad seemed to relish it. Men, women, aged from teenaged to old, had wooden stakes about twice the diameter of a clenched fist driven into their bodies; in between the legs, and out through the mouth or shoulder. Then the stakes were planted in the ground vertically so that the victims' own weight and struggling pulled them farther onto stake. It was said if the impaling was done "skillfully," the condemned could live for days in unbearable pain before they died.

The jungle of impaled humans extended at least five hundred paces from the castle gate. They were all mercifully dead or unconscious along this path, Brunhild noted. Some were rotting corpses, skulls with hollow eyes and skin sloughing off of muscle. The smell was horrible and inescapable. Brunhild had, of course, seen death before, including violent ends to human life that she had caused. But never had she experienced death on this scale of numbers and cruelty. She looked back at Ingólfur, whose ashen face showed his level of distress. What Vlad did to lesser ones was not their business, but it gave an indication of the type of soul with which they were dealing.

They halted before the great wooden gate of Poenari Castle. There was no moat: the hill and the narrow path providing ample defenses.

A man along the ramparts, visible as little more than a helmeted head, yelled something in a language Brunhild did not recognize. She called up a quick translation spell.

"...goes there? Identify yourselves and be quick about it. There are arrows aimed at each of your breasts."

Vlad is being paranoid, Brunhild thought, *but with reason*. His younger brother aimed to usurp him and turn this land back over to the Ottomans. Since it was at the nexus of the Christian West and the Islamic East, this land had been fought over repeatedly for the past five centuries or so, most recently between the Ottomans and the Hungarians.

"Tell your master that Brunhild of the Valkyrie and Ingólfur of Iceland are here to meet with him," Brunhild called out, the translation spell ensuring the man would understand. She kept her voice level, not sure if the threat about the arrows was a bluff or not.

The man laughed. "What woman would have business with the Prince of Wallachia?"

Brunhild looked at Ingólfur, who returned her look of frustration. Dealing with lesser ones was always such a chore.

Brunhild fingered her necklace from which hung her talisman. Not *Mjollnir*, for it never leaves *Volhöll*, but a temporary one, still ancient and still powerful. The persuasion spell was strong. "Tell your master that Brunhild of the Valkyrie and Ingólfur of Iceland are here to meet with him," she repeated. "You will be well rewarded."

Ingólfur wondered if it was his imagination or if the stone walls shook with her voice. His horse stamped the ground and whinnied nervously.

"Yes, I will tell my master," the man yelled, fear lacing his voice, and his head disappeared.

"Now we will see if Vlad is accommodating," Brunhild said with a sarcastic chuckle, returning to the ancient language. They could get into the castle, fight their way past any guards, but she would rather be welcomed and face Vlad rested and not weary from battle.

The sun had come from behind the clouds and it was growing warm sitting on horses in the open. The smell of the decaying bodies around them seemed to increase. Ingólfur looked sicker and Brunhild found her throat tightening. She wondered how long they should wait before they simply attacked.

Eventually, the gate opened slowly with loud creaks, as if protesting having to move. When it was fully open, Brunhild could see that two men had pushed open each side. A third man in chainmail, helm, and carrying a spear walked out slowly. His metal armored feet clanked on the paving stones.

"You will follow me," the man ordered imperiously.

Brunhild held her temper and encouraged her horse to move forward, assuming Ingólfur would follow. The horses' hooves made hollow clomping sounds on the same paving stones as they passed inside the castle wall. Brunhild looked up and saw the murder holes in the ceiling, and wondered if she was foolish not to have a protection spell invoked. Vlad had to know what the purpose of this visit was, and he couldn't be pleased. But killing two adept ones leaders would bring the wrath of all the separate guilds down upon him. This was his chance to live, he must realize.

The man in armor walked into the dusty courtyard. The smell from outside seemed not as strong, but in here the odor of animal and human waste was mixing incongruently with the smells of cooking. Brunhild was used to the clean mountain air of *Volhöll,* and the cacophony of smells was almost as overwhelming as a rune. She wondered briefly if that was Vlad's plan.

Dismounting, the Valkyrie stood tall, her blond hair hanging to the small of her back, her blue eyes darting around the courtyard looking for threats. On the ramparts and parapets were armed and armored men, but none were making threatening gestures.

Ingólfur dismounted lightly and held the reins of his horse. There was a standard wooden beam for tying up one's steed, and both adepts draped reins over it. Ingólfur spent a few moments making sure his horse was secure. Brunhild left the reins loose and spoke to her animal. Ingólfur swore the beast nodded in response.

"You will follow me," the armored man again ordered. Brunhild resisted the temptation to do something to him to teach him manners. A fortnight without speaking would humble him. Adept ones quickly learn to suffer fools lest they give away what they are. The situation was worse for women.

The two visitors followed the guard into a large hall that was just off the courtyard. At one end sat Vlad III Dracul, Voivode of Wallachia and head of the Transylvanian Guild. He was sitting in an ornate chair upon a dais. To his left in a smaller chair was a young woman with the dark hair and eyes Brunhild had come to expect of the local folk. She was quite pretty, especially by lesser ones standards, and Brunhild wondered if she was Vlad's wife or consort.

Tapestries hung from the ceiling at the entrance to the room. The pictures woven into the fabric depicted barbarities to both men and beasts. They were as long as two men and nearly as wide as a man could reach out with his arms. Brunhild wondered why a man would want to surround himself with so much suffering. There were at least ten armed men here, some with swords, some with pikes, and two, standing on either side of Vlad, with both. These also seemed to be the largest and strongest of the warriors.

The doors behind them slammed shut, and the only light entering the chamber came from high windows. Vlad seemed to like it dark.

Brunhild strode purposefully into the chamber, her eyes taking in all even as she looked only at Vlad. Her skirts rustled as she walked, and her leather turnshoes made soft clapping sounds with each step upon the stones. She knew Ingólfur was matching her stride for stride. She could hear him beside her and felt him building his strength. If Vlad attacked they needed to be ready.

Vlad just sat, looking at them impassively. If he was preparing an attack, Brunhild could not sense it. His black eyes showed no emotion and his thin mouth was curled into a slight smile. He wore no crown but his long black hair hung thick to his shoulders. The mustache under his hawk nose was a black growth across his face, and his chin protruded as was common in this part of Europe.

The man leading the visitors stopped before the dais and bowed low. "These are the people of whom I told Your Highness," he said in a loud yet respectful voice. It has lost all of its earlier swagger.

"Return to your post," Vlad growled low. His voice was smooth, like silk upon water.

The man bowed lower with a tinkle of armor and then backed away. He turned just before reaching Brunhild, and she caught the look in his dark eyes through the eye slit in his helm: he was afraid.

The Valkyrie kept walking until she was closer to the dais than the guard had dared approach. Ingólfur was by her side.

"Greetings, Vlad Dracul," Brunhild said strongly using the ancient language. Their business was no concern of the warriors gathered in the room or the young girl. "I am Brunhild, head of the Valkyrie Guild, and this is Ingólfur of the Icelandic Guild. We would speak with you." Vlad may be a prince and lesser ones rightly feared him, but as guild leaders, Brunhild and Ingólfur were equals. Brunhild would not cow to this man.

"Why do the heads of two of the most powerful guilds in Christendom travail so in order to speak to me, the head of a small,

7

unimportant guild?" Vlad kept the slight smile on his visage, but his voice was full of malice.

Ingólfur spoke, his voice higher pitched yet strong. "There was a Great Conclave of the guilds, Vlad Dracul."

"And why was I not invited?" Vlad asked, affecting an injured sound in his voice.

"Because you were the subject of the Conclave," Ingólfur added.

"Was I?" Vlad exclaimed, looking almost pleased with himself. "And where and when was this Conclave about me?"

"Paris," Ingólfur stated, "six months ago. Those who could not attend in person attended by far seeing. That included those across the ocean." Mentioning those guilds, so far away in lands the lesser ones of Europe had yet to discover, should communicate to Vlad the seriousness of the Conclave. But Brunhild still thought Ingólfur was talking too much.

"I was occupied battling the Ottomans," Vlad said dismissively.

"Yes," Brunhild confirmed, "we know." Vlad was a man of unique ambitions. Normally adept ones did not wish to involve themselves in the affairs of lesser ones, much less become leaders in their regimes. And those who sought power among the lesser ones were not interested in learning to become an adept one. Yet Vlad was both, the head of his guild by right of being the strongest, most powerful member, and the Prince of Wallachia by birthright and conquest.

"And yet, here we are," Vlad sneered. "And still I do not know why I have the honor of hosting two such powerful guild leaders."

Ingólfur stepped forward. "We have reasons to believe, Vlad Dracul, that you are engaging in necromancy, which has been forbidden since the time of Atlantis."

"And what control should the ancient and long-dead priests of Atlantis have over us?" Vlad demanded loudly, standing and throwing aside his cloak to grab the hilt of a knife.

The warriors, who had been standing as still as empty suits of armor, stirred. The two beside Vlad set their pikes against the wall and placed their hands on the hilts of their swords. Even though they couldn't understand the conversation they could certainly understand Vlad's tone and actions. Brunhild wondered if it was her imagination or if the young girl cowered. She, too, couldn't have understood what was happening unless she spoke the ancient language. But she probably knew Vlad's actions and voice were not friendly.

Brunhild looked at the knife Vlad touched. This was not a mere weapon. It was his talisman, and the blade had probably touched blood, and very recently.

Ingólfur opened his mouth to say something, and then thought better of it. Brunhild got the feeling he was going to protest Vlad's statement.

"You are ordered to cease, and turn over any documents in your possession dealing with necromancy to us for destruction," Ingólfur said instead, his voice still strong. Brunhild noted his hand was at his belt, where he kept his talisman. She casually touched her necklace, feeling comfort from the power that flowed from her talisman into her body.

"And if I do not?" Vlad growled.

"Then the wrath of all the guilds, European, Asian, African, and across the great ocean, will be brought down upon you, Vlad Dracul," Ingólfur said almost as a whisper, as if it were not a threat but a fact.

"You will be killed," Brunhild clarified. "No matter how many adept ones and warriors it takes."

Vlad's black eyes blazed as he looked at the two others. No one spoke for a long moment while Vlad glared at the two adept ones and they looked at him, awaiting an attack.

Brunhild saw motion out of the corner of her eye and turned quickly, hand on her necklace, arm out for an attack as a tapestry began to wrap around her, tightly and quickly, enveloping her in thick fabric. She fell over with a painful smack against the rock floor, no longer able to stand as her legs were pinned together. She heard Ingólfur shout a word that must have been in his native language and saw him topple over, too.

9

Brunhild wondered for a moment how the tapestries got there so fast and came unfastened from the wall. She and Ingólfur had been at least ten paces from them. Moving fabric with air was well known to most guilds, but from the time Vlad had touched his talisman to the time the tapestry had engulfed her seemed too short.

But she had other things to worry about now.

Vlad stood and walked down the few steps of the dais, cackling with laughter. The two warriors beside him followed, drawing their swords which hissed as metal escaped scabbard. The young girl chose that moment to flee from the room, her skirts swooshing and her long dark hair swaying as she nearly ran.

"You don't know the power of what I am doing," Vlad said in a soft yet somehow terrifying voice. "Bring on your armies and your adept ones. I'll defeat them all."

"You cannot believe that," Ingólfur cried, struggling against the tapestry holding him. "If you kill us they will come for you. This is your last chance to live, Vlad Dracul. Surrender or die."

"So be it," Vlad spat. Then he turned to the guards. "Kill them."

Brunhild's hand was still on her talisman, trapped there by the suffocating tapestry. She could put up a protection spell to defend against blades, but that would do nothing for Ingólfur and would only delay the inevitable as she would tire and the spell would wear off. The warriors were raising their long, straight swords to cleave off the adept ones' heads. Brunhild knew she had to act now or die. Her right hand was being held by her side, she couldn't move it in the crush of fabric. But she could still spell. She shot flames from her hand, ignoring the pain as the fire splashed back against it and her clothes. But they burned through the tapestry in the wink of an eye, and Brunhild directed them at the nearest warrior.

The orange flames lit up the room as they slammed into the warrior just as he was bringing down his sword. Spasmodically, he jerked with a painful scream and the sword blade missed

Brunhild's head, slicing off some blonde hairs but crashing into the stone floor with a spray of sparks.

The tapestry was on fire but it also mercifully became loose as it lost its unity. Brunhild used a strength spell to blow the flaming fabric apart from her.

The warrior who was about to behead Ingólfur instead swung his blade at Brunhild. She heard its hum as it cut through the air. She ducked backwards and hit him with a powerful airbolt, crashing him and his armor against the wall where he slumped. But something hard hit her and knocked her back. Vlad had attacked, his hand on his knife, confirming that it was his talisman.

Ingólfur was still trapped and another of the room's warriors was rushing to him, holding his pike with the obvious intention of impaling the Icelander. Brunhild could hear armored feet quickly approaching and knew between Vlad and the remaining eight warriors she would have a hard time escaping, let alone killing Vlad.

Ingólfur, taking his cue from Brunhild, also burned off his tapestry. Still lying on the floor, he shot the fire at the warrior about to run him through with a pike.

Brunhild ignored the pain from the burns on her hand and thigh where her skirt had burned briefly. She pivoted to face the approaching guards and fire arced from her hand, the heat of it almost burning her face as the flames smacked into the warriors. They screamed and dropped their weapons as fire sought gaps in armor and attacked skin and cloth.

Ingólfur was standing now, retreating, and looking weak. He'd been burned badly when he lit the tapestry on fire.

As she watched in amazement, Vlad used his talisman's blade to slice the throat of the warrior she had burned. He put his face to the gash as the blood sprayed into his mouth. When he stood again, blood dripping from his pointed chin, she could feel his power had increased alarmingly.

Vlad pointed at Ingólfur, and Brunhild knew the prince was about to attack. She shot an airbolt at Vlad, knocking him temporarily aside and saving Ingólfur, who still had three warriors to contend with.

Vlad stood, his eyes showing his hate and anger as their blackness seemed to be bottomless pits. He raised both his hands, the left hand holding the bloodstained knife, and both Brunhild and Ingólfur felt their air disappear. Brunhild gasped, knowing she didn't have long to live. She tried to pull back the air but Vlad was too strong, the necromancy having made him so. Brunhild's vision started going gray as the life was leaving her.

The door to the room burst open and sunlight filled the room. Vlad was momentarily stunned by the brightness of it and covered his eyes. Brunhild felt air on her face again and sucked in a deep breath while hearing Ingólfur do the same. But she feared this was more warriors to battle, and she still had not long to live.

She didn't hear armored feet slapping the floor but horse hooves. Her horse was galloping into the chamber. Brunhild noted an arrow in its haunches and blood staining its alabaster coat; it had fought its way in. Brunhild shot flame out the door, stopping anyone from following the beast into the room. She was rewarded with screams of anguish from the courtyard.

Brunhild grabbed the saddle and pulled herself up in one smooth motion. Vlad stood amazed by the spectacle as the horse still charged toward him. The prince shot fire at the beast but Brunhild deflected it, and suddenly hooves were on Vlad's chest as the horse reared up and crushed Vlad under it. Vlad tried stabbing the horse with his talisman and knife, but Brunhild fired an airbolt at his hand and knocked the talisman away and, judging by the cracking sound, broke every bone in his hand. She pulled her horse off of the necromancer and heard his rattling breath. Vlad could heal himself but the guilds would return, and in force. His life was forfeit.

"Let us leave," Brunhild called to Ingólfur, who nodded as he bounced onto the horse, wrapping his arms about Brunhild's waist. When more of Vlad's men attacked, as Brunhild assumed they would, she and Ingólfur would lose this battle and be killed. Better to live and report back to the guilds and mount an attack of many adept ones and warriors.

The horse pivoted and galloped out of the room—Brunhild and Ingólfur had to duck under the door's opening—until it hit the open courtyard, where it bounded into the sky. Brunhild heard someone cry, "Kill the Impaler and we shall be free!" before a group of armed men rushed the room. Vlad had ruled by fear and now his own protectors no longer feared him. Ingólfur noted sadly that his horse was dead, probably killed as a precaution when Brunhild's went on the attack.

The white horse flew over the wall of the castle and dropped into the narrow valley below.

The excitement of battle over, pain from her hand and thigh became intense, so Brunhild healed herself and assumed Ingólfur was doing the same.

"His documents?" he asked.

"We'll go back and find it after his subjects . . . overthrow him."

Ingólfur whispered, "Yes." Both adept ones needed to heal and rest.

Brunhild patted the neck on her horse as it landed in the valley. She spent some of her own meta force healing the animal after she pulled the arrow from its hide.

"How?" Ingólfur asked.

Brunhild just smiled. Every guild had its secrets.

Chapter One

Seattle, Washington
March 19, 1968

I had a first-class ticket on West Coast Airlines from San Francisco to Spokane with what was supposed to be a short layover in Seattle. But my flight out of Seattle was canceled due to weather problems—Spokane was fogged in—and because it was a weather problem, the airline stated they weren't responsible for getting me to my destination. They even suggested I rent a car and drive.

"It's only about two hundred eighty miles," the chipper girl behind the counter said with a pasted-on smile.

As if that were likely to happen. I had to use a persuasion spell to even get a seat on the next possible flight to Spokane. I did not want to be stuck in Seattle for the day and especially not overnight. Through the glass of the airport concourse I could see it was a nice sunny day. But that is the exception in Seattle, as I knew from personal experience. That, and there were too many echoes from my past here.

After securing my seat in tourist class (and being told "the F27 doesn't have a first-class section," the "F27" being the name of the airplane) I found a pay phone and called the number I'd been given. This meant feeding a lot of coins into the coin receptacle. Damn machines, can't use spells on them to get them to cooperate, and the long-distance operator was unsympathetic...and also

15

couldn't be influenced by a spell due to her distant location: inverse square law.

After boarding, I found my seat was in the back of the plane against the rear bulkhead. It was a small propeller-driven aircraft that seemed to hold about thirty passengers and had high wings. When the pilot gave the required, "How you doin', folks?" announcement he called it a "turboprop." The rounded, middle-aged lady sitting next to me wanted to talk—"Is business or pleasure taking you to Spokane today?"—but I subtly touched her hand and she fell mercifully asleep. I kind of felt bad about it, but that was easier than making up lies the whole way across the state.

The plane climbed out of Sea-Tac Airport into the azure sky with a droning throb of propellers. As it turned east, it passed Mount Rainier. I was in a seat next to a small window and had a great view. I smiled looking over the white-mantled mountain that dominated the landscape. I swore I could feel the power of the volcano even sitting in the plane.

The Cascade Mountains were lovely to fly over, covered in snow with the occasional iced over alpine lake reflecting the morning sun. I gawked at the beauty of it and was thankful it was a beautiful clear day, at least over the mountains.

But then, abutting the eastern slopes of the Cascades were low clouds that covered the flat landscape in a dismal gray blanket. We crossed a river I decided must be the Columbia and a small city I decided must be Wenatchee before the cloud cover became thick enough to obscure the ground. I stopped watching and closed my eyes, resting. I'd gotten up early to catch the flight out of SFO. Now I was going to be late in arriving, getting to Spokane around lunch time instead of the planned mid-morning.

Landing in Spokane an hour later, I was finally able to get off the plane as everyone in front of me, and that was the whole damn aircraft, seemed to be taking their time getting their carry-ons and shuffling out the small door and down the few steps to the tarmac. I gasped as I stepped outside–it was cold. It was still March, the day before the equinox, in fact, and while San Francisco wasn't exactly warm, it wasn't anywhere near that cold. There was a short walk into the new, albeit small, airport terminal. You walked from the short concourse into a domed common area, then out into the baggage claim. As far as I could see there were two concourses labeled A and B. I wondered how primitive I would find Spokane compared to San Francisco, and again why Vaughan and Brown had sent me on this trip.

A dark-haired man in a blue business suit was holding a white paperboard sign with hand-lettering that read "MR. SMITH." He was standing near the luggage carousel looking bored. I noticed his hair was cropped short and neat. These days you could pretty much sum up a man's politics by the length of his hair. Another man, younger, also in a suit but this one gray and his hair just slightly longer, was fidgeting next to him looking about nervously. "Smith" wasn't the name I was using, but it was the agreed-upon code name.

"I'm Smith," I told the man with the sign, my hand on my talisman. He wasn't an adept, but I had no doubt he was armed.

"Do you have checked luggage, sir?" he asked, lowering the sign. His voice was crisp and efficient. I wondered if he were ex-military and if so, how he avoided being in Vietnam at that moment.

"Yes, I do," I said simply. "Black hard-side case."

"If you would identify it, please, sir," he stated, his grey eyes glancing over at the carousel full of black hard-side luggage.

I smiled. "Of course." *Anica has acquired an interesting warrior*, I thought as I saw my bag round the corner. "There it is." I pointed, and the younger man rushed over and grabbed it, lugging it back to our group. I tended to over-pack, so the suitcase was a bit heavy.

"We have a car waiting, sir," the older man said.

"Fine," I replied. He led me out a nearby door and there was a long black Cadillac idling on the curb. I could smell its exhaust and hear the deep rumble of its engine. The car had sides that were flat as a wall and seemed to go on forever, but they were splattered with dirt and fresh gray slush. *It's probably a pretty impressive car when it's clean*, I thought.

I sucked in a sharp breath. "We're not in California, anymore, Toto," I said, laughing. I had just warmed up from my last exposure to the elements. I could see my breath, a phenomena I'd rarely experienced in my life.

The younger man was putting my suitcase in the trunk, and the older holding the back door to the car open for me. I slipped in and was thankful for the warmth inside, although the leather seats were cool and seemed to suck the heat out of me right through my clothes. The door closed and both men got in front, the younger driving. He piloted the land yacht away from the curb. There was still snow on the ground but the road was bare.

"How long of a drive?" I asked. The older warrior turned in his seat, looking at me, and held up a red pack of cigarettes. I shook my head, and he put them away. *At least he was smart enough to ask first*, I thought. I'd healed the scars long ago, but the Pavlovian response I have to cigarette smoke would never heal.

"About thirty or forty minutes," he said, turning back around to sit straight.

I shrugged and watched the landscape roll by, again wondering why Louis Brown and Michael Vaughan had sent me. They usually handled issues with the Transylvanian Guild. Yes, I was the American Meta Association's "fixer": the one adept the leaders could count on to fix problems. This made me, in practice if not in fact, third in command of the guild. But this routine trip to see the head of the Transylvanians wasn't my usual fare.

Maybe Brown and Vaughan were grooming me for a higher position in the guild. Brown was getting older—he wasn't that much younger than Kader, who had to be in his sixties—but Vaughan was only maybe five years older than I. That would make him around forty, still young enough to head the guild for a long time.

Or maybe Brown and Vaughan felt I needed a milk run after dealing with that upstart in Alabama, who thought he could break the southern adepts away from the AMA because they didn't like taking orders from a Negro such as Brown. I was amazed that there was anybody, let alone adepts, who somehow thought skin color mattered. As that Negro civil rights leader had said a few years ago, "content of their character, not the color of their skin." Or something like that. *But, hell, it's 1968*, I thought. *Can't we get over these stupid, old ideas?*

The driver pulled the car onto the freeway and we drove through what must have been the small city of Spokane. The train ran right through the middle of the downtown, it appeared, on elevated tracks. There was a predominate red-brick church not far off the freeway to the north. To the south was a hill with buildings that looked like hospitals. A white police cruiser passed us, and I still had to fight my almost instinctive urge to hide. If I hadn't become an adept I would probably be in jail right now, or worse.

I decided to concentrate on the Transylvanians.

In 1950, Francis Kader, then head of the AMA (and the adept leader who formed it out of the many diverse guilds in America after World War II) ceded Northern Idaho and Western Montana to the Transylvanian Guild. They were refugees from Soviet-dominated Eastern Europe. There'd been no problems for eighteen years with this arrangement. Members of the AMA that were living in the area—and there were few because it was sparsely populated—had no problems with the Transylvanians. Our guilds were at peace, according to documents Kader had signed with the Transylvanian leader Anica. When Vaughan and Brown became co-heads of the AMA about four years ago, they had renewed the peace treaties with both the Transylvanians and the Valkyrie. Every year or so Vaughan or Brown, or both, would come to visit Anica (as far as I knew, she used no last name) to ensure there were still no problems. For some reason this year, they sent me; and for some reason, they sent me the day before the vernal equinox conclave. I didn't mind missing it, but there was usually some good booze there.

I saw the sign signifying the border with Idaho about twenty minutes after passing out of Spokane. It seemed at the border the pine trees got thicker, as if they preferred to grow in Idaho. I smiled at that. We pulled off the interstate and drove down a narrow, snow-covered road surrounded by evergreen trees;

deciduous trees are pretty spotty in the Northwest. At one point we passed what appeared to be a fairly big lake, which was frozen over in the chill of this winter weather. After winding and occasionally slipping through snow-covered streets—the older man had to tell the younger driver to slow down—we stopped in front of a large one-story, ranch-style house. I could see its rear faced a lake that was also covered in ice. The house was isolated, with tall pine trees around the yard. The nearest neighbor was probably a quarter of a mile off.

The older warrior jumped out and opened the door for me. I looked down. The sidewalk leading to the house's front door had been shoveled and I could see the white evidence of salt. But there was about a two-foot gap between the car and the bare concrete. That gap was full of slush. I was not going to step in that and ruin my expensive shoes.

"Sorry, sir," the warrior stated.

"Could you please move the car closer?" I asked, looking at him. I tried to keep the annoyance out of my voice.

"Yes, sir," the warrior said, closing the door. The driver spent a few minutes moving the car back and forth until he was satisfied it was close enough. I simply sat and waited. I wondered if they'd do that to Anica, who paid their salary.

The door was pulled open again, and this time the car was close enough I could step out onto the bare sidewalk. The sky was covered in gray clouds that seemed to want to drop lower, and the cold cut through my suit jacket. Again, my breath was white clouds. I walked quickly to the house's front door, not caring if the warrior kept up.

He did, and he opened the door for me. I stepped into the embracing warmth of the house. The interior was clean and tastefully furnished in a classical style, as if the '50s and '60s never happened. There was a newer-looking television with a large screen—maybe twenty or so inches—against one wall.

Anica stood from a leather wing-back chair and walked toward me, her high heels clicking on the hardwood floor.

"You must be Mr. Smith," she said, holding out her delicate hand. Even though she was probably in her late forties, she was still an attractive woman. I looked into her deep brown eyes and smiled while I took her small hand in mine. I could feel her power as we touched.

"Yes," I said. "But that's not the name I use."

She chuckled and her free hand brushed back her long, luxurious dark hair from her shoulder. She was dressed conservatively out of style, looking more like June Cleaver than the way women were beginning to clad themselves in loud colors and short skirts.

"I'm called Peter Branton," I explained, releasing her hand.

She smiled knowingly and met my eyes with hers. "Yes," was all she said.

Of course "Peter Branton" was not my real name, either. Adepts don't use their real names for many reasons, the most critical being another adept who knew your real name would have power over you. I'd chosen that name by pointing randomly in the Seattle phone book in 1949. In the ensuing nearly twenty years, I'd pretty much accepted it as my name.

"Won't you sit down, Mr. Branton?" Anica said cheerfully as she again sat in her chair, crossing her long legs.

I found a nice comfortable-looking couch and settled into its brown leather embrace. "Thank you."

She smiled at me and I was again struck by how lovely she was. *If only she were ten or fifteen years younger*, I mused.

"Well," she said, "are Louis and Michael busy?" She was referring to Brown and Vaughan: I wondered if I caught just a hint of hurt in her voice.

"No, Teacher," I replied. "But I have their full authority to speak in their place." And the telephone number for Suite 1313 at the Huntington Hotel in San Francisco memorized.

She nodded. "That is fine." I still wasn't sure she wasn't upset that an underling had come and not Brown, or even Vaughan.

I decided to start as Louis Brown had instructed me. "Do you have any issues that need to be addressed by our guild?"

She gave what appeared to me to be a bittersweet smile. "We have issues, but none I think your guild could help with."

"Perhaps we could," I said, trying to stay cheerful. Brown said to offer them assistance with whatever they needed…within reason. The question was, what was the definition of "within reason"?

"Well," she started, "I foresee the end of our guild."

I blinked. That seemed pretty serious. "Why?"

She leaned forward and locked those intense brown eyes on me. "We cannot recruit new members. We have not had a new apprentice for five years."

"Why not?"

"In Romania, before the war, we could always draw apprentices from the local population. We were always and still are a small guild. But also, some would come from other parts of Europe, drawn by our power."

I nodded. The Transylvanian guild had long kept secret the source of their power. Kader hinted once that he knew, but would never tell.

"You have to understand our history," Anica said softly. "Transylvania and Wallachia, now part of Romania, are our traditional homes. Since the 12th century, those lands have been disputed, conquered, paid tribute to the Ottomans, liberated, divided, reunited, and now are under Soviet domination. It is a bitter history for our people."

I didn't know if she meant the Romanians as a whole or her guild.

"We fled the Communists and were in danger of going extinct when Francis Kader offered us these territories in North Idaho and Western Montana to settle, for which we are eternally grateful and indebted to your guild. We enjoy the mountains and the space and the sparse population, too. It reminds us bitter-sweetly of our homeland."

I nodded. If she felt the need to run through their history that was fine with me.

"But as much as we love it here, we cannot find new members. Under the terms of our agreement with your guild, those who wish to apprentice and live here can join either guild. Since Houser was deposed, all wish to join the AMA."

Which made sense: to join the biggest and most powerful guild in the world rather than a small albeit powerful guild that was tolerated in the AMA's territory.

"It is frustrating," she sighed. "For there must be those who would like to join and have the ability to join in our homeland, yet they are trapped behind the Iron Curtain."

I nodded, trying to look sympathetic, but I didn't have any idea how the AMA could help them. The geopolitical nature of the world was not something even the AMA could control. Yet, unlike in times past, we were affected by it. If nuclear war started, even being an adept would not save you (as being one saved me from having to fight in the Korean War).

"Forgive me," she continued. "I know your guild cannot force potential apprentices to join our guild. I don't have a solution to this problem, and I can't expect you to have one either."

"Perhaps," I offered, "we could work on a solution together. I will bring it up with Brown and Vaughan. Maybe we can get members for you out of Romania."

"Yes," she said, almost smiling. "It would be simple to spirit them out of Eastern Europe. In Berlin, perhaps. But how would you identify them, or they find us?"

I nodded: I saw her problem. New adepts were either found when they started showing potential and become powerful enough to be felt by other adepts, or they found the guilds by asking their local fortune teller or palm reader. Me, I picked the wrong pocket. A pocket that, it turned out, was the right pocket since the owner was a local adept, and saw in me the potential to stop being a petty criminal.

If the Transylvanian guild found a potential recruit, they would have to tell them about the AMA since, for one, they would find out eventually, anyway, and then perhaps leave the guild after it had expended resources training them; and secondly, since adepts do end up in the news media occasionally, they probably would have heard of the AMA anyway.

"You've had a long journey," Anica was saying, interrupting my thoughts. "Would you like some refreshments?"

"Yes, that would be nice," I replied happily. I hadn't eaten since leaving Frisco that morning.

"We can relax in the dining room," she said standing. "It overlooks the lake, which is unfortunately frozen over."

I stood and followed her, again noting her lithe body and long dark hair. I wondered if she dyed it; most women her age did. She wasn't using a glamor because I would see through that.

In the dining room was a long wooden table with wooden chairs around it. Again, the style was old-fashioned and classic. A small, simple chandelier hung from the low ceiling. The walls were covered in green textured wallpaper that was, like the room, tasteful and reserved. Large windows looked over an expanse of snow-covered lawn up to the flat-as-a-sheet ice covering the lake.

"Which lake is this?" I asked, trying to make conversation.

"Lake Coeur d'Alene," she replied, as if I'd said something stupid.

I didn't know; I'd never heard of it. It had a beauty though, looking like a small alpine lake surrounded by pine trees that were softly painted with white snow. Even on this overcast, gray day it was lovely. "I bet in summer it's beautiful."

"Yes, it is," she said with a smile, as if forgiving me for my earlier ignorance. "Please have a seat."

"It's small," I noted still looking out the large window. The far shore, demarked by a stand of pine trees, was maybe a hundred yards away.

"This is just one arm of it. It's actually rather large."

"Oh," I said; didn't seem important.

The table was bare except for plates and flatware on simple white placemats. I sat so I was facing the window and Anica sat to my left, her back to the wall facing what must be the kitchen. Suddenly I could smell something delicious, and hunger sprang upon me like an anxious puppy.

A young woman, a slightly shorter version of Anica, walked in carrying a steaming tray. I took a moment to admire her shapely legs under her miniskirt. Her blouse was a splash of garish colors, and her long dark hair was straight, almost to the hem of her skirt. She would not look unusual on the streets of San Francisco except for her necklace. It was obviously holding her talisman draped on a long, thin chain. Here in Coeur d'Alene, Idaho, she was like a wild flower growing in inches of snow. I could feel she was an adept, but not as powerful as I. She smiled at me. I guessed she was in her mid-twenties.

"Mr. Branton," Anica was saying as I smiled back at the girl, "this is Miss Vojir. She's been with our guild for about nine years now."

That would be, I calculated, about 1959, or the start of the Houser regime in the AMA. Anica had said they hadn't been able to recruit new members since 1963, the end of the Houser regime.

"You had better luck finding apprentices when Kader was deposed and Houser ran the guild?" I asked.

Miss Vojir looked at Anica. Anica smiled at her and said, "Yes. Some preferred our guild to one run by…" She paused as if trying to think of a word, then continued, apparently unable to "…that man."

I nodded. Those five years were very difficult for most everyone in the AMA. I barely survived them, sure Houser would kill me at the first excuse he could fabricate—which, I had to admit now, was a bit paranoid. Houser couldn't kill every adept in the guild loyal to Kader or he'd have had a very small guild.

Miss Vojir set down the dish of food—I had no idea what it was. It appeared to be some sort of meatball soup, and that was confirmed when Miss Vojir started ladling it into bowls. After setting the bowls in front of Anica and me, she pivoted and went back to the kitchen.

"It's *ciorba de perisoare*," Anica explained as she picked up her spoon. "Traditional meatball soup."

I nodded and picked up my spoon just as Miss Vojir—I wished I knew her first name—returned with bread and cheeses.

She again set them on the table and left. I watched her go, probably letting my gaze linger too long on her backside, legs, and beautiful hair.

"Mr. Branton," Anica said sounding stern.

I turned back to her. "Will Miss Vojir be joining us?" I asked, maybe too much hope in my voice.

"No, she will not," Anica replied simply.

I wondered about that. It would make sense, including her serving us, if she were an apprentice. But nine years is a long time to be an apprentice. The usual period is closer to five years.

Small talk among adepts is rare. We don't talk about our pasts because if someone learns too much about you, they might trace you back to your origins and learn your name. Politics and current events of the lessers tend to bore us, and don't even get me started on the silliness of sports.

"Is San Francisco as wild as it appears on the television?" Anica asked me as I enjoyed the soup and amazing bread.

I shook my head to delay talking until I'd swallowed. "Parts of it, yes. The hippies had seemed to have almost taken over Golden Gate Park and the Haight-Ashbury neighborhood. Last year's 'Summer of Love' pretty much drove the hippies out. Now it's just a crime-ridden nasty part of town with a lot of under-aged runaways and people strung out on drugs. But most of the city is pretty normal. Except, that is, for the occasional anti-war protest that will spill out into more areas."

Anica looked unhappy. "Yes, there have been war protests at Gonzaga. Don't these young people know we have to fight Communism?"

"Gonzaga?" I asked.

"The Catholic college in Spokane."

I shrugged. It would make sense Anica would be anti-Communist. I, like most adepts, tried to stay out of politics, but I could see how living under Communism would be pretty miserable, even for an adept. "I don't understand it, either," I said, trying to make peace, hoping we'd move to another subject.

I thought somebody dropped a dish. I heard a tinkle of broken glass, but it was followed by what sounded like a distant gun shot. Anica made a yelping noise and I looked at her. Blood was flowing down the front of her dress, staining the tasteful blue to dark red. It seemed to take me ages, but in reality was probably less than a second, to realize she'd been shot and the bullet had come from the woods across the lake and had broken through the window.

I dove over and knocked Anica to the floor as the window shattered, letting in frigid air and the sound of more gunfire.

Vojir rushed into the room. "What's happening?" she cried.

"Get down!" I yelled. "Put up a protection spell."

She dropped to the floor and her hand was on her necklace as she invoked the spell.

I couldn't put a spell around Anica. She touched herself and the bleeding stopped, but she passed out from the effort. *At least she is breathing*, I thought. She was alive, for now.

I raised my head to look out the window, hoping I wouldn't lose it. Two men were stalking across the ice. They were dressed in loose white clothes that made them nearly impossible to see. At first I didn't notice any weapons, but then I realized they, too, were camouflaged with white cloth. They were long guns, and even I knew they were rifles designed for shooting long distances. I don't know how they missed Anica's head, which was the logical place to shoot an adept so they couldn't heal themselves. The men had stopped firing as they moved across the ice. There was just enough snow on the ice that they were leaving tracks from the woods from which they had emerged.

"Damn," I spat. Anica was going to be no help, even though it appeared she was the target. "How powerful are you?" I asked Vojir, looking into her wide brown eyes.

"Not as powerful as Anica," she whispered, as if that would keep the men from seeing her. I could tell she was on the verge of crying.

"Of course not. Can you go invisible?"

She shook her head emphatically. Invisibility was an AMA specialty, I remembered.

27

I looked out the window again. Invisibility wouldn't help much out in the snow, anyway: you'd leave footprints.

The men were about half-way across the lake. I hoped that the ice would give and plunge them into the water, but no such luck. Besides, men like that probably wouldn't be walking on ice unless they knew it was safe. Their lives were dangerous enough.

Ice is made out of water, and our guild knew the secret to manipulating water.

"Keep your protection spell up and stay down," I whispered to the younger woman. I went invisible—Vojir gasped, and I wondered if she thought I'd teleported away—and I stood in the window and pointed with my right hand while gripping my talisman hard with my left. A young adept recently found the secret to making spells and staying invisible, something that was impossible before. It was sort of like walking and chewing gum and juggling cats all at the same time, but it was possible. The ice beneath the men's feet started to bulge. They scurried away from the moving ice, but that was my plan. The ice cracked and tilted before them and they ran right into it, sliding into the frigid waters with small splashes. One of them fired off a shot and I heard it impact the wall behind me. *That was too close for comfort*, I thought.

But still, that was pretty easy as the men fought to try and pull themselves back onto the ice. I watched their flailing get slower and clumsier as cold attacked them inexorably. I grimaced and let the invisibility spell dissipate. I looked down at Vojir as she watched, amazed, as I must have seemed to materialize in front of her. We exchanged a quick, nervous smile.

"It's okay now," I said softly.

That's when I heard more gunshots. These weren't the pop-pop-pop of slow-firing long guns, but the rapid pounding of machine guns. The sounds were coming from the front of the house.

I looked at Anica and she was still unconscious. Miss Vojir was cowering on the floor and shimmering slightly, which indicated she had a protection spell up.

I rushed to the room where I'd first talked to Anica. The windows were all shattered, and glass on the furniture and the floor. I saw the older warrior outside lying in the snow, blood staining the white crimson while it melted it. I wondered where the young warrior was who drove the car. I could see the car parked on the curb. The driver's side window was gone. He was probably dead where I couldn't see him, I decided.

Two more men, these in all black, including balaclavas covering their faces and the short black weapons they held, were walking quickly toward the house. I didn't know much about guns, but I knew enough to know these were probably the machine guns I'd heard.

One of the men pointed his finger at me and they both raised their weapons. I ducked and went invisible again just as bullets smashed into the wall behind me. A pop and sizzle behind me indicated the television had been shot.

I said a very bad word in the ancient language. Lesser warriors usually weren't a problem. But taking on two with machineguns by myself would be challenging. At this point the two in the lake had frozen to death, I assumed. I wanted one of these left alive. There wasn't time to wonder who had sent warriors to kill Anica, so I wanted to interrogate one of them to see what I could learn.

I stood, invisible but still vulnerable to bullets: adepts can't use a protection spell while using other spells or even moving. I was smart enough not to stand in the same spot as I shot flames out the window. It hit one of the men and he screamed and dropped to the ground, rolling in the snow. The flames almost immediately were extinguished in a fog of melted snow, but he was still lying down, steam rising from his body.

The other warrior opened fire toward where he'd seen the flames emerge, but by then I'd dropped back to the floor. I hoped this was the last armed man I'd have to deal with. I was getting tired.

I got to my knees. He was very close so I shot an airbolt at him. It knocked him on his back a few feet from where he had stood. Vaulting out the broken window and ignoring the cold but wincing a moment at the thought of what the snow was doing to my shoes, I noticed the man I'd hit with flames was starting to get up on his knees. I hit him with an airbolt aimed at his head and he crumpled to the ground, dead or just unconscious.

The other man was trying to get up, and pointed his gun right at me and fired. I felt something hit me in the shoulder, as if someone had slugged me very hard. I twisted in pain and nearly fell over. *How did he see me?* I wondered. Then I realized: I was leaving tracks in the snow, and my breath was visible. He was firing again but missed, because I had twisted sideways in response to being shot. That probably saved my life.

I hit the man who just shot me with an airbolt. He grunted as he was knocked back down into the snow. I slapped my hand against my wound and healed myself until I no longer felt blood pumping out. The invisibility spell dispelled as I walked to the man and grabbed the gun and tossed it aside. I burned my hand on the barrel that I had grabbed and wondered briefly why it would be hot. Ignoring the pain, I put my expensive shoe on his chest and pointed at him.

"If you want to live you will tell me who you are and why are you here?" I growled. I was angry, and the pain wasn't cheering my mood.

He looked at me as if he didn't understand. "*¡No comprendo!*" he cried, holding up his hands, gloved palms facing me. *That sounded like Spanish*, I thought. I used a translation spell and repeated my threat.

"I am Jose Martinez and I am Cuban," he said, his dark eyes wide with fear. They were all I could see because of the balaclava.

"Why are you here?" I growled, and pushed my foot harder into his chest. It probably didn't hurt much, but it likely was frightening for him. I kept my finger pointed at him threateningly and hit him with a truth spell.

"We were assigned to kill the female adept, Anica."

I frowned. Actually, that was obvious but, "Why?" I asked.

"I don't know. Just following orders from the DGI."

I wondered what the hell the "DGI" was, then I heard sirens. The house was isolated, but someone must have heard gunshots and called the cops.

"Who gave you those orders?"

The man shook his head almost violently. "I don't know, only the team leader talked to them."

"Who is the team leader?" I demanded.

"One of the snipers," the man pleaded. "Talk to him!"

I decided that was all the information I was going to get out of him. I hadn't said I wouldn't kill him, but said he if wanted to live he'd tell me what I wanted to know. I assumed he wanted to live. Too bad.

Chapter Two

Coeur d'Alene, Idaho
March 19, 1968

I made sure the other warrior was dead—he was breathing, as evidenced by the mist coming from his nose, so I took his air away until it stopped—and went back in the house just as a police car slid to a stop at the curb. The cops jumped out, guns drawn, and gaped at the carnage. They must have known this house was a guild house. I ignored them.

I don't like killing people, even lessers, and even in self-defense. I suppose I could have let the men out front live to be taken captive by the police. But attacking a guild had to have consequences, and people needed to know those consequences were severe.

Back in the dining room, I looked out the opening where the window had been, and all I could see was bodies floating among pieces of broken ice. I'd get no answers out of either of those men. It seemed the water was freezing around the bodies already. Miss Vojir was standing against the wall, shaking and crying. Her eye makeup had run down her cheeks, giving her a strange, tragic appearance that I somehow found alluring.

Anica was still unconscious but she'd moved. I hadn't noticed the blood splattered in an oval shape on the green wallpaper behind where she sat.

"She woke up, healed herself more, and fell back asleep," Vojir reported, her voice cracking.

I nodded. There was little else she could do in her state.

Miss Vojir turned and nearly fell into my arms, and started crying hard. I held her, enjoying the feeling and the warmth—the house with broken windows was as cold as the exterior now—and ignoring the pain in my shoulder that I needed to finish healing, and the three additional sirens that stopped suddenly once they sounded very close.

Then the doorbell rang. I released Miss Vojir and walked to the front door, opening it to find a policeman on the doorstep. I noticed three chevrons on his sleeve.

"Sir," he began, sounding like he was almost begging. "I know this all is probably guild business, but we need to make a report."

I smiled and ignored my usual tendency to prevaricate with any cop I encountered. "You might want to fish the two out of the lake behind the house," I said.

His eyes grew wide.

"Oh, and maybe call the FBI," I added. "Those men are Cuban. Said something about the 'DGI.'"

His eyes got even wider. I could tell this was going to turn into a mess.

* * * *

It was a mess.

Vaughan caught the next flight to Spokane; he had a layover in Salt Lake City. Anica woke up eventually, but was still in pain. The bullet had passed right through her body. It looked to me as if, had the bullet been a few more inches to the left, it would have gone through her heart and killed her almost instantly, not giving her time to heal herself. As it was, it had probably ripped apart a lung and broken some ribs. She was having trouble breathing, and would probably take a long time to heal.

I was able to heal completely, but the bullet was still in my shoulder. I'd probably have to have a lesser doctor take it out at some point.

Miss Vojir—I learned the first name she used was Ernestine, of all things—made some phone calls, and more warriors and adepts for the Transylvanian guild rushed to the house. Repairmen were putting plywood over the openings of the broken windows since glass that large had to come from Spokane and would take a while.

Police divers (I assumed) pulled the bodies and the weapons out of the lake. Two FBI men—also from Spokane—showed up in dark suits and ties, and spent time talking to the police, who hadn't moved the bodies from the front lawn. They'd found the younger warrior dead inside the Cadillac.

I invited the FBI men inside the house with Anica's tacit approval, and told them everything I knew. Both were clean-cut white men with serious looks on their face. One introduced himself as "Special Agent in Charge Morris Shaw," and he looked to be in his fifties. The other was quieter, younger, but still just as serious. They looked shocked when I told them about the "DGI."

"What is that?" I asked.

"The *Dirección General de Inteligencia*," Shaw said. "Sort of the Cuban KGB."

Even I knew what the KGB was. "Why would Cuban spies attack a Transylvanian adept in America?" I asked, almost to myself.

"We were going to ask you the same question," Shaw stated simply. "This guild came out of Romania, correct?"

"Yes," I replied. "Why would that matter?"

"Romania is Communist and Cuba is Communist. That might have something to do with it."

I shrugged. I couldn't see how there could be a connection between a Communist island in the Caribbean and a Communist country in Eastern Europe. "That seems unlikely," I said, as if I knew.

Shaw looked at me and shook his head. "All these Communist countries, except China, North Korea, and Albania, are under Soviet domination, and they all work together to subvert democracy." He paused a moment, letting that sink in.

I didn't see how killing Anica could subvert democracy.

"This is above my pay grade," Shaw finally said. I could almost see fear in his eyes. He knew something big was up.

Vaughan arrived that night. The guild had to use a different car, as the Cadillac was a bloody mess and the police were still doing whatever it is they do at a murder scene. It was dark by the time he arrived, but the police were still there and their flashing red and blue lights were making the scene look more macabre than it was. I suspected Vaughan used a persuasion spell or two to get into the house. Shaw was also still there, but he'd sent the younger agent back to the office to "Call this in to D.C."

Vaughan's blond hair was just beginning to gray at the temples. His blue eyes were still quick to sum up the situation in the house, with the bullet holes in the walls and the shot-out television.

Anica was resting in her chair. Vaughan rushed to her and took her hand in his in a tender gesture. I was sort of surprised; I didn't think they were lovers: she was significantly older than he.

"How are you feeling?" he asked.

"I'll live," she said without mirth, "but I need to heal more."

"Then why don't you?" he asked. "You're safe now."

She shook her head. "I need to know what is happening."

He turned to me. "What is happening?"

I told him all I knew. When I mentioned the "DGI" he looked surprised. "Damn, the *Dirección General de Inteligencia*?"

"That's what the FBI said," I replied, looking at Shaw. He'd apparently heard of it, but he had worked for the CIA up until '63. That was how he survived the Houser regime.

"It makes no sense," Ernestine said, nearly crying. I had this overwhelming desire to walk over and hold her. I'm sure the fact that she was young and beautiful had nothing to do with it.

"It might," Shaw said. "But I can't talk about those things." He looked at Anica. "I'm sure investigators will come from D.C. Do you mind speaking with them?"

This was unusual. Governments usually left adepts to their own devices, and we took care of our own with varying degrees of success. But when I told the cops the assailants were Cuban, that got the government into our business. Vaughan had given me no clue if he was unhappy about that.

"Yes," Anica said softly, "I'll speak with them, but I don't know much of anything."

Shaw looked as if he didn't believe her, as if she knew why Cuban spies were trying to kill her.

Shaw finally left, leaving only adepts and warriors in the house. The adepts could finally talk in private.

"No, it's okay you told the police," Vaughan said to my question. "In this matter we may have to have the help of the government. Cuban assassins? Makes no sense."

I told him what Shaw had said about Communist countries working together. Vaughan nodded. "He's right about that."

"But why would any Communist country want to kill me?" Anica asked.

"And why the risk of doing wet work in the U.S.?" Vaughan said. "It must have taken huge resources to get those men here. I'd be interested to see what kinds of guns they were using. I bet none of them can be traced back to a Communist country."

"Wet work?" I asked.

Vaughan looked a little embarrassed. "Sorry, Company slang for assassination."

Nobody spoke for a moment. Then finally Vaughan broke the silence. "Branton?"

"Yes, Teacher?"

"I want you to work with the FBI on this. Get as much information as you can from them, and tell them whatever they want to know…within reason."

"Yes, Teacher."

"I have contacts still at the CIA. I'll see if I can get some information there."

"Thank you," Anica breathed. I could tell she was still in pain.

Vaughan smiled at her. "Our guilds are still at peace. An attack on your guild is tantamount to an attack on ours."

"Again, thank you."

"You need to rest, Teacher," Ernestine said softly.

Anica nodded but looked worried.

"The place is surrounded by warriors and adepts," Vaughan added. "It's safe."

"I don't know if I'll ever feel safe here again," Anica said softly.

Ernestine helped Anica out of her chair and down the hall to her bedroom, I presumed.

Vaughan and I looked at each other. There were two Transylvanian-paid warriors in the room, but they might as well have been furniture. One was overtly holding a nasty-looking black weapon. But their presence meant I couldn't ask Vaughan the real reason he wanted to expend guild resources on a Transylvanian problem.

Ernestine returned after about half an hour. She was still in her miniskirt and garish blouse, but she'd washed her face and reapplied makeup. I had to admit that she was very beautiful. I especially liked her long dark hair. Hitting on her at that moment struck me as unseemly, but I could always find an excuse to come back to Idaho later.

She sat in a chair, crossing her legs that her miniskirt barely covered, and looked at Vaughan and me. "She's resting."

"Good," Vaughan stated.

There was little more to talk about, so Vaughan and I left. The police were just packing up, and a man in a suit and trench coat tried to ask us some questions. Vaughan glared at him and growled, "Ask the FBI." Even I felt the persuasion spell Vaughan used. One of Anica's warriors drove us to a nearby motel. The accommodations were clean but basic. I guess that was the best that I could expect in Northern Idaho.

* * * *

Shaw's office was in a ten-story building in Spokane's downtown area. It looked brand new, and had arches at the bottom that rose up to the third floor. It also seemed to serve as a courthouse.

Shaw had a window that looked over a river that was flowing, but you could see there was ice in it. It had been about a week since the attack. I'd found a nicer hotel in Spokane. There was an old hotel downtown that was supposed to be a luxury property, but it had seen better days. I ended up in a chain hotel near the airport which, unfortunately, was a long drive to get anywhere. Thankfully, Brown had sent a warrior who rented a car to drive me around. Vaughan had returned to San Francisco.

The "people from D.C." had come, questioned Anica and me, and left without a word. They seemed to be hiding that they were as perplexed as we were at this attack.

Shaw was showing me 8x10 color glossies of weapons and dead men. "As I suspected, nothing can be traced back to a Warsaw Pact country or Cuba. The sniper rifles were Austrian, the SGG 69." He pointed to one of the pictures. I looked at it as if I could discern something. Looked like a picture of a rifle to me.

"Fires a 7.62 by 51 millimeter supersonic round," he said, just confusing me. "Your Anica is very lucky." That I understood. "Usually they aim for the head," he continued. "Either they were unfamiliar with the weapon or misjudged the distance, maybe because of the snow. That tends to make judging distances harder. In either case, they missed her head and hit her in the chest. Bullet must have gone clean through and hit the wall. We found it when Anica let us in the house the next day.

"Lucky you people can heal yourselves. A normal human would have died of their injuries pretty quickly."

I nodded, adding that to my reasons I was glad to be an adept.

Shaw handed me another picture. It looked like a pistol with a long barrel and a box in front of the trigger. "You were shot with a French nine millimeter M.A.T. 49 submachine gun. Subsonic round but still deadly. Good thing they hit you in the shoulder." He'd seen the ripped suit jacket and the blood on my shirt, both expensive and both ruined.

"And all four were carrying 1911s."

"What are those?"

"American pistols," Shaw explained. "They probably bought them in America along with all their ammunition. It was all NATO spec gear, including their clothes, right down to the skivvies."

I didn't understand that last sentence so I ignored it. "How would Cubans get the Austrian and French weapons?" I asked.

"Oh, there are black-market arms dealers where you can get pretty much whatever you desire. And these weapons were sanitized."

I didn't know what he meant. "How do you mean?"

"Serial numbers filed off so they can't be traced."

I nodded. Vaughan had said that the weapons probably couldn't be traced. "What about the men?"

Shaw took back the weapons pictures and laid out four 8x10 glossies of naked dead men. None of them had any obvious signs of trauma, except one was missing some hair. That must have been the one I lit on fire. All had brown or black hair, brown eyes, and light brown skin.

"We took fingerprints, and the CIA actually had files on two of them. Yes, they are DGI, and have been seen in Miami."

I shuddered. Did Castro and the Russians have spies all over the U.S.? That seemed to be a disadvantage free countries had. I was sure it would be very hard to be a spy in a Communist country.

"Anything else?" I asked. I'd learned nothing that helped me find out why Cubans were trying to kill Anica.

Shaw shook his head. "I've told you everything I know. I dealt with people like you during the war. I know you can make me tell you everything, so I hid nothing...nothing that I know, at least. There is stuff going on at higher levels of government they don't tell me."

"Did the people who came from D.C. tell you anything?"

Shaw looked frustrated. "Again, that's all above my pay grade. But frankly, I think there's nothing more to learn. Your Anica seems to have no idea why this happened."

"Do you believe her?"

Shaw looked at me. "I'll be honest. It's hard to know whether to believe any adept. I know you all have your own agendas. But I've been completely honest with you," he concluded.

I wondered if that were true. I could hit him with a truth spell and find out, but that would probably make further cooperation difficult. Vaughn had talked about how hard it was to work with lessers. I had to agree.

"Thank you," I said.

Shaw nodded and looked as if he wanted to say something.

"What?" I asked.

"You were very lucky. These are highly-trained and motivated individuals. They were probably trained by the Russians. By all rights, Anica should be dead, and so should you. It was a classic set up: the sniper team to take out the target, the assault team to finish the job if the sniper failed. They had walkie-talkies for communication; Japanese-made and probably bought in America, if you're wondering."

I nodded, listening.

"Frankly, we're amazed," Shaw continued, "that the Communists would expend this effort and these resources, on U.S. soil, even, to kill an adept leader. It's just...inconceivable. There must be more to this than there appears on the surface." He looked at me as if I could explain it all.

"We are as confused as you are," I stated, which was true. In fact, there was a growing knot in my stomach. Something big was happening, and my guild and I were behind the curve on finding out about it. I knew Vaughan and Brown would assign me to find out.

* * * *

Ernestine greeted me at the door to the house. The exterior showed no signs of the violence that had happened there a week before. The Cadillac's window had been fixed, and I assumed the interior cleaned. I'd have been tempted to get a new car, but maybe the Transylvanian guild wasn't as rich as mine.

Ernestine knew I was coming and was wearing a short skirt, a pretty pink blouse, and tasteful yet alluring makeup. I had to admit she looked lovely. I knew she'd developed a crush on me, which was understandable since I'd saved her life. While it would have been fun to start a relationship with her, it would be difficult because of the distance and the fact that we were in different guilds.

"Hi!" she exclaimed and gave me a tight and inappropriately long hug. I finally managed to pull myself from her arms. She looked at me with a gaze I couldn't mistake the meaning of. *Damn*, I thought. I knew she'd sleep with me if I just said the word.

"Is Anica in?" I asked needlessly, but I needed something to let her know I was there on business.

Ernestine looked a little disappointed but smiled. "Yes, she's resting. She'll be out in a moment."

"Thank you," I said, looking around the living room of the house. The television had been replaced and the bullet holes in the walls patched and painted over. Like the exterior, there were no signs of the shoot-out that had happened.

I sat on the same couch I had sat on the week before as Ernestine walked down a hall.

A few minutes later she returned with Anica, who looked strong and pretty. I stood and shook her hand. "Greetings, Teacher."

"Hello Mr. Branton," she said, and sat on the couch.

"Are you completely recovered?" I asked, still standing.

She shook her head. "Just when I think I'm completely healed, something new will spring up. That man from the FBI said the bullet probably sent shock waves through my soft tissues, so I'll continue to have problems until I find all the damage it did."

I nodded. I'd had a lesser doctor in Spokane take out my bullet and then I healed myself, spending a day in my hotel room resting. But mine hadn't been fired from a high-powered rifle, nor had it hit anything vital.

"Anything my guild can do to help?" I asked. Vaughan had told to me say that.

Anica shook her head, smiling. "No, but thank you. I'll be fine soon, I'm sure."

"I wanted to ask you some questions, Teacher," I stated. I had plane reservations for the next day to go back to Frisco. This time through Salt Lake City like Vaughan, which seemed the long way but that was how the airline operated.

"Yes?" she asked softly, locking her brown eyes on mine.

"Do you know why the Cubans would want to kill you?"

She shook her head. "As I explained to the FBI, I still have contacts in Romania and know the situation there. It doesn't matter if it was the Cubans, the Poles, the Romanians, or the Russians, this attack probably originated with the KGB."

"Then why would the KGB want to kill you?" I asked. I knew the KGB was the Soviet Union's equivalent to our CIA. I had no idea what "KGB" stood for. Probably something in Russian.

"That I do not know," she stated simply. "I'm no threat to them."

I studied her face. I sensed no subterfuge. She honestly didn't know why this attack had happened.

"There's nothing you know that they might want to keep secret?"

"How could there be?" she exclaimed. "I left Romania just after the war. My guild knew what was coming and we left. The Soviets were worse than the Fascists." I knew by that she meant the Nazis. I'd visited a library in Spokane and looked up Romanian history in an encyclopedia. The Germans hadn't invaded Romania, but had dominated it. The Americans had bombed some oil fields that were supplying the Nazi war machine. When Romania switched to the Allied side just before the end of the war, the Germans bombed Bucharest, the capital. Then the Soviets invaded and installed a Communist government that still ran the country. Currently a man named Nicolae Ceausescu, who had come to power three years ago, was the leader of the nation.

I looked at her and I looked at Ernestine. Both were watching me with their beautiful dark eyes. I almost chuckled, but was sure they would misinterpret it. I was thinking: *here are two beautiful women, and Anica is too old and Ernestine is almost too young.*

Instead, I said, "Thank you, Teacher."

"Thank *you*, Student. I owe you my life."

All I could say was, "You're welcome, Teacher."

* * * *

I was happy to be back in San Francisco. In Suite 1313 of the Huntington Hotel, I explained to Vaughan and Brown everything I knew, which wasn't much. I'd spent the airplane trip thinking about it. Why would the Communists want Anica dead? Because she'd escaped Eastern Europe? But she couldn't have been the only one. I doubted the KGB was going to expend those kinds of resources to kill every person who escaped Communism. Before the Berlin Wall had been built, East Germany was hemorrhaging people. No, it didn't make sense unless Anica wasn't telling the truth…and that made no sense.

The suite had been destroyed and rebuilt at least twice, once in 1943 and again in 1958. Since then it'd been fairly peaceful. Brown seemed to have classic taste, as there was dark wood wainscoting and cream-colored wallpaper. The carpet was shag, as was the current style, but the furniture was mostly leather. One camel back couch, I'd been told, belonged to Kader's predecessor.

Almost like furniture, there was Brown's personal warrior against the wall. He held a black deadly-looking weapon I'd heard called an "Uzi."

Brown greeted me warmly as he always did, his black face starting to wrinkle and his hair nearly all white. Vaughan was younger, brusque, and wanted to get to business. I reported all I knew, leaving out what Agent Shaw told me about the guns, other than they were "sterilized" and couldn't be traced. I was pretty sure Vaughan and Brown wouldn't care about what types of guns were used.

"Sanitized," Vaughan stated.

"What?" I asked.

"I'm sure Agent Shaw said the guns were 'sanitized,'" Vaughan intoned.

"Yes," I said, slightly embarrassed. "You're probably right."

Vaughan leaned out of his leather chair and handed me a yellow piece of paper. I recognized it as the paper telegrams are delivered on, with evenly spaced punched holes down each side for some reason.

"This may just be coincidence," Vaughan said, his blue eyes looking at me. "This was delivered yesterday."

I read the telegram. Under the date and time, and a location of "LANGLEY, VIRGINIA"—and a bunch of letters and numbers that I had no idea what they meant—was:

PLEASE RECEIVE MESSRS HELMS & KARAMESSINES ON 3/31 AT

10:00 AM STOP MATTER MOST URGENT TO US AND YOUR GUILD STOP

The thirty-first was Monday: two days from now.

"Who's 'us'?" I asked. And why did Langley, Virginia sound familiar?

"It may be 'U.S.' and not 'us,'" Vaughan explained. "Helms was my last boss at the CIA. I never met Karamessines or worked with him, but I heard about him at the CIA. Also, Langley is where the CIA headquarters is now located."

"Oh," I said softly. That's why it sounded familiar. "First the FBI and now the CIA? We must have stumbled into something big."

Brown looked at me with a worried expression. He was getting old enough that in guilds of the past—and in other guilds, I heard—Vaughan would be challenging him for sole leadership of the guild. But this guild, the largest in the world, was different. When Brown wanted to retire, Vaughan would step into his place and I would probably step into Vaughan's position. Brown would go fish or do whatever he wanted. I knew he liked to read.

"As Mike said," he indicated Vaughan as only he could get away with calling him "Mike," "it may be coincidence, or it may be related to the attack on the Transylvanian Guild."

"The FBI agent, Shaw, said they contacted the CIA and that the CIA had files on two of the assailants indicating they were Cuban spies," I reminded Brown and Vaughan.

"So maybe this is about that," Vaughan said.

"I guess we won't know more until Monday after you meet with them," I said.

"I want you in that meeting, Student," Brown stated.

I tried not to smile to give away how happy I was to be included. "I'll be here," I said.

We talked a little about less important matters and I excused myself. I had a room on the twelfth floor of the Huntington, one of the larger suites. I changed out of my business suit and into more casual but still classic and expensive attire, while watching an episode of "Star Trek." While I enjoyed that show sometimes, it seemed hit or miss based on the quality of the writing. This one was a miss, set on 20th century Earth with some alien and a blonde chick trying to save the planet from the stupid humans. The episodes with time travel annoyed me. How could such a thing be possible? I grumbled and turned it off and took the elevator to the lobby. I caught a taxi in front of the building. It was already dark out this soon past the equinox.

"Where to?" the driver asked curtly.

"Haight-Ashbury," I replied, sitting back in the seat.

I saw him smirk in his rearview mirror before he pulled the car away from the curb. The Huntington is on Nob Hill and Haight Ashbury is south and downhill from there. The driver swung his yellow Ford sedan around and drove. I'd lived in San Francisco three years now, having moved from Los Angeles, but I had visited on a regular basis since I joined the AMA as an apprentice in 1949 at age 16. The city was no longer the small, intimate town it once was. It seemed all innocence left about the time the Vietnam War heated up. That's when the hippies showed up, taking over the Haight-Ashbury district and the Golden Gate Park directly to its west. The year before had been declared "The Summer of Love" and young people from all over the country descended on San Francisco. There was even an insipid pop song about if you're going to San Francisco to wear flowers in your hair.

The men all had their hair over their ears and in some cases down to their shoulders. It seemed required for the women to wear their hair long and straight. Shoes were optional and flowers were everywhere, as were drugs and illicit sex. More and more people came lured by the promises of easy access to drugs and sex. They over-ran the area and were sleeping in Golden Gate Park. It seemed few knew what a shower or bathtub were for.

But it all seemed to coalesce around opposition to the war in Indochina and the draft. People had protested the Korean War, too, but not like this and not on this scale. The newspapers were calling it the "counter-culture."

I looked out the window. Sometimes it seemed as if it would be nice to halt so-called progress and not have changes happen quite so fast. Some pointed to the assassination of President Joseph P. Kennedy, Jr. as the end of a time of innocence. I didn't know. The hippies said "Don't trust anyone over thirty," and here I was thirty-five, and already the hippies struck me as ridiculous.

Cars lined the edges of the streets, bumper to bumper; seemed everyone wanted to own a car now but there was no place to park them but on the hilly streets, and traffic in the city was sclerotic. In front of the taxi was a sea of red tail lights. *Would almost be faster to walk*, I mused.

"Any place specific you want to be dropped off?" the driver asked. I think he assumed I was a tourist wanting to check out the nightlife in the wildest part of town.

"Do you know the Purple Chrysanthemum?"

He looked at me as if trying to determine if I were joking. "It's a dive. There are a lot better places than that. How about the Carousel Ballroom? The Grateful Dead are playing there tonight."

I couldn't stand the music of the group called "The Grateful Dead," so that wasn't much incentive to change my destination. And the Carousel Ballroom wasn't even in Haight-Ashbury. Plus I had reasons for where I wanted to go. "The Purple Chrysanthemum, please," I repeated.

"Your funeral," he said. He pulled out a pack of cigarettes and had a tube in his mouth before I noticed and ran a persuasion spell on him to keep him from lighting it.

He stopped in front of the night club, I paid the fare and a small tip—if he was going to think I was a tourist I might as well act like one—and walked up to the doorman. He was a big guy, as required, with what seemed more fat than muscle. His whitish head was shaved, which probably meant he suffered from male pattern baldness. He looked at me with gray eyes, his tattooed arms crossed over his multi-colored T-shirt.

"Two dollar cover and two drink minimum," he said, looking at me. He must have thought that would drive me away, being a tourist. I could feel the bass of the music through the concrete sidewalk. I dreaded what it was going to be like inside the establishment.

"Thanks," I said and walked by. I paid my two dollars at the window where a girl with long, multi-colored hair stamped the back of my hand.

"There's a two drink minimum," she said not bothering to hide how bored she was.

"Thanks," I said again and entered through the heavy door. The music assaulted me like a barrage of noise. The band on the stage was amazingly loud for a trio of scraggly-haired men. I was sure the place was in violation of the fire code judging from the number of bodies writhing on the dance floor. It was dark and the only lighting was flashing and changing multi-colored lights that battered the eyes. Even so, I could see there were a few men without shirts dancing in the throng of flesh in the center of the room. There may have been some topless women, too, but with most of the hair both male and female reaching the back, it was difficult to be sure.

There were girls, topless, dancing in square cages. They both had designs painted on their svelte bodies. I'm not an expert, but I guessed both of them were on some drug of some sort.

Booths lined one wall and I sought the one farthest from the stage.

Between two waifs of girls who didn't look older than fifteen sat the man I was looking for. He ran the Chrysanthemum, and either paid off the cops or somehow otherwise kept them out of his business. There were marijuana joints on the table in plain sight and paper with printed patterns on it. I had heard just touching LSD-laced blotter paper could get you high. I didn't know if that was true.

The man, with thick brown hair down to his shoulders and a beard going gray nearly half-way down his chest, looked at me and shook his head unhappily.

"What the hell are you doing here, man, this ain't your scene?" He had to yell over the music and still I could barely hear him.

"I need to talk," I said simply—well, as simply as I could while nearly screaming.

He shook his head again and the hair must have tickled one of the girls, because she giggled and playfully hit him in the chest. I wondered what and how many drugs she was on.

"What the hell's in it for me, man?" he yelled back, not moving, his arms still around the girls...one blonde and one brunette. He liked variety, and there were plenty to choose from, I understood. The Haight-Ashbury was full of runaway teenagers.

The only commodity I could offer him was information. I decided to give him a taste: "What do you know about the Cuban DGI?"

That seemed to get his attention, and he looked around as if to see if anyone overheard. As if they could in that cacophony.

"Excuse me, girls," he said and pushed a disappointed blonde out of the booth so he could exit. I could see she was wearing a tiny little flowered cotton dress, like the hippie women wore only much shorter. He kissed her with a long and passionate kiss, then bent over the table and kissed the brunette the same way. Apparently satisfied, he jerked his head toward the rear of the establishment, indicating I should follow him.

As I walked away I watched as the blonde got back in the booth and picked up a joint, lighting it and inhaling the sweet smoke. Between marijuana and tobacco, the whole place was in a haze that seemed to blur the psychedelic colors the patrons wore. Maybe that was part of the allure.

Chapter Three

San Francisco, California
March 29, 1968

My contact took me back behind the stage and to a small office. The pounding of the bass was in the background and more felt than heard, but the office still seemed almost sepulcher-quiet after that noise in the bar.

He sat in a wooden chair with a groan. The man was actually older than I, and the drugs and the hard life were aging him quickly. He didn't offer me a place to sit and there were no other chairs. If I hadn't been worried about keeping my clothes clean, I would have leaned against the wall.

He pulled out a cigarette pack, looked at me, and put it away. We'd already had that discussion and yes, I would use a persuasion spell to keep him from smoking.

"Damn, this is a young man's game," he said, throwing down the cigarettes and opening a drawer in his beat-up desk. He pulled out a bottle of whiskey and filled two shot glasses with the brown liquid, handing one to me. I threw it back, feeling it burn as it went down my throat.

"The Haight-Ashbury's changing. There's a lot of money going to be coming in with these hippie bands getting record deals and the hippies moving out to the country. Even the Dead left last year. And now everyone wants in. I mean, look at this bull," he said, showing me a piece of paper that had the amateur look of being mimeographed in black and white only. With it was a small reel-to-reel tape spool. I read the name of the band both on the paper and a hand-printed label on the plastic tape reel: "Carlos Santana Blues Band."

"This Santana guy is a damn dishwasher at the Tick Tock's Drive-In over on Third Street. And he wants to play in my damn bar?" He almost spat.

"Did you listen to the tape?" I asked. I was thinking of saying they couldn't be worse than what was playing in the bar at that moment.

"Bah!" he exclaimed, dismissing it. "What's this about the DGI?" he asked as he filled his glass again.

I hung onto mine, thinking that would mean he wouldn't refill it. He liked cheap booze, apparently, and I didn't. "What do you know about it?" I asked.

"The Cuban equivalent of the KGB, although necessarily a lot smaller and less capable. They have the drug trade on the East Coast locked up."

"Pardon?" I asked. This was news.

"Yeah, pot out of Mexico, coke out of South America, heroin out of Asia, it all goes through Havana, man."

He must have forgotten he didn't have to keep up the hip affectation with me.

"I thought it was done by organized crime."

"Yeah, sure, but the DGI gets it to the U.S., and the mafia distributes it."

"Why would they do that?" I asked almost to myself, but he answered anyway.

"A source of hard currency they need and a chance to undermine the capitalist American Imperialists."

I said a bad word in the ancient language. He just watched me. *That explains why there'd be DGI men in Miami*, I thought.

"What's your interest in the DGI?"

I looked at him. This was the trade-off part. "They were doing wet work in Idaho." I decided to use Vaughan's phrase to see if I could get a reaction.

He leaned forward in his chair. "You're freakin' crazy, man. When?"

"Ten days ago; the nineteenth."

"Why would they do that?" he asked.

"I was hoping you'd tell me," I stated.

"Who was the target?"

"The head of the Transylvanian Guild."

He ran his fingers over his beard as if he were thinking. "That makes no sense. Were any of them captured?"

I shook my head. "I killed them all, but not before one told me they were DGI."

He again just looked at me. "Hell, this is messed up, man."

"You have any sources that could shed some light on this?" I decided not to tell him what Shaw had told me, that the DGI could have been operating at the behest of the KGB.

He shook his head. "Probably not. I could talk to some East Coast people, Miami and stuff. But everyone's pretty tight-lipped. I'm not the big player I used to be, you know that. I'm tryin' to go legit."

"Awful lot of drugs and young girls around," I said off handedly.

"You threatening me, man?" he said with deep menace in his voice. He'd had a violent past but he didn't worry me. He must have forgotten what I was.

"Nope," I said lightly. "Just making an observation."

He spent a few beats of his heart glaring at me, and then poured himself a third whiskey. "I'll tell you this. If the Cubans are risking wet work on U.S. soil, it must be for something important. The target can hurt them, badly."

"Them or the Russians?" I asked.

"Hell, it's all one big happy freakin' commie family. Something that woman knows has the Commies worried."

"And that's what doesn't make sense," I stated.

"Beats me," he said. "Unless you want some merchandise, I need to get back to my business before my employees steal me blind."

"Merchandise?" I asked stupidly.

He glared at me as if I were an idiot. "Acid, maryjane, horse, blow, uppers, downers, you name it, I've got it."

I chuckled mirthlessly. "I thought you were going legit."

"This is legit. I'm a business man."

"Right," I said trying to keep the sarcasm from my voice. "No thank you."

I left the Purple Chrysanthemum and the ear-splitting racket behind and strolled down the street toward the intersection of Haight and Ashbury that gave the district its name. Street lights and storefronts gave off plenty of illumination.

There were young, able-bodied men sitting on the sidewalk. A few were begging but most didn't even have the gumption to do that. No telling how many were on what drug. The streets were crowded, mostly with young people affecting hippie attitudes and a few older folks looking bewildered. Those were tourists, I surmised. A pretty, young, blonde girl in a brown poncho was asking passers-by for spare change. I turned her down and she said, "That's cool, man, you have a beautiful day." Being a hippie seemed to be a mostly white phenomenon; I saw few blacks on the streets.

I passed a tattoo parlor and stores selling tie-died T-shirts and glass items, the use for which I had no idea. There was the free store which gave away other people's throwaways. Well, you get what you pay for and if you pay nothing. . . . I walked by two guys in orange robes pounding on tall thin bongo-like drums and chanting something about "hairy Krishna." There was a smoke shop that probably sold a lot of roll-your-own paper. A wooden Indian was guarding the entrance but someone had dressed it in hippie garb: a flowered dress and a peace sign painted on its cheek. When I was a kid wooden Indians were ubiquitous in front of smoke shops: carved wooden Indian statues with crossed arms and full headdresses, usually. They seemed to have fallen out of favor lately, however. I wasn't sure which was more disrespectful to Indians: the wooden Indian itself, or that someone had vandalized it.

A hirsute young man got in my face, waving something that looked vaguely like a newspaper. "Buy our revolutionary newspaper!" he demanded, as if yelling would make me want to buy his rag. "Twenty cents."

"No, thank you," I said politely.

"What, you like living in ignorance of the fascist state of America?" He was so close to me I wrapped my hand around my talisman and was about to hit him with a spell.

"I'm not interested," I said louder, giving him one last chance before I hit him with, oh, perhaps a fear spell.

He stepped back and looked at me. "We're gonna destroy America in the revolution, and then people like you will have to *learn*." He was trying to sound threatening, but to me he was just silly.

"Yeah, good luck with that," I growled and stepped around him. Adepts don't normally give a hoot about lesser politics, but I liked the United States and didn't think I'd like living in the world that young man dreamed of.

Outside the Drogstore Café, a pretty brunette girl who couldn't have been more than twenty-five, wearing jeans and a knitted top and sandals, was talking to an older man, conservatively dressed, who looked upset. I caught a bit of what she was saying: "Why shouldn't we make love to those we love? And we *all* love each other. Love can change the world. It's a revolution, man."

The man scowled, looking even more unhappy, and said, "Don't call me 'man.' I'm your father, damn it."

I passed out of earshot before I heard her reply.

At the corner of Haight and Ashbury were two motorcycle cops sitting on their machines looking bored. My usual response to cops was to make sure I wasn't noticed by them. But they were ignoring blatant law-breaking so I needn't worry. I could see they had little choice. They were out-numbered, and it would probably start a riot if they wrote a jay-walking ticket. I knew the cops occasionally came through Haight-Asbhury in force and rounded up under-aged kids, but these two were alone. One did catch my eye and gave me a look of disdain, thinking I was a gawking tourist. I ignored it.

A taxi drove by slowly and I hailed it down. Climbing in the back seat I said "North Beach." If the driver knew the city he'd know what part of the North Beach I wanted to go to.

Apparently he did.

* * * *

I'd woken up Sunday afternoon with a hangover that took a healing spell to cure. The problem was bars and cigarette smoke were synonymous. If I wanted to drink, I had to tolerate the clouds of tobacco smoke that every bar had, and that just made me drink more. I'd been at an after-hours joint on Polk Street until almost 6:00 A.M. Polk was a wild part of town and there were a lot of people living what was starting to be called "alternate lifestyles." The bartender was a drag queen, and at the encouragement of the patrons he put on a show about four in the morning. Amazing that a balding, middle-aged man could dress up like a Las Vegas show girl with a wig, makeup, the slinky outfit and the outrageous headdress and actually pull it off. *Almost as good as a glamour spell*, I thought sarcastically.

I spent the rest of Sunday in my suite at the Huntington, reading the newspapers and thinking about the problem. Anica claimed she didn't know why the DGI or any of the Commies would want to kill her. The CIA was coming for a visit tomorrow and I would be amazed if that was a coincidence. The drugs the DGI were supposedly importing to the U.S. didn't seem germane. Maybe the proprietor of the Purple Chrysanthemum could find out more if I pushed him.

It was a nice day so I took a walk and tried not to fret. It didn't work.

On Monday I was in Suite 1313 in my best suit at 9:45. I was wearing the new shoes I'd bought to replace the ones ruined in Coeur d'Alene. Brown and Vaughan were there, too. It was still a beautiful day, and I could look out the windows of the suite at the Golden Gate Bridge. I had to admire the skill and ingenuity that went into that structure. It truly was both beautiful and functional.

Brown interrupted my thoughts, "Any new thoughts, Student?"

I shook my head. "No. I did learn that the DGI smuggles drugs into the U.S. But I don't see how that affects our situation."

Vaughan looked surprised, but I wasn't sure if it was because of the facts I'd just related, or that I knew something he thought was a secret. He didn't clarify.

"Who are these people we are meeting with?" Brown asked him.

Vaughan sucked in a large breath as if he had a lot to say. "Helms was my last boss at the CIA when he was the Deputy Director for Plans. That's the operational arm of the CIA. Now I think he's the DCI."

"DCI?" I asked. I didn't realize at that point how much dealing with the government involved learning their acronyms for everything.

"Director of Central Intelligence," Vaughan clarified. "The head of the CIA. Karamessines was Helms' deputy in the Directorate of Plans just before I left the CIA. I didn't have anything to do with him, as I reported directly to Helms or to McCone, who was the DCI then. In fact, I've never met him."

I shook my head. I was surprised how easily Vaughan could sound like a bureaucrat after being out of the government for over five years.

A few minutes before ten, the phone rang. Brown picked it up. "Yes? Yes, send them up, please."

The warrior and the adept that were always stationed in the lobby must have called up about the visitors.

The adept would accompany them up, since otherwise they couldn't get past the armed guards at the elevator landing. I realized I had my hand on my talisman. I wasn't sure why. What was I expecting?

The adept, a blonde woman in her late twenties, showed the men in. Both were wearing dark business suits with narrow ties. One was carrying a briefcase. I almost expected it to be handcuffed to his wrist like in the movies. Vaughan stood, as did Brown and I.

The young woman left at a word from Brown and shut the door behind her.

Vaughan greeted one of the men, the taller of the two, with a long narrow face and dark, slicked-back hair that was thinning in front. They shook hands with polite salutations. Vaughan then shook the second man's hand a little more coolly. This man wore round glasses on his prominent nose. His hair was dark and thick despite being cut short. He was the one with the briefcase.

"This is Richard Helms," Vaughan said, indicating the taller man. "And this is Thomas Karamessines. Gentlemen, let me introduce Louis Brown, my co-leader in the American Meta Association, and Peter Branton. You could call him our DD/P."

Karamessines looked at me through his glasses as if sizing me up. We shook hands all around and then sat, Brown behind his desk, Vaughan and I in leather chairs, and the two CIA men together on the old leather couch that Brown had inherited from Kader.

Helms leaned forward on the couch. "We were hoping just to speak with you, Vaughan."

Brown cleared his throat. "Your telegram said this affected our guild. In that case, Vaughan and I agreed that both of us should be here, along with Mr. Branton."

"And what is Branton's role in your guild?" Karamessines asked. He seemed annoyed I was there.

"As I said," Vaughan stated, "he's sort of our Deputy Director for Plans. If there's something that needs to be taken care of, he's the man we turn to."

Helms and Karamessines exchanged a look. Neither one appeared very happy. But they probably realized if they wanted to deal with a guild, they would have to do it on our terms.

Karamessines pulled the briefcase onto his lap and opened it. He pulled out something that reflected the light and handed it to Vaughan, who had to stand to reach it but took it from the lesser.

Vaughan held it up between his thumb and his forefinger. It appeared to me to be a steely marble like I used to con the kids out of back in Seattle, except that it was somehow more perfect, with almost a mirror finish.

"What is this?" Vaughan asked.

"A ball bearing," Karamessines stated without mirth.

"And why do I care?" Vaughan queried, handing the ball bearing to me. It was heavier than I thought it would be.

Helms looked at us seriously. "You'd be amazed how much national security rides on ball bearings. They are needed for just about everything from truck wheels, jet engines to ICBM gimbals."

"Gimbals?" I asked.

"Yes," Karamessines said emphatically. "ICBM motors are on gimbals to balance the missile. It's like trying to balance a sixty-foot, forty-ton pencil on the end of your finger while accelerating it at hundreds of feet per second per second."

If he was trying to confuse me, he did.

"And what does this have to do with our guild and the DGI?" I asked, working hard to mask my frustration.

"The DGI?" Helms asked. "What about it?"

I blinked in surprise and looked at Vaughan. He looked as perplexed as I felt.

"The Cuban *Dirección General de Inteligencia*?" Karamessines asked incredulously.

"Yes," I said. "They attacked the head of the Transylvanian Guild in Northern Idaho."

Karamessines and Helms looked at each other as if both didn't know what I was talking about.

"An FBI agent, Morris Shaw, told me that the CIA knew two of the assassins were DGI," I said, trying not to sound as surprised as I was.

"Wait," Karamessines barked. "Start at the beginning."

I shook my head and explained about the attack on Anica and how one of the attackers told me he was taking orders from the "DGI," and how Agent Shaw said that the CIA had confirmed two of the attackers were DGI agents. I decided to leave out the information about the DGI smuggling drugs.

"When was this?" Karamessines asked angrily.

"About two weeks ago," Vaughan stated.

"This FBI agent's information must have come through the DI," Karamessines stated. "I didn't hear anything about it."

"And that's a bit below my pay grade," Helms said.

I loved how both men were making excuses. I wondered if they were lying or incompetent… or both.

"DI?" Brown asked, saving me the trouble.

"Directorate for Intelligence," Karamessines explained, explaining nothing.

"So this visit has nothing to do with that attack?" Vaughan asked.

"No," Helms said, shaking his head. "We were hoping your guild would help us with another problem."

"What problem?" Vaughan asked. I could tell he was angry and confused but he was keeping his voice level.

"Ball bearings," Karamessines stated. "The U.S. has always had better ball bearings than the Warsaw Pact. This means our ICBM gimbals are more precise, and our missiles therefore more accurate."

"I didn't think accuracy was a big deal in nuclear weapons," I said without hiding my sarcasm. How accurate did a nuclear bomb really have to be?

"They are if you're going against a hardened target," Karamessines continued, either ignoring or oblivious to my tone. "So where we can have one or two missiles aimed at a target with a fair assurance of eliminating it, the Russians need three or four because their ball bearings aren't as good."

I looked at the metal sphere in my hand. I was amazed at how such a little thing could make a big difference, and despite myself I was interested.

"You said this affects our guild," Brown said, bringing me back to reality.

"National security affects everyone in America," Helms stated a little too strongly. He knew he'd just been caught in a lie and was trying to use a quibble to get out of it.

Brown shook his head. I could tell he wasn't pleased at having been fooled into this meeting. "What is it you want from my guild?" he asked softly. When Brown got angry he spoke softly.

"We have intelligence," Karamessines started, seeming happy to get to the crux of the matter, "that the Warsaw Pact is now producing much better ball bearings. Apparently a factory in Pitesti, Romania is manufacturing them, thanks to some genius engineer the Romanians apparently produced."

"Romania?" I asked. Transylvania was in present-day Romania. Was this a coincidence, too? Seemed unlikely.

"What do you want from us?" I asked, trying to sound non-committal. But I really wanted to know where this was going.

Helms spoke. "We were hoping Vaughan would agree to helping us out again by getting into the factory, getting pictures of their milling machines and their plans, and bringing that information back to the U.S. so we can determine how good those bearings are and how they are making them."

"So we can make bearings just as good," Karamessines added. "Assuming they actually are better than ours."

"A black bag job?" Vaughan asked.

"Yes," Karamessines said, looking uncomfortable, as if Vaughan had said something he shouldn't.

I looked at Vaughan and then we both looked at Brown. I could tell he wanted to show the gentlemen the door. I wanted more information. Vaughan looked as if he did, too.

"First of all," Vaughan stated, "it won't be me, but Branton."

Karamessines started to object, but Helms put his hand on his arm and the man became quiet.

"Second," Vaughan continued, "we'd like to discuss it. We're not sure if we want to. . . ." He hesitated, and then finally said, "Cooperate with the CIA."

Karamessines didn't look happy but Helms nodded. "Yes. We'll be in town a few days. We're staying at the Hilton. You can contact us there or—" he reached into his suit pocket and handed Vaughan a business card "—that's my direct number at Langley."

There were some more innocuous words and pleasantries exchanged and the two spies left, accompanied by an armed warrior.

I looked at Vaughan. "This can't be a coincidence. Are they lying?"

"Of course they are lying," Vaughan said. "Hell, they burned me when I was on a mission the president himself had ordered.

"But why are they lying to us now?" he concluded.

"Do we care?" Brown stated. "Does this affect our guild beyond our obligations to the Transylvanians?"

"We don't have enough information," Vaughan stated raising a hand in frustration.

"Exactly," I stated sharply and stood up. "We need to talk to Anica, see if she has any ideas about this. And I think we should cooperate with the CIA long enough to find out what's really going on." I realized I still had the ball bearing in my hand, so I pocketed it, the opposite pocket from my talisman.

"That could be risky," Vaughan said.

I shrugged. "What can they throw at me that I can't handle?"

Vaughan and Brown exchanged a knowing look. I ignored it.

* * * *

That night the president of the United States went on national television to say he wasn't going to run for re-election. JPK's younger brother, Robert, and a senator named Eugene McCarthy were running as anti-war candidates, and apparently beating President Johnson in the Democratic primaries. I knew Vaughan didn't like Johnson, but he wouldn't say why. Something that happened when he worked at the CIA, I assumed. I wondered if Vaughan wasn't telling me the complete truth, either. Something strange was happening, and I felt as if I were trying to put together a jigsaw puzzle in the dark, and with a lot of missing pieces. Well, Anica was coming Thursday; the arrangements had been made by phone. Maybe I'd learn more then. But I was starting to doubt it.

* * * *

The taxi stopped with squeaking brakes in front of the arched entrance to the Huntington Hotel as a cable car clanged by.

I'd gone to the airport to pick up Anica and Ernestine as they flew in from Idaho (well, Spokane). When Brown told them about the CIA's bizarre visit, Anica volunteered to come for a talk. I was happy when I heard Ernestine was also coming.

I got out of the taxi, held the door open, and Anica and Ernestine exited. The younger woman was again wearing a short dress of many colors, and as she slid out of the taxi I saw what struck me as an indecent amount of thigh. I averted my eyes, but not in time to avoid a reproving look from Anica.

The four of us met in suite 1313—Ernestine wasn't invited, so I gave her a key to my room and told her to make herself at home. Vaughan told Anica what the CIA men had told us.

Anica frowned. "That doesn't make a great deal of sense to me," she said. She was completely healed and rested from her ordeal and looking beautiful again, I noticed.

"Since Nicolae Ceausescu came to power, Romanian relations with the Soviet Union have been strained," she explained. "He opened up diplomatic relations with West Germany, and didn't break relations with Israel after the Six-Day War."

"So you're saying," Brown asked, "that the Romanians wouldn't be making ball bearings for the Soviet Union?"

She shook her head. "I just don't know. This is what my contacts still in Romania tell me.

"Also," she stated, "the education system in Romania has been deteriorating since before the war. How they would produce some amazing engineer, I don't know." She held her head up high and looked directly into Brown's eyes. "I do know this: if you can help the United States in its fight against Communism, you should."

Vaughan appeared torn and I didn't know what to say. Brown finally said, "Why?"

"Because," she stated, still looking directly at him, but her eyes growing bright with tears, "Communism is a threat to all of us. And if there is a nuclear war, no one will survive, not even adepts."

Brown didn't have an answer to that.

"I remember Kader saying there's no way to survive a nuclear war other than to not have one," Vaughan stated.

"And you think helping the CIA will help avert a nuclear war?" Brown asked.

"Yes," Anica replied

"Probably," Vaughan said.

I stayed quiet. Then I realized, "But do we really think this is about ball bearings?"

"No," Vaughan said with conviction. "But we won't find out what it is about unless we help them."

Anica looked from me, to Vaughan, to Brown. Brown shook his head. "You're right. We need to know what's happening. Are you willing, Student?" He addressed that to me.

"Yes I am, Teacher."

* * * *

Vaughan volunteered to take Anica out for dinner, as it was getting late. Brown demurred and said he'd order room service because he needed to think. I returned to my room to find Ernestine coming out of my bathroom wrapped only in a towel. Her bare shoulders were still damp and her thick, dark hair was wet. There was a funny smell in my room, almost like burning flesh. She had all the windows open despite the chill evening.

"What have you been doing?" I asked lightly.

"I'm sorry," she said softly, holding the towel at her bosom. "I had a smoke and I know you don't like it so I was airing out the room."

I looked at her. It didn't smell like cigarette smoke. I closed all the windows and turned back to talk to her.

Then she dropped the towel, which puddled at her feet, and stepped toward me, wrapping her small, nude body about mine. And I forgot all about the funny smell as our lips met.

* * * *

Warm, soft skin pulsating with life pressed against my body as I woke. I realized Ernestine was cuddling with me as I dozed. I smiled and turned to face her.

"Good morning," she said with a smile, those brown eyes seeming to sparkle.

"Good morning," I said, grinning. I had no idea what time it was, but I knew we hadn't slept much after she dropped her towel. Sometime during the night I'd ordered us a room-service dinner and she'd giggled, lying in the bed naked as I answered the door in a bathrobe and tipped the waiter, after finding my pants with my wallet where they'd been unceremoniously discarded.

I kissed her softly on the lips and relished her flesh against mine for a moment before going to the bathroom. I glanced at the phone on my way. The red message light was on. Being an adept isn't a 9 to 5 job, and when Brown and Vaughan wanted me, I needed to be available.

For some reason I didn't want to talk to anyone naked, so I slipped on a bathrobe before using the phone. Ernestine slipped into the bathroom while I waited for someone to pick up.

"Front desk," a male voice said.

"This is Mr. Branton in room 1210. I have a message?"

"Yes Mr. Branton. Mr. Brown would like to see you in his suite as soon as possible."

"Thank you," I said and hung up. I found my watch and it was almost ten. Well, I knew if Brown needed me immediately, he would have called the room and not left a message.

Ernestine came out of the bathroom naked and with a lascivious smile on her full lips.

"I have to go," I said, earning a pout from those lips.

"I should see if Anica needs me," she said, trying to cover up her disappointment.

I nodded as I started to get dressed. She found her clothes and dressed, too, and we took the elevator together to the thirteenth floor. The warrior guarding the elevator (a large bulge under his suit jacket indicating the size of the weapon he carried) directed Ernestine to Anica's suite while I went to 1313.

"Greetings, Student," Brown said as I walked in. That was awfully formal and I wondered if he was angry with me.

"Greetings, Teacher," I replied, mirroring his formality.

"Did you rest well?" he asked.

"Yes," I lied.

"Good." He hesitated, looking at me from behind his desk. He hadn't said I should sit so I remained standing. Finally he spoke, his dark eyes seeming to smolder. "I'm not sure I agree, but Mike and Anica think it's important you find out what's happening in Romania. Mike thinks the CIA is lying to us, and that alone he thinks is worth investigating."

"Yes, Teacher," I said. I didn't know whether to celebrate or dread this trip.

"I talked with Kader last night," Brown said matter-of-factly. That was either a strong far-seeing spell or an expensive long-distance call. Kader was living with the Valkyrie now, in northern Norway.

"Yes?" I asked. I didn't know where this was going.

"He wants you to come visit him on your way to Romania."

"In Norway?" I asked stupidly.

"Yes. He says it's important."

I nodded. "I'll go talk to him."

"Good. Mike will contact Helms and tell him you're going. We won't tell them about the trip to Norway."

"Understood. When do I leave?"

"As soon as arrangements can be made with the CIA, I suppose."

I was still standing. "Is something wrong, Teacher?"

Brown shook his head almost sadly. "I'm worried, is all. There's more to this than meets the eye. I might be sending you into a trap."

Which was why they were sending me and not Vaughan: I was expendable.

"Warrior?" I asked.

Brown shrugged. "I'll have Vaughan ask the CIA if you may take a companion."

"Thank you." I meant it. If this was a trap, I wanted as many weapons on my side as possible.

"We're going to have more meetings with Anica...see if we can figure out a way to get them more members. Maybe a dual membership arrangement," Brown stated. "If you'd like to entertain the young lady today, that would be helpful." He gave me a smile and I knew that he knew that was exactly what I wanted to do.

"I'd be happy to, Teacher."

"Thank you."

I took the elevator back down to the twelfth floor and to my room. Ernestine was there and dressed, and looking pretty in jeans and a peasant top, her long dark hair straightened out after I'd tangled it during the night.

"What's up?" she asked.

"Want to go sightseeing?" I offered. I thought we could hit Chinatown, Fisherman's Wharf, the Presidio, Golden Gate Bridge, Coit Tower, and maybe Mount Sutro; go by cable car whenever possible, taxi otherwise. Have lunch somewhere and then go to dinner. I knew some nice places with nice views of the city.

She practically squealed in delight. "Can we go to Haight-Ashbury?" she asked excitedly.

"Why?" I asked, trying to keep the annoyance from my voice.

"I've heard so much about it; I want to see it."

"It's not like it used to be," I said, smiling. "There're still some hippies there, but there are a lot of other unsavory types, like drug pushers and pimps."

"Please?" she whined, giving me a look that was hard to resist.

I smiled despite my unease. "Sure." I'd have the taxi drive us through on our way to Mount Sutro.

We left the Huntington together and caught the first cable car heading toward Chinatown. Ernestine was so excited she squealed with delight and kissed me right there on the car. I hoped we wouldn't get in trouble. A couple of weeks ago the president's daughter had been kicked off a cable car for bringing on an ice cream cone. I could handle any problems with easy spells, but it would be a hassle. But nothing happened, and we arrived in

Chinatown and I helped Ernestine off the wooden platform and onto the street.

Walking down Grant Avenue we passed what used to be Young Fat's before he died. It still echoed of that adept's power.

Eventually we were in the backseat of a yellow taxi sedan, a Chevy I noted, and I told the driver to drive through Haight-Ashbury. He didn't look too enthused, so I hit him with a slight persuasion spell and told him our final destination was Mount Sutro and Twin Peaks. That made him happier: this was going to be a large fare.

As usual, traffic in Haight-Ashbury was jammed. In daylight the area didn't look any better. I did notice a lot of psychedelically painted cars I hadn't noticed the other night. I didn't understand why hippies loved raucous colors so much.

The taxi stopped due to traffic and Ernestine, who had up until then been holding my hand in hers, let go and jumped out of the car, exclaiming, "Oh, look!"

"Ernestine!" I called but to no avail, she was disappearing into the crowd.

"Sorry," I told the driver and paid the fare with a good tip. I felt bad about getting him stuck in Haight-Ashbury. I got out of the car as quickly as I could and took off after Ernestine, losing her dark hair in the throng of hippies on the sidewalk. I could feel her presence so I knew I was headed in the right direction, but I couldn't see her petite form.

I was moving fast and didn't see it, but something smacked me hard in the face and knocked me back. I almost fell on my ass. At first I thought it was an airbolt, but I was amazed to see the wooden Indian in the hippie garb moving toward me. It had apparently hit me in the face.

Chapter Four

San Francisco, California
April 4, 1968

I'd never seen this type of meta before. At least I assumed that's what it was, as the wooden man inexorably walked toward me with a creak of moving wood, like tree branches in a heavy wind. It was raising its arms for another blow so I stepped back and shot an airbolt at it. I heard wood crack, but that didn't stop it. It swung again and its wooden fist pounded into my face, knocking me down and back on the sidewalk. Somewhere I heard screams and yells. A guy sitting on the sidewalk, his back to a storefront, muttered, "Wow, bad trip, man."

The Indian was bending over, its face expressionless except for the painted-on peace sign as it seemed to prepare for another attack. I shot fire at it, assuming old dry wood would ignite easily, and it did: the hippie dress went up in flames, and now the monster was a burning mass, still attacking me. It smacked me again with a flaming arm and I suffered from both the impact and the burns. Nearly screaming, I scrambled away on hands and knees. I don't think I'd ever been that scared. Still it came, oblivious to the fact it was on fire.

A motorcycle cop I hadn't noticed jumped off his bike, pulled his service revolver, and shot it into the Indian with six cracks of bullets being fired. It had no effect other than sending burning splinters of wood flying. The cop suddenly looked frightened, and was gripping his billy club but taking no further action.

People were screaming loudly now. I looked around, looking for an escape. If I could teleport away I might escape, but I could see no clear place to teleport to. Briefly I wondered what happened to Ernestine and if she were safe. I didn't sense the presence of another adept, but I didn't really have the ability to be quiet enough to do so. I just hoped she was okay.

The burning Indian smacked me again, hard, in the chest and I felt as if my feet left the ground as I was knocked into a car's side. I heard and felt sheet metal crumple and knew I'd hit the car hard. My vision was going gray. But I realized my shirt was on fire and that kept me from passing out; if I passed out I was probably dead. I pulled water from the air to douse the fire, but this took time and the Indian was on me again, even though it was moving very slowly.

I wondered if I'd survive until the wooden Indian had been consumed by the flames. It hit me again, knocking me to the sidewalk. There was an unpleasant smell and I realized my hair was burning. I used my bare hand to pat out the flames. This gave the Indian time to hit me again, hard. It almost felt as if I flew through the air and was slapped painfully to the sidewalk, the Indian still lumbering toward me.

In desperation I shot another airbolt at it. It must have been on the verge of falling apart because that hit blew it into flaming pieces that scattered over the street and also hit me, burning my skin or singeing my clothes. But it was no longer attacking.

I took a deep breath and felt for broken bones. My face was bruised, and both it and my chest were burned. The top of my head was hot, and the pain there was growing by the moment from excruciating to unbearable. I did enough of a healing spell to stop the pain and then rushed back into the crowd—which parted before me in wide-eyed horror—and called out "Ernestine!" From somewhere she fell into my arms, which hurt my chest but I ignored it. She was bawling almost hysterically.

"Are you okay?" I asked.

She nodded, still crying. "Are you okay?"

"I'll live," I said grimly.

The cop that had shot the Indian was looking at us, I realized. "What the hell is going on here?" he demanded. I assumed in all the time in Haight-Ashbury he'd never seen anything like that, and to be honest, neither had I.

Adepts generally can manipulate the four basic elements: air, fire, water, and to some extent earth. Even flying carpets are manipulation of the air under them. Teleportation and invisibility and a number of specialty spells are known by the various guilds, but no guild that I knew of could make a wooden Indian come to life and attack someone. I didn't know what it meant. It seemed I was dealing suddenly with an adept that had powers no one had ever heard of before.

* * * *

The sight-seeing tour was called off and Ernestine and I took a cab back to the Huntington. I healed myself completely and fell asleep on my room's bed in the early afternoon. Ernestine stayed in my room. I trusted her, mostly, and anything important was in my safe.

When I woke up it was getting dark, and Ernestine was looking at the room's television.

"What's going on?" I asked with a yawn. It was obvious that there was special coverage of a news event. Walter Cronkite looked especially serious on the color screen.

"Someone shot Martin Luther King," Ernestine said, nearly in tears.

"The civil rights leader?" I asked.

She nodded, and I noticed how prettily her hair moved despite myself. "There are riots happening in some cities, too."

I fought the urge to go to the window and see if there was one happening there, as if I'd see rioters marching up Nob Hill.

"Damn," I whispered. It seemed the country was making some progress on civil rights and now this. I wondered how this would affect the nation. I know as an adept I'm supposed to be above such things and hold lesser issues in disdain, but I thought the better the country was the better it was for everyone, including adepts. The guilds had their own history of racism. Prior to World War II there were Negro guilds and Indian Guilds and Asian Guilds. Another thing Kader accomplished was getting most everyone in America in one guild, the AMA. That we woke up to the stupidity of racism only twenty years before the rest of the country was nothing to crow about.

I wrapped my arms around Ernestine's lithe form and held her, watching the T.V. over her shoulder.

Then I remembered my duty and reluctantly let go of her to pick up the phone. I asked to be connected to suite 1313, and when Brown answered I said simply, "We need to talk."

"Come on up," he said.

"Vaughan needs to be there," I added.

"He's here."

I changed my clothes (I was still in the singed attire), looked at my hair that was half burned off, and decided I'd better get a crew cut until it grew back. Brown and Vaughan wouldn't care so I took the elevator up to the thirteenth floor. The warrior on duty looked at me funny, but I assumed that was due to my lopsided hairdo.

I told Brown and Vaughan about the wooden Indian attack. They both gawked at me, amazed. They, too, knew how unprecedented it was.

"Only thing I've ever heard close to that is a golem," Brown said.

"A what?" Vaughan asked before I could.

"It's a Jewish legend," Brown explained. "A rabbi makes a statue out of clay and it comes to life and does his bidding. But I assumed the story was apocryphal."

I had never heard of it and wondered where Brown had. But he liked to read a lot so he may have come across it then.

"Most of the European guilds, including the Transylvanians, can make broomsticks fly," Vaughan said. "Maybe it's related to that?"

I shrugged. We were getting into areas I knew little about.

"Where was Ernestine?" Vaughan asked.

I'd explained how she'd jumped out of the taxi and I lost her in the crowd. "I don't know."

"Could it have been her?" he asked.

I looked into his eyes and had to contemplate the possibility. "I suppose that's possible, but I don't think she's that powerful. And where would she have learned that?"

"She could be masking," Vaughan said.

"We've been very intimate," I responded. I assumed both men had assumed what was happening when Ernestine spent the night in my room.

"If she's good enough, that wouldn't matter," Brown added.

I shrugged. "I can't rule her out, I guess, but I'd be surprised. And why would she do it?"

"There're too many coincidences," Brown said with frustration on his face. "This attack is just another one."

All three of us were quiet while we contemplated that.

"Did you get ahold of the CIA?" I asked Vaughan.

"I left messages. Helms' 'direct line' goes directly to his secretary. Probably won't hear back until Monday at the earliest."

"Our business with the Transylvanians is through," Brown said to me. "Make sure they go home right away."

"Yes, Teacher," I replied. I was curious why he seemed to want them gone as soon as possible, and I was unhappy Ernestine would be leaving soon. I was enjoying her company. "We don't have enough information," I said.

"I know," Brown growled. "Maybe we'll learn more when you go to Europe."

"Maybe," I said. "I hope."

* * * *

Six days later, I flew from San Francisco to Seattle, and then boarded an SAS flight for Stockholm that flew over the North Polar Region with stops for fuel in Anchorage and Greenland. The plane was huge, a DC-10 I think they called it, and even in first class there were lots of people. I did appreciate the ability to put up my feet.

The tall, thin man sitting next to me was polite enough not to want to chit chat the whole dang flight, which was good because I was planning to sleep to try to minimize jet lag.

"Big plane," he said as he sat down.

"Yes," I agreed.

"Boeing is working on a bigger one right here in Seattle. Called the seven-forty-seven."

"Really?" I said. That was interesting. I wondered if there was an upward limit on how big planes could get. I had no idea how something so big as this DC-10 could fly, let alone something bigger.

"Going to have two decks," the man stated, "like an upper floor with stairs between."

I thought he was kidding and I laughed.

"No," he said. "It's true." He hesitate a moment and stuck out his hand. "Anthony Lynn," he said. "I practice law. I have business in Oslo."

"Peter Branton," I replied, shaking his hand.

"Business or pleasure trip, Mr. Branton?"

"Business," I said, thinking I might need a spell to keep him quiet.

"Oh, what business are you in?"

I couldn't think of anything else to say so I said, "Ball bearings."

"Interesting," he murmured as he got comfortable. "I don't know about you, but I'm planning to sleep."

"Me, too," I said.

He almost looked relieved. He was worried I might be a chatter, apparently.

After takeoff the cabin was darkened and I reclined my seat, put up the foot rest, and tried to sleep. Vaughan had dropped me off at the airport in San Francisco. I think he'd wanted to talk to me alone.

"Don't trust the CIA or the government," he said as we rode in the back of the car a warrior was driving.

"I won't," I stated.

He must have felt the need to emphasis the point. "Their job is to do whatever it takes that they perceive as protecting the United States from its enemies. They will lie, cheat, and kill even their friends and allies to achieve those ends."

"Doesn't that make them as bad as what they are fighting?" I asked.

He shook his head. "No, because what they are fighting is worse. But they will sacrifice you and your life on the altar of protecting freedom without a moment's hesitation."

Vaughan should know what he's talking about, I decided. He worked for the CIA for something like five years. He never had talked about it.

I eventually went to sleep to the drone of the plane's four jet engines.

I had to stay overnight in chilly Stockholm, and in the morning I caught a flight to Tromsø. This was a DC-9, a plane with two jet engines on the back of the plane. There were three coats of arms or shields—I wasn't sure which—painted on the engines. This was a smaller plane and the first-class section only had eight seats. It was about a two-hour flight to Tromsø which gave me time to ponder.

I was a little uncomfortable meeting Kader again. I'd only met him twice before, and I hadn't been in San Francisco in 1958 when Houser deposed him. If I had, chances were I would have died in Suite 1313. It'd only been four years since I passed my trials to become an adept and I wasn't remarkably powerful. But I'd regretted all my life since not being there. When the call went out for supporters of Kader to fight Houser, I decided to stay neutral even though I supported Kader in my heart. This ended up being good, because when Brown and Vaughan took over the guild, they were more than happy to expel or kill those who had supported Houser too directly. But there were too many who, while not supporting Houser, did nothing to support Kader, to kill or expel them all.

Houser ended up being a dictator and a tyrant. I defied him as much as I could while remaining alive. I knew he'd kill anyone who threatened him…or at least try to kill them. I didn't want to end up a rogue like Vaughan, or dead like so many others.

I first met Kader in 1954, shortly after I passed my trials to become a member of the newly-formed AMA. I would be surprised if he remembered that meeting.

The second time I met him was in 1964; he was still in San Francisco despite turning the guild over to Brown and Vaughan. I traveled from Los Angeles for the vernal equinox conclave in order to meet the new leadership of the guild. I must have impressed Brown and/or Vaughan, because a few years later they asked me to move to San Francisco. But, again, I doubt Kader remembered meeting me then, either. He was bent like a question mark and painfully thin. He'd been sick for five years with a rune that Houser, knowing his name, had placed on him. Brown, with the help of a Valkyrie named Liesl, had barely managed to keep him alive, and he looked as if he were near death, anyway. I politely if carefully shook his hand and said I was glad he was alive. Everyone at the conclave probably did the same thing.

Yet, in a way, Kader was the closest thing I had to a father. He was someone to look up to and emulate even from a distance. Maybe if I'd known him better I would have gone to defend him from Houser and gladly died for him. But no one had ever done anything like that for me.

* * * *

I never knew my father. I'm fairly certain my mother didn't, either. I like to think he was a sailor or a soldier, but he was probably a drunken lout looking for a good time. All I remember of my mother is her blonde hair framing her face, which always seemed to be in a scowl of anger or a mask of pain. My grandparents took me in—I think in order to get me away from my mother—or my mother gave me to them. I didn't know, as I was too young to remember. But they were poor and the Depression hit them hard. Soon they gave me up to the state.

I lived in a group home—no one called it an orphanage but that's what it was—with many boys and girls. When I arrived I was awed by the size of the place, three stories tall and bigger than any house I'd ever seen. But it was a lonely and painful existence until I turned five and we were segregated by sex. I was put in the room with the boys aged five to ten. Then it became downright unbearable. The biggest, meanest ten-year-olds ran the place. The adults nominally in charge either didn't care or didn't have the means to control them.

When I was seven I walked up to the biggest one of the bunch and punched him in the face as hard as I could. He and his friends beat me mercilessly and I spent several days in the infirmary. But I wouldn't stool pigeon, even though asked many times with everything from threats to pleas.

When I returned to the dorm, I punched the boy in the face again, hard as I could. He looked at me and laughed. I became a lieutenant in his gang for a while. But while this saved me from being a victim, it required me to treat others as I had been treated, and I just couldn't do it.

Faced with a near-impossible choice, I fled to the streets of Seattle. It was 1940, the eight-year-long Depression was going from bad to worse, and I was living under bridges and porches at age seven. Of course, I fell in with a gang. I was their youngest and best pick pocket after they taught me how. They said it was almost magical the way I could abscond with someone's cash. I even got to keep a little of it (more than they really allowed as I would skim some off the top). I had food and a roof over my head in the run-down house the gang had in the south part of the city, near the Boeing plant and airport. I used to listen to the planes flying overhead, propeller driven noise making the whole house rattle. When the war started this became nearly constant. I would dream of being on those planes, a pilot maybe, seeing the world.

There was booze everywhere and they didn't care that I was seven or eight years old: it was funny to see me drunk.

A couple of times they caught me skimming and there were beatings to endure, but I just figured that was part of life. The one part I could not stand was my gang leader's fascination with cigarettes. He loved to burn my skin with them. Never on the face (I had to stay innocent-looking) but my chest, arms, back, and even genitals were burned. I always came to associate the smell of cigarette smoke with agony. When I became an adept I healed the scars, but nothing seemed to heal my mind.

When I was about twelve, I was working downtown Seattle. There was a spot near the Smith Tower where the city had helpfully put up a sign reading "BEWARE PICKPOCKETS." This invariably caused every man to check his wallet, letting me know where it was...except one well-dressed man didn't. From his clothes and manner I was sure lifting his wallet would be profitable, but it would be difficult. I signaled my partner and the ten-year-old boy started crying, loudly, drawing the attention of everyone, but my mark ignored it. *He is making this difficult*, I thought ruefully. But I rarely backed down from a challenge.

I tried the bump and grab, assuming his wallet was in his coat. Before I got my hand out of his clothes, he's clamped his hand on my wrist and held it hard. He looked into my eyes.

"You're good," he said with a smile I couldn't interpret. "But I'm better."

I was looking at him, trying to figure an escape. I'd never been caught and I had a dreadful fear of the police. Would they send me back to the group home? Or to my grandparents? I struggled to pull away. My partner, the ten-year-old distraction, was running away, leaving me to my fate.

"How old are you?" the man asked.

"Let me go," I yelled, hoping someone would think it was a kidnapping in progress and come to my aid.

The man just smiled, almost kindly. But then I found I couldn't move, couldn't talk, could barely breath. I looked at the man, scared now, and he was still smiling.

"Yes," he said, confirming my fears. "You shouldn't pick the pockets of adepts."

Of course I knew about adepts even though they were somehow more shadowy and elusive than even our criminal gang. But I didn't realize that they apparently had money.

"You have potential," he said softly. People were streaming by us, ignoring both him and me, and I wondered if that were some magic of his.

He released me, reached into his pocket, and handed me a twenty-dollar bill and a card. There was an address on the card and his name…or at least the name he used.

"Come see me, let's talk."

I looked at him in disbelief but he stepped around me and walked away.

I hid the card in my clothes before the rain got it wet.

* * * *

The plane touched down in Tromsø with a bounce. Looking out the window, it seemed to be mid-winter, not a couple of weeks after the vernal equinox. Exiting the airplane and going down the steps to the tarmac, I was shocked at the cold. I hurried into the new-looking airport building.

There was no baggage claim carousel. A couple of beefy-looking guys who were dressed warmly unloaded the luggage through a large portal into the building. I waited until mine was plopped onto the pile and grabbed it.

I felt her before I saw her. In any other part of the world her blonde hair would have been striking. Here it just seemed typical. She was beautiful, about my age, and felt very powerful. She was dressed warmly, most likely because she was used to this climate.

"Hello," I said walking up to her as she stood near the exit to the street.

"You must be Mr. Branton," she stated simply. "I'm Liesl."

I blinked and looked at her. "*The* Liesl?"

She laughed—a happy cheerful sound that was almost musical. "I suppose I am," she said. "Shall we go? I have a car waiting."

I just nodded and followed her out of the building and into the cold again. I found myself wishing my hair were longer and more stylish than the crew cut I was wearing since half of it got burned off.

There was a square-shaped sedan waiting by the curb. Unlike American cars that oozed style, this one seemed to have function foremost in mind. The hub caps all had the letter "V" on them, and its paint approximated the color of oatmeal. A large man was standing next to it. I didn't see any chainmail but I presumed he was a berserker, one of the Valkyrie guild's warriors.

Liesl slid into the back seat and I followed. It was roomier inside than I expected. The berserker got in the front and drove the car into the street. It seemed the airport was not, as typical in America, a long way from the town, but nearly right in it.

"You'll be meeting with Mr. Kader at our house here in Tromsø," Liesl was saying as I looked out the window.

The buildings all seemed to have steep roofs, to let snow slide off, I presumed. "Oh?" I asked.

"And we've arranged for a hotel for you to stay in. You can probably leave tomorrow."

"I have to be in Bonn on Monday," I stated. "Today's Friday, right?"

She smiled. "Yes."

I nodded. I wasn't sure with all the time zone changes. Also, I was a little disappointed. I had hoped to see Valhalla, the home of the Valkyrie guild.

"I can leave tomorrow or Sunday," I stated as the dry fact it was.

Liesl simply gave me a lovely smile. I looked at her, amazed. She was startlingly beautiful. Rumor had it that Vaughan had fallen in love with her. I could see why.

Every member of my guild knew how the Valkyrie Liesl had helped Brown protect and care for Kader during the Houser regime. I never expected to meet her. It almost made up for not going to Valhalla.

The house was smaller than I expected, and in a dense neighborhood in the city. Most houses were right next to each other but this one seemed to have a buffer zone around it. It looked old, but that may have just been the style.

Liesl opened the door on her side of the car and I did the same.

"He's waiting for you," she said, nodding toward the house.

"Are you coming in?" I asked.

She shook her head. "This is your guild's business. We'll wait out here."

I hoped she meant in the car. It was dang cold and the coat I had brought which was suitable for "cold" weather in San Francisco seemed like thin gauze here in Tromsø. I glanced at my watch, which I'd set to Stockholm time, and I assumed it was the same time here. It was getting close to noon.

"Thank you," I said. I walked through the snow to the house and pushed the heavy wooden door open.

Kader was sitting at a table made of rough-hewn lumber. A fire was filling the room with wavering light and tepid heat. There were some chairs, but the room was otherwise sparsely furnished.

The old adept stood and smiled. His hair was almost completely gray and he had crow's feet around his eyes. He was wearing a gray suit that seemed too big for him. He extended a thin hand in greeting and I shook it.

"Greetings, Teacher," I said reverently.

"Hello, Student," he replied. "Did you have an enjoyable journey?"

"Yes," I stated. "Airlines in America could learn hospitality from SAS."

He smiled. "Yes. And how do you like Norway?"

I looked at him a moment. According to Vaughan he was 67 years old now. He looked a bit older than that, but five years under a zombie spell will do that to you. He seemed to have grown stronger since I'd last seen him, perhaps having fully recovered from his illness. At least he no longer stood as if he were shaped like a question mark.

He and the leader of the Valkyrie guild, Brunhild, were long-time lovers. Since World War II, Vaughan said, and that was over twenty years. I wondered if his mind was still as sharp as it was when he managed to defeat an immortal god.

"Sit down, please," he said, doing the same. "Lunch will be arriving soon. I don't know about you but when I travel I get hungry."

I sat and smiled. "Thank you, Teacher."

He dismissed it with a wave of his hand.

"You're probably wondering why I wanted to see you," he stated.

"I am," I said. He wouldn't even tell Vaughan or Brown.

"Where do you go from here?" he asked, surprising me.

"I need to be in Bonn on Monday. I'm to report to the CIA at the American embassy there. From there I'm in their hands, and I assume will go to Romania." When Vaughan finally got ahold of someone at the CIA, he told them I had business in Europe and asked if I could meet with them there. They said I should report to the "station chief" in Bonn, West Germany.

Kader nodded. "Brown told me all that we know about this situation. But I think there is more to it."

"So do we," I stated. "That is why I'm cooperating with the CIA, for now."

"There's not a lot to do in Valhalla," he said, again confusing me. "Don't get me wrong, it's beautiful and I love it there. But there's not even phone service."

"Yes," I said, wondering where this was going.

"Brunhild has let me read her guild's documents."

I nodded, not knowing what to say. She must really trust him. Even I hadn't seen all of our guild's documents.

"You know about Vlad the Third Dracul?"

"Of course," I replied. "He was dabbling in necromancy and the guilds decided he had to stop." Even 500 years ago it was remarkable for the guilds to agree on anything, that's how serious necromancy was. "He was killed; details are murky."

Kader nodded knowingly. "He was killed by a Valkyrie and a member of the Icelandic guild."

"I didn't know that."

"Very few do. But it's in the Valkyrie's archives. Actually, that's not quite accurate. He was killed by his own soldiers after an attack by the Valkyrie and the Icelander weakened him sufficiently."

That was interesting, I thought. That detail, lost to history or so most guilds thought, was in the Valkyrie's archives. But I didn't see how that pertained to me

That was one reason the guilds kept the ancient language alive. Documents written a thousand years ago were still readable. There'd be some slight variation in terms and syntax over that time, but if I happened to meet an adept from 968 A.D., we should be able to converse in the ancient language.

Kader hesitated and looked at me seriously. "According to the Valkyrie's archives, Vlad's documentation, called the *Book of Death*, was destroyed. However, a young woman escaped, a wife or consort of Vlad's, and there were rumors of a second copy."

"A second copy?" I asked. "No one's found it in five hundred years? Then it must be destroyed, or lost, or didn't exist."

"Possibly," Kader said softly. "The key point is, we don't know."

I nodded. If that's all he wanted to tell me, this was one heck of a detour.

"Also," he continued, "not all of Vlad's knowledge has been lost."

This surprised me and I watched his face. The fire crackled while I took that fact in. "How do you know this?"

Kader glanced away for a moment and then looked back. "I kept this out of the AMA archives because I promised someone I would."

"Who?"

"Anica."

I felt my eyebrows go up. If Anica was keeping secrets, what else might she have not told us? "What is it?"

"The Transylvanian guild knows how to use necromancy . . . a little."

"Oh?"

"Yes," he said. "There's power in blood and death. I inadvertently discovered this when I accidentally cut my leg with

83

my talisman." I remembered his talisman was a piece of a samurai sword that was perpetually sharp. "Anica later confirmed it to me. Also, I saw her kill someone to gain more power."

I looked at him, surprised. "When was this?"

"Nineteen fifty. During the Thor incident."

I felt myself growing angry. "You've known for eighteen years the Transylvanians are using necromancy and you've said nothing?"

"The Valkyrie know, too," he said sounding defensive. "It was decided to keep it quiet."

"Decided by whom?" I demanded. I was forgetting who he was in my surprise.

"Brunhild and I, in consultation with Anica."

I could only think of one thing to say. "Why?"

Kader took a deep breath. "Anica said what little necromancy they knew was nothing compared to the power of Vlad. And they only used it in emergencies because they, too, wanted to keep the secret."

"But they're…vampires." I shuddered. I realized that included Ernestine, perhaps.

"But they control it; they don't use their power that way. Or they use animals."

"But you said they did."

"Anica did, when we had to face an immortal god at Valhalla. She claimed that was the first and only time."

I sat back and looked at him. The light from the fire made him look old and haggard, or maybe it was this conversation. I didn't know. "And you believed her?"

"Yes."

"Ever since I was an apprentice, I was taught vampires, real vampires, are an abomination, and that's why Vlad had to be killed." Lessers feared Dracula because he drank their blood. Consumed might be more accurate, from what I knew. Most necromancy spells supposedly did not involve the actual drinking of blood, but used blood in potions and powerful unguents. But the direct drinking of blood was supposed to give untold power to an adept/vampire.

"It's a moot point," Kader said suddenly and strongly. "I told you to warn you that you may be facing necromancers in Romania."

"And if I tell Brown and Vaughan this?" I asked.

"I've already told Brown. He agrees with me. I assume he's told Vaughan."

I let out a breath. "Is that it?"

He shook his head. "No, there's one other thing."

When he didn't say anything for a moment I took a guess. "They can manipulate objects?"

He looked at me with wide eyes. "Yes. At least, that was the opinion of the Valkyrie who attacked Vlad. She said some tapestries moved too quickly to be moved by air, and seemed to unhook themselves from the wall.

"Why did you say that?" he finally asked.

"Because I was attacked by a wooden Indian."

He seemed to study my face a moment to determine if I were joking. When he decided I wasn't he said, "Tell me about it."

Lunch arrived in assorted brown paper bags, carried in by the berserker who'd driven me from the airport. I was telling Kader about that day on Haight Street in San Francisco. He just kept shaking his head over and over.

When we were alone again he said, "You realize what this means."

"That there are necromancers after me already," I stated, trying to keep the trepidation out of my voice.

"And that means they know the CIA is sending you to Romania, and they want it stopped."

"Which means the CIA has a leak."

"Or told them."

I shook my head.

"Don't trust the CIA," Kader warned.

"I wasn't planning on it," I replied. Vaughan had already drilled that into me.

Chapter Five

Tromsø, Norway
April 12, 1968

Liesl insisted on having dinner with me that night. The restaurant was within walking distance of the hotel, or would have been if I'd had a decent coat. I wore the best suit I had with me. Was I trying to impress *The* Liesl? Probably.

The berserker drove us there and we sat near the rear with the berserker seated a few tables away where he could watch the entrance and the kitchen door. It was a new building—I guessed built in the last year or so—which seemed unusual for Tromsø. A lot of the city seemed quite old. Liesl explained that Tromsø survived World War II better than most of Norway likely due to its remoteness.

The food was simple fare with an emphasis on seafood. Liesl warned me I'd probably want to stay away from something called "lutefisk."

"I like it, but it's an acquired taste," she said with a smile.

I ordered the chicken.

As we ate Liesl suddenly said, "Brunhild wants to retire. She and Kader want to live the rest of their lives in peace."

I nodded, since I had a mouth full of food. "Makes sense," I said eventually.

"Most likely I will become head of the Valkyrie guild," she stated. "Then I'll use the name 'Brunhild.'"

"Yes," I acknowledged. That tradition was well known: the leader of the Valkyrie was always called "Brunhild." I had no idea why.

"I'll want to continue the peace treaties between the AMA and the Transylvania Guild," she stated, looking at me intently.

"Good," was the only thing I could think to say. I wondered if she knew the Transylvanians were vampires.

"Would you please let Brown and Vaughan know?"

"Of course," I said with a smile, and picked up another forkful of chicken.

That's when the berserker exploded. There was no boom, no crack of explosives. It was as if his body just decided to disassociate. Blood and viscera were splattered about the small dining room, women screamed, and I realized there was blood all over my suit jacket. There were parts of bone and flesh and entire limbs flung everywhere.

Liesl reacted faster than I did. She dropped to the floor and turned the table on its side for protection before I'd managed to get out of my chair.

"What the hell was that?" I asked dropping behind the protection with her.

"I don't know," she growled, trying to look around the table.

"Did someone throw a grenade?" I asked stupidly.

"No," she said, her voice tight with stress. "I don't think so."

Two men walked through the front door of the restaurant from the dark and cold outside. They were dressed all in black and had balaclavas pulled over their faces. Neither one had a weapon but both had talismans in their hands. These were adepts, I realized, and could feel their power. Had they used some sort of new meta to kill the berserker?

The downside of turning over the table was they knew exactly where we were. One pointed and said something in a language I didn't understand, but which sounded vaguely Russian. Flame leaped from his finger and smacked into the table, splashing fire around us. The table started smoldering and smoking and I was surprised the wood wasn't on fire.

"Come out!" the other one called in passable English. "And we won't kill you." He was taller and skinnier than the one who shot the flames.

Liesl and I exchanged a look. She was the second most powerful adept in the Valkyrie guild (a very powerful guild) and I was the third most powerful adept in the AMA (perhaps the only guild stronger than the Valkyrie). We weren't going to be that easy to kill. Plus I didn't believe them, anyway

I had my talisman encased in my left fist when I shot lightning at the shorter man who was shooting flames. He was knocked back and his chest was smoking, but he didn't go down. *That shot should have killed him,* I thought.

"Very naughty of you," the taller man called out. "Please do not make us hurt you."

Liesl again looked at me. "Airbolt, flames, air," she stated crisply, making a pulling motion. I knew what she wanted me to do. "Now!"

We both stood and I shot an airbolt at the man talking. It slammed him into the wall next to the door. Liesl shot flames at the one I'd hit with lightning but it seemed to have no effect. He'd gotten a protection spell up in time.

Didn't matter. I shot flames at the speaker just as he was recovering from my airbolt and he had to put up a protection spell. We pulled the air from them. I almost smiled at the look of terror in the shooter's eyes.

Then they pulled the air from us. They'd abandoned their protection spells to pull our air away. They were strong enough to do it, too. This was remarkable.

For the first time Liesl looked worried. These two were stronger than we suspected. I was breathing faster as the air got thinner, and it turned into a tug of war of atmospheric gases. I looked up for some reason and saw an air vent directly above us. I gave up the tug of war and pulled air from that vent, hearing the metal crumple in the duct as I sucked the air out of it. But Liesl and I could breathe. I shot the most powerful lightning spell I could at the speaker and he, not expecting it, went down.

The fire shooter tried to flee out the door but Liesl got him with her own lightning, and he was knocked outside and into the street. All our air returned.

Liesl looked at me, and I at her.

"Who the hell were they?" she cried. I could tell she was upset by her use of profanity.

I shook my head. "Necromancers," I said. "And how did they know I was here?"

I suddenly realized my suit was ruined. Also, lessers were climbing out from under tables, looking around to see if it was safe. I walked up to the speaker, turned him over. He was dead, as I intended. The one outside was face down in snow. Neither was going to answer questions. There was a dead dog on the sidewalk, its blood spreading on the concrete. It may have been a stray or it may have been a beloved family pet. I didn't know, but it was obvious the necromancers had killed it to increase their power.

* * * *

Kader hadn't gone back to Valhalla. Brunhild showed up a couple of hours later. I imagined, but didn't know for sure, if it was on a flying white horse.

There were three well-armed berserkers surrounding the house where Kader and I had met. Now Bruhild and Liesl were also there. I'd gone to my hotel room, cleaned up, changed clothes, and a fourth berserker drove me to the house.

"You were attacked in San Francisco, too?" Kader stated.

"Yes, Teacher."

"And you think it's necromancers?" Brunhild asked. She was still a handsome woman, her blonde hair mostly gray now, her face showing her age. But she held Kader's hand as if they were teenagers.

"I don't know what they did to the berserker," Liesl said. "I've never seen meta like that."

"Could it have been technology?" Kader asked looking at me.

"I don't think so. There wasn't a 'bang' like a gunshot or an explosion. He just… came apart violently." And bloodily, I didn't add. I don't know how much blood there is in a human, but it seemed to have painted the walls in that restaurant. I felt sorry for the proprietor.

Brunhild and Kader exchanged worried looks.

"Do you know something, Teacher?" I asked carefully.

Kader shook his head. "No, I've never heard of anything like that, either."

I had no choice but to believe him.

"Where do you go from here?" Brunhild asked.

"I'm scheduled to fly to Bonn tomorrow. I meet with the CIA at the American embassy on Monday. I could fly out Sunday if need be." I kind of hoped not. I suddenly didn't feel safe in Tromsø.

"Somebody wants you dead, Student," Kader said angrily.

"Apparently," I stated simply. I felt a growing knot in my stomach.

* * * *

I made the mistake of leaving my shades up in my hotel room, and the sun came up around four in the morning, waking me up. The meeting with Brunhild, Kader and Liesl ran until nearly midnight, and I didn't get calmed down and asleep until nearly two. Once the sun woke me up, I couldn't go back to sleep. Almost getting killed, again, does mess with your sleep cycles, I guess.

I got up, exercised, dressed, ate a simple breakfast of bread and cheeses in the hotel's restaurant, and waited for my ride to the airport with the berserker in that square car. It was a long wait.

I flew back to Stockholm, and then I took another small plane to *Flughafen Köln/Bonn*. From there I took a taxi into Bonn to the hotel the CIA had recommended: the Hilton, of course.

The Second World War had left its scars on the entire European continent. Germany was divided into free West Germany and Communist East Germany or the Democratic Republic of Germany. All of Eastern Europe was under Soviet domination and in something called the "Warsaw Pact" which was a counter to the U.S.'s NATO which stood for "North Atlantic Treaty Organization." That was pretty much all I knew about it. I was sure it was more complicated than that.

Since World War II, Bonn had been the capital of West Germany. The former capital, Berlin was a divided city as the nation had been parceled out. The demarcation between the two countries was where the "occupation zones" were after the war—the Soviet zone becoming Communist.

Tensions seemed to have calmed since the Berlin Wall was erected by the Soviets and an unstable peace developed...or maybe that was just my perception. But it seemed ten years ago there were always worries the Communists would attack Western Europe. I remembered when the Korean War started, there was speculation that it was a diversion for a Soviet move on Western Europe, but lately it seemed the action had moved to Southeast Asia and the Vietnam War.

The taxi dropped me under a portico in front of the Hilton. It was about four stories tall and yellow in color. My room faced west and overlooked a river and a bridge, and I watched the sun go down.

The next day was Sunday, and having nothing to do I did a little on-foot sightseeing. The bridge I'd seen over the river—the Rhine, actually, I found out—was named for President Joseph P. Kennedy, Jr.

There didn't seem to be a lot in Bonn older than about twenty years, because that's when the city was almost leveled during the war. I did come across a very old church. It was made of grey stone and had one very tall tower with a steep and tall roof. A sign in German and English explained it was built between the 11th century and the 13th century. I could feel its age. It had seen a lot in its eight hundred years of existence. I watched families walk along the sidewalks—men in blazers, pretty wives in dresses and sensible shoes, obedient kids, most of them blond, it seemed. The outrageous fashions of San Francisco were occasionally present (it was too cold for miniskirts, I assumed) but most of the people seemed to be nice, middle-class, conservative types enjoying an early-spring sunny day.

I didn't know why the CIA recommended the Hilton. It was a long and expensive taxi ride to the U.S. Embassy. At one point we passed an immaculate park. If there were hippies in Bonn they kept them out of the parks.

The embassy was not one building but a compound. Getting past the gate and the two uniformed and armed guards wasn't a problem after showing them my passport and they checked a list of names. They apparently had been told to expect me. The main building was a post-war monstrosity block of a building with all the style of a child's wooden block. I walked in the main entrance, showed my passport to the guard at the door (in a very handsome blue uniform with red stripes on his pants), and I was directed to a desk where, again with a check of my passport, they issued me a visitor's badge to wear on my suit jacket and told me to wait. Someone would be with me shortly, I was assured.

Apparently "shortly" meant a good forty-five minutes. I took a seat in the large hall. The place was full of echoes as its walls and floor all seemed to be marble. There was a steady stream of people coming in. Many seemed to be asking about visas to visit or live in the U.S. Some, the better dressed ones, were there for business and were given badges like mine and left to sit as I was. Most were led away after a few minutes.

Finally, a young man wearing a white shirt and tie and no jacket approached me.

"Mr. Barton?" he asked nervously.

"Branton, you mean?" I retorted, looking up at him.

"Oh, yes, of course, sorry."

I just sat and looked at him. He didn't seem to know what to do.

"Would you come with me, please?" he finally said.

"Be happy to," I said with mock sincerity. I stood and he tried to look at me but couldn't.

He silently walked away and I followed, catching up to walk beside him. We went to an elevator and he punched the "down" button. This slightly surprised me because we were on the ground floor.

The elevator opened and its interior was as opulent as the foyer, with marble flooring and dark wooden walls. It even had soft music playing: innocuous stuff that seemed designed to put you to sleep. We both entered, me following him.

As the doors closed I said, "This embassy seems huge."

"Yes," the young man said, seeming to be happy to talk about something to cover the insipid music. "It's the largest U.S. embassy in the world. West Germany and Western Europe are important in the containment of Communism, so we have quite a large staff here. And there's support staff for that staff to run the movie theater, school, stores, and bowling alley. There're four hundred houses to hold embassy personnel. The locals call it 'Little America.'"

The elevator stopped and the doors slid open. In marked contrast to the upper floor, this level was Spartan, with a tile floor—still highly polished, though—insulated pipes running along the ceiling, and walls seeming to be made of cinderblocks and a green color never seen in nature.

I followed the man off the elevator and down the hall, listening to our footfalls echo off the barren green walls.

"Ambassador McGhee," the man was saying, "has tried to make it very home-like for the Americans working here and to truly make the embassy representative of America to the German people."

I found this all very uninteresting. "What do you do here?" I asked.

"Technically, I'm a cultural attaché, but in reality I work for the DI."

"Dee-eye?" I asked.

"Directorate of Intelligence at the CIA. I'm an analyst."

Yes, I remembered Helms, or was it Karamessines, mentioned that during our meeting in San Francisco. I nodded as we came up to a big metal door that blocked the hallway. Standing beside it was a serious looking man in a green uniform with an anchor and globe on his left breast pocket, and "USMC" stenciled over that. Despite the drabness of his uniform, his black boots were polished almost to the point I could see myself in them. He had a black pistol with brown checked grip on a belt at his right hip. I wondered how many armed guards this place needed, this being the third I'd encountered. He looked straight ahead and didn't react as the young man punched numbers into a keypad on the door and turned the handle.

The door opened on a large office. Like any other office, there was the staccato banging sound of typewriters and the murmur of people talking, punctuated by the occasional ding from a typewriter having reached the margins. A teletype machine was rattling in one corner spitting out yellow paper. Most of the walls were lined with doors or filing cabinets with combination locks. There were magnetic (I assumed) signs on each one stating whether it was open or closed. Bright overhead fluorescent tubes made the place almost dazzlingly bright after the dim hallway. Every person in the office was young, male, and dressed almost exactly like my companion with dark slacks, white shirts, and narrow ties with no jackets.

I followed my escort in and he led me to a side office. There were no labels on the doors.

"Sir," the man said, leaning in the doorway, "Mr. Barton is here."

"Branton," I corrected.

A voice said gruffly, "Send him in."

The man backed out and indicated I should enter. I slipped past him into the office.

The office was nicer than the rest of the establishment; with actual white plaster walls instead of block, carpet, and lighting that was still harsh fluorescents, but somehow more indirect. There was a wooden desk and two wood and leather chairs in front of it. Behind it sat a man with a scowl on his face. He ran a hand through thinning red hair and pushed up his horn-rimmed glasses.

"Branton?" he asked.

"Yes," I said.

"Come in, please, and shut the door."

I did and then sat in one of the chairs facing the desk. It was actually not uncomfortable.

The man looked at me. "I don't know where Karamessines came up with this hare-brained scheme."

I didn't say anything.

"I'm Douglas Rhoden," the man said, looking at me with intense blue eyes. "I'm chief of station here. You're the adept, I assume."

"Yes," I replied. I was reasonably impressed he used the correct term and not "meta."

He nodded without saying anything for a moment.

"I'm supposed to get you into Bucharest, Romania under diplomatic cover," he finally said.

"I see."

"You'll be travelling on a diplomatic passport and an assumed name. You have a problem with that?"

"No problem," I stated.

"Good. Once in Bucharest you'll be briefed on your mission. It's a strictly 'need to know' basis op."

"Op?" I asked.

He took a moment, perhaps deciding if I were serious. "Operation."

"Oh," I said. It made sense after he explained it.

"You'll be posing as a diplomatic attaché with the FSS."

"Eff-ess-ess?"

"Foreign Service Staff," he explained. "The cookie-pushers at State don't like us to make our operatives FSOs."

I understood approximately none of that sentence so I ignored it. "How I will I be travelling?"

"You'll fly from Cologne-Bonn Airport to Bucharest on, unfortunately, TAROM."

"What is that?" I asked with trepidation.

"Romania's official airline." When I didn't react he said, "Hey, could be worse, could be Aeroflot. And even so, you will be flying on Sov equipment."

"Sov?"

"Soviet. Probably a Tu-134."

Vaughan had warned me these people had their own language. "I assume that's an airplane."

He chuckled. "Yes, a Soviet-made airplane."

I nodded, not knowing what he found amusing.

Rhoden spent the next hour handing me documents, including airline tickets on TAROM, and a diplomatic passport that was black instead of blue, said "Diplomatic" on the cover, and was in the name of "Richard Jackson." He seemed to think there was some joke in that, because he chuckled as I read the name.

There were already stamps in the back of the passport showing Mr. Jackson had traveled from the U.S. to Bonn.

There was no picture so we had to have one taken with a Polaroid instant camera. The resulting unflattering picture was cut out, glued into the document and a seal pressed into it.

"This passport confers upon you diplomatic immunity," Rhoden said seriously. "Don't give it to anyone, don't lend it to anyone, and don't, for God's sake, lose it."

I nodded.

I was given cash, both American dollars and Romanian currency called the "lei."

"Due to Romanian restrictions, someone from the embassy will be at the airport to pick you up," he explained.

"Sounds good," I stated, not knowing what else to say.

Finally I was given a large blue canvas bag that had its zipper locked closed.

"What is this?" I asked.

"It's a diplomatic pouch," Rhoden explained. "The Romanian authorities can't inspect it...which reminds me, they will inspect your luggage, so I suggest we keep your passport and anything that can identify you as Mr. Branton."

I hesitated to do so because I wasn't sure I should trust Rhoden or anyone at the CIA. But the diplomatic passport sounded like a better passport, anyway.

"When you are done with your mission, return here and we'll exchange passports. Do not keep that passport."

I would if I felt like it, but I didn't tell him that. "Okay."

"Any questions?" he asked.

I shook my head. "No."

"Good. And please, don't foul this up, whatever it is."

Rhoden looked at me finally, as if trying to sum me up. "Do you know what happened over the weekend in Berlin?"

"No," I said. "I've been travelling." Not that I paid much attention to lesser news anyway.

Rhoden shook his head. "There are Soviet-funded radical student groups in this country getting bolder and bolder every day. Friday in Berlin they blocked access to a newspaper building because they don't like what it prints. I've got agents all over this country trying to contain them, and what do they ask me to do? Babysit a meta that's going to do some work for the DD/P."

I just looked at him, unhappy that now he did use the insulting term "meta." I was about to say something when he started talking again.

"I hope you're worth it," he said. "You understand what's at stake here, don't you?"

"To be honest, I don't know," I said. Since I wasn't sure what the mission was how could I know? Ball bearings seemed too mundane for all the trouble the CIA was putting me through.

Rhoden looked at me as if he didn't believe me. "You realize the Soviet Union is paranoid. If they aren't the biggest shark in the ocean, they feel they'd better control the other sharks. And they hate and fear the Germans. They are hanging onto Poland and the rest of Eastern Europe to have a buffer zone between them and the Germans. They keep Germany divided so it isn't a threat. And they think the U.S. is just like them, so naturally, they think we are plotting their demise as they are plotting ours."

He hesitated, to see if any of this was sinking in, I guess.

"And while they have allies in Western Europe and America that they can fund and direct, because of the police state situation in Russia, we cannot have similar operations there. We are at a distinct disadvantage, and I'm afraid it may just be a matter of time."

"Before what?" I asked.

"We capitulate to them. The Finlandization of the West."

I didn't know what he meant by that, but I got the gist: the U.S. surrenders to the Soviets. Again, that didn't sound like a pleasant place to live.

"Better get some rest," he said, interrupting the silence. "Your flight is early tomorrow, and I understand TAROM flights aren't the most comfortable."

I took that as my cue to leave and walked out of the office and back into the din of the main room. I noticed most of the men were looking at me as if they expected me to glow in the dark or something.

The young man who'd led me to the room jumped up and offered to escort me back to the foyer. I said no and he said it was required.

After turning in my "VISITOR" badge, I walked out and past the two uniformed guards at the gate and waved down one of the taxis parked in front. I got in the back seat and said "Hilton, please," not giving the driver a second glance.

The driver nodded and drove off. I sat back and relaxed, holding the diplomatic pouch on my lap. I leaned my head back and closed my eyes. For some reason the meeting with Rhoden had exhausted me.

I'm not sure how long I kept my eyes closed. I might have even dozed off. Then the taxi made a sharp left turn and I opened them quickly. I didn't remember any sharp turns on the way there. I looked around but didn't recognize a thing. The street had turned to cobble stone and was very narrow.

"Driver," I said, "this isn't the way to the Hilton."

He looked at me in his rear-view mirror. I saw the look in his eyes. I wasn't a person to him; I was a piece of meat.

"Stop the car," I said stupidly. He grinned at me in a manner that wasn't even close to friendly.

I thought about teleporting out of the car, but one of the first things I was taught was never to teleport out of a moving vehicle. It wasn't explained why.

I hit the driver with a persuasion spell. "Stop the car!" I probably made the spell stronger than needed out of my sudden fear. He slammed on the brakes and I was nearly flung into the back of the front seat. I tried to open the door but it was locked; in fact, the handle moved so easily I assumed the mechanism had been unhooked. I was looking for a place to teleport to when something sharp hit my arm. The driver was holding a pistol with a very big barrel. In my arm, poking out of my suit jacket, was a dart.

I said a bad word in the ancient language and tried to teleport out of the car, but my brain would not work properly...I couldn't run the spell. The world seemed to be spinning as I tried to find a place to teleport to. Then my vision went blurry and I could no longer sit up, so I lay down on the car seat to rest for just a moment....

* * * *

I have no idea how long I was out. They could have flown me to Moscow for all I knew. I was in a bare room illuminated by one bare bulb hanging from the ceiling. The paint on the walls was blue and starting to peel. The floor was wood, rougher than I thought it should be. I was handcuffed to a chair and the chair was nailed to the floor. I couldn't teleport. My talisman was missing—I felt that immediately—but it was nearby. I thought I could hear a highway: the ululating drone and growl of passing vehicles.

The one window in the room was covered with cardboard that had been taped to the wall. I had nothing better to do than wait. They had handcuffed my hands so I couldn't reach any other part of my body. Did they know I had a wire for picking locks in the skin under my arm? My ankles were tied to the legs of the chair. My suit jacket and tie were gone, and my sleeves had been rolled up. I wondered about that.

My persuasion spell worked on the driver, but I had failed to add "Don't shoot me with a tranquilizing dart," as if I'd considered that possible. Still, he must have had a strong will to do that under the influence of the spell I'd used.

It seemed hours later but since I had no watch, it could have been much shorter. The taxi driver walked in and started speaking German. I pulled up a translation spell.

"...you have spells to understand, so I know you can understand me, yes?"

"Yes," I replied in the same language. I almost just said "*Jawohl*" and didn't bother with the spell, having seen an episode or two of "Hogan's Heroes."

He looked at me. "Why are you in Bonn, Mr. Barton?"

Before I thought about it I said, "Branton." Then I realized maybe it was a good thing they had the name I used wrong. The fact he'd said "Why are you in Bonn" made me think maybe I still was.

"Yes," he said, as if my name didn't matter. "Answer the question, please."

I looked at him. He didn't look German, but he seemed to speak it flawlessly. His hair was dark and shaggy, not as long as a hippie's but not as short as most men still wore theirs. He had a thick black mustache and seemed to need a shave. He wasn't a big man but seemed more wiry than muscular under his loose shirt. Did he seriously just think I would answer questions?

"Who the hell are you?" I demanded.

Anger flashed for a moment in his eyes and he gave me that same look, as if I were nothing: not human, not a person, just meat. "That is not important," he stated. "Why are you here, Mr. Branton?"

I again just looked at him. It did sound like I was still in Bonn, but maybe that was a ruse. I wasn't sure if I should be honest with this man or not. The CIA never said "Don't tell anyone," but in working with spies, keeping secrets seemed to be part of the job. Hell, even Rhoden, the Bonn CIA Chief of Station, didn't know the full extent of my mission. But should I tell this man without any reason?

"Sightseeing," I said.

He gave me that same look, which was starting to worry me. "I know I can't torture you," he said simply as if discussing the weather. "Or at least not without wearing through your protection spell first."

Then I realized what the problem was. He wasn't afraid of me. He'd taken my talisman, bound my hands, and knew he could wear me out.

"Or I could just give you some pharmaceuticals that would make you very cooperative. But the….side effects, shall we say…are unpleasant and permanent."

"Who are you?" I asked. I was growing frightened.

"A contractor," he stated again. "A mercenary. I've done work for you Americans, too. This time you were out-bid."

"Where am I?" I asked, trying to keep the fear out of my voice and not entirely succeeding.

"You're safe, for the moment." Again, he just looked at me as if I were nothing. After a moment he said, "I'll return shortly to see if you are feeling more cooperative." He walked out of the room's only door and shut it.

I looked around. I had scant hope of a rescue. I was sure the taxi I'd gotten into looked just like hundreds of others, and no one at the embassy suspected a thing. In fact, it was probably stolen. I didn't know if I'd been out twenty minutes or twenty hours. Rhoden probably thought I was on my merry way to Bucharest.

The chair I was handcuffed to was made of wood. I tried to rock back and forth in it, thinking maybe it would break, but no such luck. It was pretty firmly put together. Nor could I reach the wire I had under my skin to pick the lock. It seemed helpless.

I decided to tell him the truth. It wasn't out of cowardliness, but cold logic. He knew how to break through my defenses. It could take a while but eventually he would. I would eventually be forced to tell him whatever he needed to know, I was sure. Between drugs and physical torture, there was no doubt in my mind. So I might as well save myself the pain and possible permanent damage and tell him. I also decided it was my best chance to live through this.

Then an idea hit me.

Again, I have no idea how long it was until he returned. He wheeled in a metal tray on wheels like doctors use to hold instruments, except one instrument was a power drill with a nasty looking bit used to make large holes. He plugged it in and pressed the trigger twice to make sure it worked. I tried not to wince at the sound. There were also two glass syringes full of liquid. It surprised me that the liquid was clear, like water. I think I sort of expected it to be some nasty green color. I was sure he was letting me see it, hoping it would frighten me. It did.

"Are you feeling more cooperative," he stated.

I nodded.

"Good," he whispered, but looked disappointed.

"But first, I have one question."

He looked annoyed. "Yes, of course you do. I sleep very well, thank you."

I almost found that amusing. But instead I said, "What would it take to out-bid the ones who out-bid the Americans?"

He looked genuinely surprised. "You couldn't afford it."

"Between me, the CIA, and my guild, I doubt it."

He chuckled. Then he shook his head. "No, you couldn't, believe me."

Well, I guess it was worth a shot. "What would you like to know?" I asked, hoping he'd realize I was cooperating fully.

"Why are you in Bonn? What are you doing for the CIA?"

"They want me to go to some place in Romania called Pitesti to look at a ball bearing plant that is supposedly making amazing ball bearings."

He looked at me, still as if I were just a plant he was about to prune. "Lies will not work, Mr. Barton."

"Branton," I said almost angrily. "And I'm not lying."

"There is no ball bearing plant in Pitesti," he said, looking over his tray.

I sighed. "Then I was lied to, too."

"Pity," he stated. He picked up a syringe and tapped it to get the air bubbles out of it.

I tried something out of desperation. I teleported up and out from the chair about three inches. The handcuffs cut painfully into my wrists, but my feet were free of the ropes. I was as surprised as the man holding the syringe. I kicked him hard as I could while using a strength spell, aiming for his groin. I swear I felt something pop when the toe of my shoe landed between his thighs. He howled in pain and dropped the syringe, which shattered on the floor, splashing the liquid across the wood. He bent over, grabbing his crotch. I kicked him again but unfortunately at an oblique angle and probably did no damage. He stood up straight and looked at me, anger raging in his dark eyes. He swung his fist and smacked me across the jaw. But I had the protection spell up in time and all he did was hurt his hand.

He yelled profanities in a language I didn't understand. Believe me when I say I knew they were profanities.

Then I noticed something. The jar of my teleportation must have loosened the bracelet on one of the handcuffs. It was off my right wrist. I didn't have time to get at the wire, but I swung that fist has hard and fast as I could at his jaw, the strength spell still active. It connected and I didn't know who it hurt worse, him or me, but I was rewarded with a crack of bone and blood ejecting from his mouth, along with a tooth or two. He spun around as if he might fall but instead just stumbled a bit. I pointed at him and shot a weak airbolt at his head. All my spells were weaker than they would normally be because I had no talisman, but the airbolt knocked him down and out. He crumpled to the dirty floor.

Chapter Six

Unknown
April 16, 1968

I had to rip my shirt (and not think about what I paid for it) to get to the wire. I was hurrying lest he regain consciousness as I ripped the wire out of my skin, ignoring the blood, and unlocked the other handcuff. Vaughan had warned me many times to keep in practice so it only took a few moments.

I stood up and took a moment to stretch my tight muscles. Adrenaline was starting to wear off and I could feel my arms and legs start to ache. I was tempted to shoot him full of whatever was in the other syringe but I didn't want to kill him and I had no idea what that would do to him. I bent down and touched his neck, and knew he'd sleep for a while. I needed my talisman.

I was apparently in a house in the country. Looking out the window, I saw fields and other houses far away. It made sense he'd want privacy. There was a highway, possibly a freeway, not far away, but the noise of passing vehicles probably just enhanced his privacy. I found my clothes, talisman, diplomatic passport, and the diplomatic pouch cut open. Inside were some papers marked as CONFIDENTIAL and TOP SECRET, and a *Playboy* magazine. I wondered about that as I looked at a green-eyed, dark haired woman, apparently fully dressed and only shown from the shoulders up, leaning up against a man in a yellow sports jacket. She was doing something with the dark handkerchief in his pocket, and I wondered if that had some secret meaning. There was also a pistol—a real pistol, not the dart gun—but I had no use for that.

I returned to the room where he was still snoozing like a baby. I found the handcuff keys in his pocket and handcuffed him to the chair with the one still-working handcuff, but left his body lying on the floor.

I hit him with another spell, and he woke up and looked at me.

I was angry so I didn't waste time with small talk but just hit him with a truth spell and a holding spell. He could only move from his neck up voluntarily.

"Who are you?" I demanded in German.

"Dragomir Bochinsky," he said, almost as a wail. He looked afraid. I wanted him to be.

"Who are you working for?"

"I am a major with the *Departamentul de Informatii Externe.*"

"What the hell is that?"

"Romanian intelligence service."

Oh, man, I thought. This was getting crazy.

"Are we alone?"

"My partner may return at any moment," he said. I knew it was the truth because I still had the spell on him.

"I thought you said you were a mercenary."

"A lie, to make you more afraid."

I shook my head. It worked. "Why did you kidnap me?"

"Orders," he said. "Procure, interrogate, liquidate."

I assumed "liquidate" meant kill. That made me feel angrier and scared.

"What do you know of my mission?"

"Nothing," he said. "Just that lie you told."

So he really did think it was a lie and as far as he knew, there was no ball bearing plant in Pitesti.

"Where are we?"

"Germany. About fifteen kilometers outside of Bonn."

That was the first good news I'd had all day.

I touched his forehead. "Sleep." And he did. I briefly considered killing him, but I couldn't justify it even if he was planning to kill me.

I had to get out of there before his partner came back. Knowing how to drive would have been helpful (I'd seen the taxi parked outside).

I looked for the nearest neighboring house, and seeing one that looked only a mile or so away, I grabbed all my stuff and ran for it.

When I was maybe a hundred feet from the kidnap house, cutting through a green field of some crop, I heard the gunshots. I put a spell on myself to make me run like an Olympic athlete, but I knew I couldn't outrun a bullet. I turned, and another dark-haired man was shooting at me with a pistol. There were muzzle flashes and I could hear the sound, but as of yet, none had hit me. He was too far for an airbolt or fire, so I pointed to the ground at his feet. The soil climbed up to his waist and pulled him down until only his head was out of the pile of dirt. I smiled, turned, and ran.

* * * *

At the neighboring farm house, it took strong spells to keep the residents from calling the *Landpolizei*. I was pretty sure the CIA wouldn't want the local constabulary wrapped up in this, and I didn't want to deal with the authorities, either.

The farmer drove me to the U.S. Embassy in his roundish hatchback with a Volkswagen emblem on the grille. I'd never seen a car like it in America, but that didn't surprise me; I'd seen lots of unfamiliar cars in Europe. I gave him twenty American dollars, out of what Rhoden had given me, for his trouble and petrol.

It took persuasion spells—and maybe the fact they didn't want a man with a blood-soaked shirt and a ripped open diplomatic pouch standing in the embassy foyer—but I got back in to see Rhoden. He stood as I walked into his office.

"What the hell happened to you?"

I slammed the door shut. "Give me one good reason not to put you under a truth spell."

He glared at me as if daring me to do so. I was damn close to doing it. Then he saw what I was holding.

"What the hell happened to the pouch?"

"My kidnappers ripped it open." I tossed the *Playboy* on the desk. "You might want to report this has been compromised."

He let out an exasperated sigh. "Kidnappers?" he asked incredulously.

I told him about the taxi driver and my altercation, and finally what Major Bochinsky told me.

"*Departamentul de Informatii Externe*?" Rhoden asked. "You sure that's what he said?"

"Yes. He said it was—"

"I know what it is," Rhoden interrupted. "The Romanian version of the KGB."

I sat down. "The CIA has a leak."

He laughed derisively as he sat, too. "We have leaks, they have leaks. Do you really think there are all that many secrets we can keep from the Communists?"

"I don't know," I stated. "This is the third time I've been attacked since I agreed to go on this…trip—for lack of a better word—to Romania."

"I don't know what to tell you, Branton. I know nothing about your mission other than I was to get you from Bonn to Bucharest because you had some business in Europe. Otherwise they were going to brief you out of Langley.

"As for that…" he picked up the Playboy as if it were infested with germs. "You can't get those behind the Iron Curtain, and some guys need…entertainment."

"I'm sure they read them for the articles," I said ruefully.

He actually laughed at that.

Eventually he said, "It's obvious your mission has been blown, whatever it was. Will you stay in town while I get instructions from Langley?"

"How long will that take?" I asked.

He shrugged. "It's mid-morning there now. Depends on how long the wheels have to turn before a decision is made. Probably be tomorrow morning our time at the earliest. I'll code it highest priority."

I nodded. "I'll stay until tomorrow, but I'm not guaranteeing I'll go to Bucharest or anywhere else other than home."

"I understand." He picked up the phone on his desk. "I'll have an embassy car drive you to your hotel," he said with an almost kind smile.

"Thank you," I replied.

I left with my own passport. A car was parked near the front gate and a young man asked if I was Barton.

"Branton," I corrected, and he apologized and drove me back to the Hilton. I got to my room and put secure and alarm spells on the doors and windows, then relaxed...but only a little. At that moment, I thought of a good reason I should have killed my assailant: to ensure he couldn't come after me again.

I wondered about calling Brown to see what his thoughts were. If it were midmorning in Washington D.C. it was probably early morning in San Francisco. Or maybe I should wait and see what the CIA said tomorrow and act on my own. If I wanted to move up in the guild I couldn't run and cry for help with every setback.

I shook my head and laid on the bed in the small room.

Something was going on and I didn't know enough. The CIA wanted me in Bucharest for a reason, but apparently not to infiltrate a ball bearing factory in Pitesti. The Romanians didn't want me there, and neither did some necromancer adept or adepts. But apparently they didn't know why I was going there, otherwise why interrogate me? Anica knew something for which the Communists were willing to kill her to keep it quiet, but she swore she didn't know what.

I didn't have enough information and that frustrated me.

And thinking of Anica made me think about Ernestine. I missed her, despite myself. It would have been comforting to have her there at that moment. But of course, it would have been highly impractical to bring her along on this trip.

I let out a long, frustrated breath through my nose and picked up the room service menu. Thankfully the hotel had a restaurant.

* * * *

The next morning I took a taxi, after noting the driver was blond with blue eyes, and went back to the embassy. The same young analyst escorted me to the CIA's area. It probably had a name, but they weren't sharing that with me.

Rhoden looked up with exasperation when I walked in. "You need to call Karamessines," he said. "They want you to proceed with the mission, but they won't tell me a thing. Whatever you're working on, it's big."

I was frustrated with all the mysteries. "Then why send a lone adept?" I asked with a growl.

"You'll find out in Bucharest," he stated. "At least that's what they're telling me."

"If I go," I said. I still hadn't made up my mind.

Rhoden looked at his watch. "It's around three in the morning there. Even Karamessines needs to sleep sometimes. He'll be ready for your call at noon our time."

I looked at my watch. That was almost three hours away. "Have a book I can read?" I asked sarcastically.

Rhoden snorted. "Like movies?"

I got the feeling Rhoden wanted to keep me happy. The embassy movie theater was showing a film called *The Sand Pebbles*. According to the marker board, the first showing was at 5:00 P.M. and a second showing at 9:00 P.M. They showed it to me, alone, at ten in the morning. I imagined some poor projectionist being roused out of bed to show me the movie.

I did not completely understand the historical basis of the film, which was set in China in the 1920s. The politics on the boat were interesting. It reminded me a bit of the politics of my criminal gang, where the young kids did all the work and the older kids and adults enjoyed the benefits. But I didn't even get to see the whole movie, as Rhoden's errand boy came and got me so I could call Washington at noon.

They took me to one of the side offices, and inside was a desk, a wooden chair, and a green metal box about as tall as me with two phones built into it. Rotary dials and handsets were at the top and middle of the box. The top handset was off the hook.

110

"That's the phone?" I asked.

Rhoden nodded. "It's a KY-3 encryption phone. Karamessines is waiting." He pointed to the off-the-hook handset.

I picked it up while Rhoden left the room and shut the door. From the sound of it closing, I got the feeling the door was solid and the room was sound-proofed. I sat in the room's lone chair.

"Hello?" I said.

"Mr. Branton?" a female voice said.

"Yes," I replied, wondering who the heck that was.

"Please hold for Mr. Karamessines." The sound quality was amazing. It didn't sound at all as if I were calling another continent. Some sort of CIA technological wonder, I guessed.

"Branton?" a male voice growled. I could tell this was the man I'd met in San Francisco a couple of weeks ago.

"Yes," I said again.

"Listen, Branton, you've probably figured out the ball bearing story was cover."

"Yes," I said again.

"It's imperative for national security that you go to Bucharest and cooperate with the Chief of Station there."

"Why?" I asked.

There was clear-as-a-bell silence for a few moments. I don't think he was prepared for that question. "It's an issue of national security."

"I'm an adept," I stated. "We don't care about national security." That wasn't totally true in this age of nuclear weapons, but he needed to give me a better reason than that.

Again silence. "There is something going on in Romania that affects both your country and the guilds."

"What?"

"What?"

"I said, 'what?' What is going on in Romania that affects the guilds?"

The connection was so clear I heard him sigh on the other side of the world. "We know more about the guilds than you probably imagine. The FBI has kept tabs on them since its inception. And every now and then we do get an informer."

That was news to me. I just kept listening and let him talk.

"We know about necromancy. We believe elements in the DIE have found Vlad Dracul's *Book of Death* and are planning to use its power to steal secrets from the U.S. Government and other NATO allies."

"What's the dee-eye-ee?" I asked.

"The *Departamentul de Informatii Externe*," he stated with exaggerated patience. "The group you said kidnapped you yesterday."

"Oh," I said, feeling a little stupid. "But, again, how does that affect the guilds?" He wasn't going to call on my patriotism, I hoped. I liked living in the United States and not a Communist country, but I could probably live in, oh, Australia, just as easily.

"Because," Karamessines said, "if a nuclear war starts, being an adept won't save you. And even if that doesn't happen, we know how the guilds feel about necromancy and think you would want it stopped."

He had me there, on both points. Guilds banned necromancy for a reason: it was too powerful. One guild using necromancy could rule all the guilds. Vlad tried it but was killed before he was able to bring his plans to fruition. It was generally well-known that anyone who dabbled in necromancy would be killed by the other guilds. Apparently, the Transylvanians had managed to hide that they used it for these five centuries. Again, I was surprised Kader and Brunhild agreed to cover it for them.

And I didn't want to live in a world devastated by nuclear war, either. It seemed helping the U.S. was the most probable way to prevent that.

But I couldn't understand why they just couldn't have told us that in San Francisco two weeks ago.

"I'll make you a deal," Karamessines was saying. "Go to Bucharest, talk to the Chief of Station. If you don't want to help at that point, we'll fly you to San Francisco, our expense, or anywhere else you wish to go within reason."

"Okay," I said.

I think I stunned him because he was suddenly silent.

"But," I added, "I need to tell my guild leadership so they know why I'm going, and if I don't return, they can search out the necromancers."

"No!" Karamessines said strongly. "If it is revealed that we know about this, it would compromise sources and get people killed. That's why even Rhoden doesn't know: compartmentalization."

I had no idea what he meant.

"One condition," I stated.

"What's that?" he asked.

"I want to fly first-class. No tourist class."

Again he sighed. "That's not a problem."

"Thank you."

* * * *

Plans had to be changed and re-arranged, since I'd missed my TAROM flight that day. I was booked to Bucharest the next day. Apparently there was no first class available. "All Communist countries are classless societies, don't you know that?" Rhoden said sarcastically.

This time they didn't bother with the diplomatic pouch, but I still had the diplomatic passport.

That night in my hotel room I wrote a letter on hotel stationary to Brown and Vaughan. I wrote it in the ancient language, which was as good as any encryption system since only adepts would be able to read it. I told them everything I knew up to that point, and suggested if I didn't make it back, there should be a Great Guild Conclave to decide what to do about the possibility of necromancers in Romania. I knew that was unprecedented: hadn't been one since 1476 when it was decided to stop Vlad. But this was an unprecedented development.

I wanted to write a letter to Ernestine, but I didn't know the address in Coeur d'Alene. Long gone were the days you could put "Transylvanian Guild, Coeur d'Alene, Idaho" on an envelope and be assured they'd get it. Now they had "zip codes" and you had to use the correct state abbreviation. I sucked in a deep breath. I wasn't in love with Ernestine, but she was the first woman to come along in my life that seemed to like me for me, not because I was an adept or high in the guild leadership.

I slept fitfully that night, alarm and secure spells in place.

I arose early and took a taxi to the Bonn-Cologne airport. When I told the driver my airline was TAROM he gave me a look that seemed a mixture of pity and awe.

The TAROM ticket counter was small and, unlike the rest of the immaculate airport, shabby. The dark-haired and unattractive woman behind the counter didn't seem to speak English so I tried German (translation spell) and finally Romanian. She looked at me as if she didn't believe I wanted to go to Bucharest.

"You must make arrangements with *Agentia de Turism*," she snarled.

"I'm not a tourist," I countered and showed her my passport.

That changed her attitude slightly. "Embassy must pick you up at airport," she said, still sounding cross.

"They will," I said.

"Good."

The flight was late and I waited around for it to leave. Finally I went with a group of people out onto the tarmac and up to the plane. It reminded me of the plane I'd flown from Stockholm to Tromsø with two engines on the back of the fuselage under the high tail. But somehow it looked more primitive and less-well put together. The nose was pointy and there were two pods on the wings whose function I couldn't imagine. Rivets protruded from the skin everywhere, and the inside was no better. There were four seats across, with an aisle down the middle and a shelf overhead. Plus the plane was dirty, inside and out.

By luck, I ended up being one of the first people on the plane. "Sit down!" a stewardess in an unstylish blue uniform demanded. I glared at her. She would have been pretty if she didn't have such an angry look on her face. There wasn't assigned seating so I sat in the nearest seat, in the front row. I could tell this was going to be a fun trip.

The stewardess stared at me as if my very existence was an affront to her. She strode over. "You can't sit there!"

I looked up at her. "Why not?" I asked, trying to keep my voice calm.

"You can't sit there," she shrilled, louder.

I spent a moment wondering if she was worth the effort to hit her with a spell. I decided not. I stood up, moved back one row, looked at her questioningly, and when she didn't respond, sat down.

About twenty minutes after everyone else had boarded the plane, a large man in a gray suit showed up. The stewardess was very obeisant with him, taking his coat and hat, and speaking with him in a pleasant voice. He dismissed her with a wave and a grumble.

She shut the cabin door and the plane finally moved. I wondered who this man was who had the power to keep a plane waiting for him and more remarkable, make that stewardess polite.

It was only a three hour fight. I had learned a long time ago I could endure pretty much anything if I knew it was going to end.

* * * *

Seattle's Queen Anne Hill might as well have been Mars in my existence. The tall hill on the north side of Seattle, between downtown and the Ship Canal, was off-limits according to my gang's leader. I didn't know if it was because there was another gang operating there or for some other reason. But the address on the card the man gave me was on Queen Anne Hill according to the city map I'd ripped from a public telephone booth's phone book.

I took the city bus that seemed to strain to get up the steep street on the south side of the hill. It let me off near the top where there was a big high school. My education had ended when I left the group home in second grade. I had to walk a few blocks to find the address. I elicited more than a few stares. Most of the people I encountered were dressed well, and by the cars I saw I could tell this was a moneyed part of the city. The war had just ended and I thought I saw a brand new Cadillac.

The man's house faced north with a view of downtown Seattle and, if it hadn't been overcast, Mount Rainier. (Eighteen years later it would be one of the last places Francis Kader was hidden from the Houser regime.)

I stopped and looked at the house. It was made of red brick and was large even for this neighborhood. *It must have cost $20,000*, I thought. I double-checked the address to make sure I had the right residence. I almost chickened out, but decided there must be a reason the man wanted to talk to me. Oh, I'd heard of men who like young boys and would prey on the vulnerable. But this man didn't have the slimy demeanor those other men did. And besides, I could protect myself, I was sure. I may be small, but I was wiry and tough for a twelve-year-old.

I walked up the concrete walk that cut through the immaculate lawn. *Real live grass*, I thought, not the scrubby yellow tufts of it that was around the house where the gang lived. *I'd love to run barefoot through it*, I mused. Or at least I would in the spring when it would be green, not the gray tinge it took on in winter when it got plenty of rain but not enough sunshine.

I walked to the door and pressed the doorbell. Nothing happened for what seemed a long time. I was about to press it again when a younger man, maybe in his twenties, answered the door.

"Yes?" he asked, giving me a derisive look. I'd worn the best clothes I had but they weren't good enough, apparently.

I didn't know what to say or do, so I held up the card in my hands, suddenly ashamed of my chewed off and dirty fingernails. "A man gave me this. Said I should come and see him, here, at this address."

The younger man gave me a questioning look, then stated simply, "Wait," and closed the door. He took the card and I was worried I wouldn't get it back.

It was a chilly December day and I didn't have a very good overcoat. I'd stolen it off a clothesline a year ago and now it was too small for me. Rain was falling in a constant mist as it often does in Seattle's winters.

The door opened again and it was the man whose pocket I'd tried to pick.

"Oh," he said with a smile. "I'd just about given up on you."

"I was busy," I stated. It was the truth. My gang leader had never heard of a day off and since we usually worked in pairs it was impossible to shirk. I had to bribe my partner with the twenty this man had given me to let me take off and him not tell.

"Would you like to come in?" the man asked opening the door. I got a glimpse of luxury I'd never known existed outside the rare movie I saw.

"Yes," I said enthusiastically. Then I remembered to add, "Please."

He opened the door and I stepped into the warmth. Someone must have been baking because I could smell bread like in the bakeries we'd pinch lunch in, but it smelled better.

"What's your name?" the man asked as the door closed.

I looked at him. "Are you a meta?"

He smiled. "We prefer the term 'adept.' And yes, I am."

"Then I ain't gonna tell you my name."

The man nodded. "That is probably wise."

The younger man came in. He'd removed his suit jacket and I saw a gun in a shoulder holster. For a moment I worried he was a cop.

The adept just smiled again. "This is my personal warrior, Maxim," he explained.

A rather rotund woman then entered, looking harried. "Mr. Pickard, lunch is growing cold. I must insist you eat."

The adept just chuckled and winked at me. "Would you like to join me, young man?"

I could only nod. It was if I'd stepped into a movie or was awake in a dream.

"Well, I'll have to set another place," the woman said with a harried, exasperated look and scurried off.

The three of us—the adept, the warrior named Maxim, and I— walked into a dining room that was bigger than my grandparent's house, it seemed. There was dark wood wainscoting and flowered blue wallpaper and a large glass or crystal chandelier hanging from the high ceiling. A massive wood table was under the chandelier and the woman was setting a third place. The adept, Mr. Pickard apparently, indicated I should sit there.

Lunch was soup, which after being outside felt so good, and some of the bread I'd smelled baking with lots of butter. I don't know if I'd ever had butter before. It was heavenly.

Mr. Pickard looked at me. "You may be wondering why I wanted to talk to you, my boy."

I just looked at him. I was grateful for the meal but now came the payback. Everything in life had a payback, I had learned early.

"I think you could be an adept," he said. "And a good one, at that. You show natural talent. I can feel your power even as you sit there."

I had no idea what he was talking about. I did know I could sweet-talk the spots off a leopard if needed. That had saved me more than one beating or night in jail. But be an adept? That was a whole different proposal. Although looking around at the wealth this man obviously commanded, being an adept sounded like a good thing.

"Now, you're probably around thirteen," he said, then raised his hand as I was about to correct him. "First lesson, no personal information."

I nodded, almost afraid to speak then. "Most apprenticeships start between sixteen and eighteen, and rarely because you pick an adept's pocket." He again chuckled. He seemed a genuinely happy person.

Again, I couldn't think of anything to say.

He turned to Maxim. "Do you think we could put him up on a cot in your room?"

"Sir," Maxim said, shocked it seemed. "I think that would be inappropriate. I do have lady friends, you know."

"Oh, yes," Pickard said with a sigh. "I should have never installed that outdoor entrance to your room." He smiled.

He turned to me. "Did you enjoy your lunch?"

"Yes, sir," I said, trying to emulate the warrior.

"It's 'teacher,'" he said. "Come back tomorrow. I have a room you can sleep in but it will take me until tomorrow to clear out my...junk and make it acceptable for you. If, of course, you wish to become my apprentice."

I looked at him. Was it as easy as all that? I could live here in this house? I'd sleep on the floor if need be (I slept on a thin, dirty mattress back at the gang's hideout). I could eat food like this and learn to be an adept and not have to be afraid anymore and be happy like this man.

But, I suddenly wondered, what was in it for him? "Why you doin' this?" I asked.

He looked at me as if the question surprised him. "Bringing in and training a new, powerful adept will increase the power and prestige of my guild and my position in it. And it will be nice to have someone to talk to besides Mrs. White and Maxim. You could live here, with me, until you are old enough to start your apprenticeship in a few years. In the meantime I'll teach you to read and other things you'll need to know."

I sat up straight. "I can read!" I said with perhaps too much pride. And I could. "It's just that I don't know some of those five-dollar words."

The adept smiled at me again. "Of course, and I can help you with that. I'm a born teacher, but I don't suffer fools gladly. Don't worry, son, you're safe, now."

I nodded, wanting to believe him. "Okay, I'll come back tomorrow," I said. It was only one more night in the hideout, in the gang. And if anyone could protect me from the gang, this man could.

I reluctantly left just as the mist turned into a cold winter rain outside. Maxim walked me to the door. He grabbed my collar as I tried to step outside. "You like it here, boy?" he asked.

I nodded, suddenly frightened. Maybe he wasn't a cop but he acted like one.

"You steal from Mr. Pickard and you'll be back on the streets, understand?"

I nodded again. I had no intention of blowing this deal by doing something that stupid.

"Good," Maxim growled and let go of my collar. I stepped outside into the rain.

I had to wait for a bus to take me back downtown to find my partner tarrying in a candy shop. No idea how much candy he managed to steal.

We returned to the hideout. It would have been better if I'd spent the night on the streets like I did before I fell in with the gang. I'm not sure why I didn't. Force of habit, maybe. My partner squealed when my gang leader wondered why we had no money.

"Where did you go?" he demanded of me. He was an adult and at least a foot taller than I.

I didn't reply.

The beating and the cigarette burns lasted only an hour or so. But I knew it would end and the next day I'd be with the adept, and if I didn't fail at that—and I'd make damn sure I wouldn't—I'd never have to take another beating in my life.

Chapter Seven

Bucharest, Romania
April 17, 1968

The flight was long and miserable, but the man in the gray suit got impeccable service, better service than anyone else got. In fact, he got the only service anyone received. The stewardess didn't even seem to mind when he put his meaty hand on her butt and moved it up and down. My master, Mr. Pickard, taught me better than that. Even lesser women deserved respect. I was very tempted to play a trick on what was obviously a government or airline official, maybe big hairy spiders coming out of his seat. But I didn't want to reveal that I was an adept.

The plane finally landed on a rough runway outside a smoggy, gray city. The airport looked as if it had been built after the war and then never touched again. Getting off the plane, stepping onto the stairs to go down to the tarmac, I was shocked to see what even I recognized as machine guns and bigger weapons surrounding the airport. The tarmac, rather than being one smooth piece, seemed to be squares of concrete joined together. There were weeds growing through the joints between the slabs.

The interior of the airport terminal was dim because most of the lights were off. I didn't know if the bulbs were burned out or they were turned off to save electricity...or both. Immigration personnel were invariably rude except to the man in the gray suit. A thin young man in a uniform glanced at my passport, looked at me, and spent a moment looking at my eyes. Then he stamped the back of my passport and waved me through without a word. I got my luggage from a pile of bags and headed for the way out, demarked by faded signs.

Near the exit to the street a young man in a dark suit, white shirt, narrow tie, and with a short haircut was holding a sign saying "RICHARD JACKSON."

"I'm Jackson," I said. He had dark eyes hidden behind wire-framed glasses.

"Hi, Clayton Wynter, U.S. Embassy. I have a car waiting."

"Great!" I said, trying to sound enthusiastic, and followed him out, noting he didn't even offer to help with my bag.

The car was an older American sedan. It was black but had a few dents in the sheet metal; I wasn't sure if it pre-dated the war. The engine was running and a man was sitting behind the steering wheel.

Wynter said, "We can't talk in the car...the driver is a local and probably reports everything we say to the *Securitate*." Without explaining what that was, he got in the back seat and left it up to me to put my bag in the trunk, then I, too, sat in the back, and the driver piloted the car away and onto the empty roads. Most airports are surrounded by vehicles: cars, taxis, and buses. All I saw this time was one dilapidated old bus that looked as if it hadn't been cleaned in its entire existence.

"You'll like it here," Wynter said. "Not a lot happens in Romania."

I thought we weren't supposed to talk in the car so I just nodded. Maybe he was trying to make the driver think the CIA didn't do much, or that we weren't CIA...or whatever. I was having trouble caring.

I looked out the window of the car at the dreary-looking city. I'd never been behind the Iron Curtain before. Like the airport, it seemed everything had been built after the war and never touched again. Sidewalks were crumbling, as were the facades on buildings. The streets were lined with huge, multi-story apartment buildings that were rectangular in all dimensions. It looked like a miserable way to live unless you lived on one of the upper floors. That was assuming there were elevators. Everything I'd heard about Communist countries made me think that perhaps there weren't, or if there were, they rarely worked.

The one thing that looked fresh and new were the propaganda signs that seem to be put up every couple of blocks; heroic pictures—art, not photographs—of a man I assumed was Ceausescu. There was stylized art of men working in factories, women with babies, or soldiers looking off toward any threat. Red was the predominant color of these signs. I didn't bother to bring up a translation spell to read them; what they said was pretty obvious.

Despite the cold, children were playing in front of many of the buildings on rusty playground equipment that had been placed on ground that was barren or sported a tuft of brown grass here and there. The children looked a bit on the thin side, and their clothes appeared to be old and often ill-fitting. I wondered if they got a lot of hand-me-downs like we had at the orphanage.

Wynter must have noticed where I was looking. "Ceausescu is a bit of a maverick," he said. "He's almost dropped out of the Warsaw Pact and has openly traded with the West. Still, for the locals, there's not a lot of food, clothes, or consumer goods unless you have hard currency to use on the black market."

I remembered my contact at the Purple Chrysanthemum saying the Cubans sold drugs to get "hard currency."

"What the heck is hard currency?" I asked, forgetting we weren't supposed to talk with the driver present.

Wynter studied my face, perhaps to ascertain if I were serious. "Usually that means American dollars," he said. "Or British pounds, West German deutsche marks. Pretty much anything that's not the worthless stuff the Communists print up."

I nodded and assumed this was common knowledge and not a secret.

"Ceausescu, for a Communist leader, has fairly good popular support. However, his Decree 770 has reduced that some."

"What's that?" I asked despite myself.

"He has restricted access to birth control and abortion to women who've already had at least four children and are over the age of forty-five."

I turned and looked at Wynter to see if he were serious. "Why would he do that?" I asked incredulously.

"He's worried about the aging population and not enough replacement children being born."

I shook my head. Why would someone wish to control people to that extent? Maybe it was a good thing I was going to help the U.S. contain Communism. My own feelings on abortion were that if it were readily available when I was conceived, I probably would never have been born, which made me a little more than squeamish about the whole deal.

Watching the town slide by the car window, I was also struck by how few cars there were. None were on the street and none were parked anywhere. One black car careened down the boulevard seeming oblivious to physics and safety, honking its horn as it raced by us.

"Must be some official," Wynter said, seeing my astonished face. "No one else can afford Russian cars."

The U.S. Embassy in Bucharest was a lot smaller than the one in Bonn. It was behind high walls with only one gate that slid open as the car pulled up. There were two uniformed and armed men guarding the entrance. They were wearing the same uniforms I'd seen in Bonn, with the dark blue jacket and pants and a red stripe going down the pant leg, except the younger one didn't have the stripe. That seemed strange to me. I thought uniforms were supposed to be, well, uniform.

The older one waved the car into a small courtyard before the main building. It almost looked like a smaller, albeit cleaner and better maintained version of the apartment blocks we'd seen.

The foyer was smaller than and not as nice as in Bonn. Since I was on a diplomatic passport I didn't need a visitor's badge, apparently. I also learned there were apartments in the Embassy for personnel, such as the ambassador's residence and rooms for visiting dignitaries. I was given what I assume was the smallest one of those where I unpacked a bit and freshened up from my three-hour TAROM flight ordeal and then called a number that Wynter had given me on the room's phone. He came up and escorted me to the CIA section. Like in Bonn it was in the basement, and like in Bonn there was a guarded door with a keypad for typing in a code for entry.

The room was almost as big as the one in Bonn. I found out later that was because in West Germany, most of the CIA operatives are connected to the military and not the embassy. In Romania, the entire "station" was located at the embassy.

Wynter took me to the office of the Chief of Station, a man Wynter told me was named Phillip Sorensen.

Sorensen looked at me through thick, dark-rimmed glasses. He was wearing the CIA uniform, as I came to think of it: white shirt, narrow dark tie, and no suit jacket, although I could see one hanging from a hook on a coat tree in the corner. His office was a slightly smaller version of Rhoden's. He'd turned off the overhead fluorescents and had a couple of strategically placed lamps on instead. It gave the room a shadowy and dark look.

"You're Jackson?" he asked, looking exasperated.

"Yes," I said, sitting down in one of the two chairs before the desk.

"Close the door on your way out, Wynter," Sorensen said, looking at the younger man.

"Yes, sir," Wynter replied, almost but not quite keeping the disappointment out of his voice as he walked out.

Sorensen again peered at me. I noticed his close-cropped hair was starting to thin and gray. He seemed older than Rhoden yet I assumed this was a less important assignment.

"What do you know about Vlad the Impaler?" he asked, interrupting my thoughts.

I told him everything that was common knowledge about Vlad III Dracul. I left out what Kader had told me.

When I finished Sorensen shook his head. "And the guilds killed him because he was a necromancer, correct?"

"Yes," I said. No use in denying it. "Necromancy is, to the guilds, sort of like nuclear weapons. It's too powerful to allow it to be in one man's hands, or any one guild." I didn't tell him that some adept/priests in Central America practiced it in pre-Columbian times, but they were isolated enough that the European guilds let them be. "So either all guilds would have to practice it, something we find repulsive, or no guilds," I continued. "For three thousand years anyone who used necromancy was killed by the other guilds. Vlad was the last to try." He didn't need to know about the current Transylvanians. In fact, I may have said too much.

"Apparently until now," Sorensen said.

"Yes," I agreed. "I've been twice attacked now by adepts I can only assume are necromancers. I was also kidnapped by the Romanian intelligence service in Bonn."

"Yes," Sorensen said, "Rhoden informed me. We debated aborting your mission since you've been compromised. But we're hoping your...talents will let you complete it."

I hoped so, too. "So what is it you want from me?" I asked. "Karamessines said you'd have the final information I needed, something about 'compartmentalization.'"

Sorensen pulled a thin file from out of a locking filing cabinet (with a magnetic sign stating "OPEN") and opened it on his desk. "This reveals methods and sources; I can't let you see it."

I tried very hard not to roll my eyes, but this secrecy made me wonder how these people ever managed to accomplish anything.

"There's a city not far from Vlad's old citadel—"

"Poenari Castle?" I interrupted.

Sorensen appeared slightly surprised I knew that name. "Yes, Poenari Castle. The city is called Pitesti. We believe the necromancers are operating there."

That's where the ball bearing factory was supposed to have been. "Where?"

"Pitesti," Sorensen repeated.

I shook my head. "No, where in Pitesti?"

"That we don't know. But it's not a very large city."

I nodded. If I went there I could probably feel them. Unfortunately, they would probably feel my presence, too.

"We think Vlad wrote something called the *Book of Death* detailing his necromancer spells," Sorensen was saying. "And somehow it's turned up after five hundred years."

I didn't say anything about there maybe being more than one. "So essentially you want me to find the necromancers and stop them from doing whatever it is they are doing?"

"Only," Sorensen stated, "if what they are doing threatens U.S. national security. But we have reason to believe they are working with the DIE to do just that."

"By using necromancy to learn military secrets?"

"Yes, both ours and our NATO allies. Then they are probably sharing this with other Warsaw Pact countries, including the Soviet Union."

"And if they aren't doing anything to threaten 'national security,' then what?"

"They are the meta guilds' problem, then," Sorensen said. "We don't care. But our intelligence says otherwise."

I nodded, thinking. "Guilds working with governments is not unheard of," I stated. "Or individual adepts." It never seemed to work out well, starting with Merlin and King Arthur. "But usually," I continued, "it is a strategic move to somehow gain power over other guilds. I don't see how working with the DIE helps the necromancers. Everything I've heard and learned about them indicates they are strong enough on their own to take over the guilds."

Sorensen just looked at me. "All I can tell you is that's what our intelligence says."

"What's the source of that intelligence?"

"I can't tell you," he stated simply.

I let out an exasperated sigh. "Fine. But here's my problem: if there are necromancers, even one, in this city…what's its name?"

"Pitesti," Sorensen filled in for me.

"Then I probably cannot defeat them myself. I will need to bring in more and stronger adepts, depending on how many of them there are." The guilds would want to clean out this infestation as quickly and as thoroughly as possible.

"How long will that take?" Sorensen asked with trepidation.

"The guilds will move quickly. This is one thing they don't fight about." There hadn't been a Great Conclave of the Guilds since 1476, but there hadn't been a necromancer threat since then, either. For almost five hundred years necromancy had been the quiet reserve of a few Transylvanians while the other guilds thought it was extinct.

"There's one thing I'm confused about, though," I said.

"What's that?" Sorensen asked, looking at me through his glasses that made his blue eyes seem preternaturally large.

"I was told that Romania was sort of in the dog house with the rest of the Communist nations because it maintains relations with West Germany and Israel. Why would they be trying to get NATO secrets for the Warsaw Pact?"

Sorensen chuckled. "Don't believe everything you read in the *New York Times*."

I didn't know why he said that, but he continued speaking.

"Ceausescu uses those relationships to bring in hard currency or other goods. He gives exit visas to Jews or ethnic Germans in exchange for cash or, at least in one case, a farm."

"So," I speculated, "he's playing both sides?"

"To an extent. Ceausescu is always trying to increase his prestige among Warsaw Pact nations and the West. This scheme is right up his alley. He can get secrets from NATO and then trade them to the Sovs or other Communist nations for more prestige."

I remembered that "Sov" meant the Soviets.

"He must be very happy about what's happening in Czechoslovakia right now," Sorensen concluded.

I frowned. "Why? What is happening in Czechoslovakia?"

"About two weeks ago the Czechoslovak Socialist Republic government announced an '*Action Programme*' of reforms and made moves to disassociate itself from the Soviet Union and the Warsaw Pact."

"How does that affect Romania?" I asked. I wasn't quite following all of this and was finding I wished I paid more attention to lesser politics.

"It has to take some pressure off of Ceausescu and his own independence streak."

I shook my head. I didn't see how that mattered.

"There's one other thing," Sorensen said closing the file.

"Yes?"

"We received a telegram from San Francisco. Your guild leader, Brown, would like you to contact him right away."

I tried to hide my surprise. "Did it say why?"

"No," he said as if that were a stupid question. And I guess it was. Guild matters were guild matters and not for lesser eyes. "Be aware that, unless encrypted, every phone line or other electronic communication out of the embassy is most likely tapped and monitored by the DIE."

"I wasn't planning on using the phone," I said with a smile.

He looked at me questioningly but I refused to explain further.

* * * *

I returned to my apartment and made sure the door was locked. It was a small room, more like a hotel room than an apartment. There was a television in the corner on a metal stand. I turned it on out of curiosity and it was showing programs from the Armed Services Network. The quality was low both in production values and the picture. Another channel seemed to be the official Romanian state television station. It was in black and white. And those were the choices. I was glad I wasn't interested in looking at the television.

It was late afternoon in Bucharest but I had no idea what time it was in San Francisco. We had gone over another time zone from Bonn. I'd never realized that time zones were such a bother having lived most of my life in only one. I guessed it was probably early morning for Brown.

It would have helped if I'd had an object of his but I didn't. The far-seeing spell needed to be powerful to reach half-way across the world. I saw Brown. He was seated at a table in what I assumed was his suite in the Huntington eating what looked like breakfast. I could see his warrior standing quietly behind him. The sight was fuzzy and wavy, like the Armed Forces Network looked on the television.

Brown looked up and I was sure he saw me because he said, "Branton."

"Yes, Teacher," I confirmed.

He reached into his pocket and must have touched his talisman, and the scene became vividly clear, as if I were in the room with him, not two continents and an ocean away. His breakfast smelled good.

"Branton," Brown said. "We don't know if this is important but we have information."

"Yes, Teacher?"

"Ernestine Vojir has disappeared."

I looked at Brown for a second. "You mean she's missing?"

"Yes. Anica called. Shortly after you left she simply vanished in the night from Anica's house. Anica's guard that was on duty said he saw nothing. The Transylvanians can't use invisibility, so we don't know how she got out without being seen."

I didn't say anything. I was surprised and worried.

"It may not mean anything," Brown said. "Or it may mean something. We have no idea what."

And neither did I.

I told Brown everything I knew up to that point, some of which was in the letter I'd sent.

"This sounds dangerous, Student," he finally said.

"Yes, Teacher," I replied, not knowing what else to say.

"If you find a clan of necromancers, perhaps you should come home and we'll try to convene a Great Conclave to deal with them."

"My only worry is," I said, "that this may need to be dealt with quickly. If they are stealing secrets from the U.S. and its allies, then a nuclear war could result."

Brown sighed and frustration was etched across his face. "Get as much information as you can then contact me," he ordered.

"Then we can decide on a course. Saving the guilds is the primary concern."

"But that may require saving the United States," I stated.

"Yes, but it may not."

Having no more to report, I broke the spell and leaned back in my chair and rested. It was a difficult spell and the further you did far-seeing the more difficult it was due to the inverse square law. Double the distance and you quadruple the effort needed.

The news about Ernestine was disturbing. What had she been doing in my room at the Huntington that required her to shower and open all the windows? Was she practicing necromancy, perhaps on an animal? And to what end? And where was she when the wooden Indian attacked me? Was she causing that attack? If she were a necromancer, and in league with the Romanian clan, that would explain a lot. Maybe the CIA didn't have a leak, but the Transylvanians did.

And my personal feelings for her were wrapped up in this whole thing. I thought I'd found an adept I could fall for and who would love me, not for my power but for me. I sighed sadly and hoped I was wrong and there was some logical explanation for her disappearance, but I doubted it.

Maybe I'd find answers in Pitesti.

* * * *

The next morning I went and saw Sorensen again. He looked at me questioningly as I plopped into one of his office chairs.

"How do I get to Pitesti?" I asked.

He smiled grimly. "There's four ways," he said in a manner indicating I wouldn't like any of them.

"Yes?" I asked prodding.

He counted them off on his fingers as he talked. "You can drive. The roads aren't very good, and even though it's only about one hundred twenty kilometers, the trip will take two or three hours depending on construction delays."

"Construction?"

"Yes, the Romanians are building a highway to Pitesti; supposed to be as good as an autobahn or an interstate highway."

"How far is one hundred twenty kilometers?" I asked.

"About seventy five miles," he responded.

That sounded miserable, I decided. Plus, I couldn't drive and I didn't know how willing Sorensen would be to loan me a car and driver. "What else?"

"There's the bus," he stated opening another finger and touching it with his other hand. "Overcrowded, slow, and this time of year, cold."

This was starting to sound as if there were no good choices. "What else?"

Another finger. "TAROM on an old, creaky An-24 turboprop. But it only takes about an hour, assuming the plane runs on time…and doesn't break down. And nothing in Romania runs on time."

"And the fourth?"

Last finger. "The train, but would still be crowded, dirty, and slow since it would stop at every village between here and there. Of course, so would the bus," he added.

I shook my head. "When I'm in Pitesti I may need to make a hasty, unscheduled departure," I said, hoping he'd agree I needed a car. Actually, I didn't need a car to make a hasty departure, nor to get there, really. But I wanted to keep my use of meta to a minimum in case I ran into a clan of necromancers.

"Then you should drive," he stated. "But 'hasty' is not something I'd recommend on Romanian roads."

"I don't drive," I stated.

Sorensen looked at me a moment to determine if I was serious. I just looked back trying to look serious. It was true. My master didn't drive but had Maxim chauffeur him everywhere. He said driving was "beneath" adepts, like using guns. Besides, I had too much reading and studying to do to waste time learning to drive, he'd say with a wink. I really did love that old man.

However, I was ready to use a persuasion spell on Sorensen if need be.

"Lucky for you," Sorensen grumbled, "Karamessines told me to cooperate with you fully."

I smiled. "You know those armed guards I see everywhere?"

"You mean the marines?"

"I guess. Could you supply me one of those, preferably well-armed but in civilian clothes?"

Sorensen shook his head with a chuckle. "Sorry, no. They are under the ambassador's command."

"Then how about one of your CIA hot-shot spies?"

Sorensen shook his head. "You've been watching too many movies. Most of these guys are analysts. Any field people I have are NOC."

"Knock?"

"Non-Official Cover. Basically means they are on their own. I only hear from them at regularly scheduled intervals to ensure they are still alive. They are all tied up with their own operations."

"Just not a Romanian," I asked, trying not to sound whiny. Maybe I could use a persuasion spell to get a marine or a "NOC," but that sounded like it would take time, and I needed answers fast.

"I have just the person for you," Sorensen said with a mischievous smile.

* * * *

Unfortunately, one couldn't just hop in a car and drive to a city seventy-five miles away. Maybe Romanians could but not foreigners. The Romanian government had to be informed and permission obtained. I wasn't too happy about informing the Romanian government that I was traveling to Pitesti. But since I was officially a diplomat, an excuse had already been fabricated for me to go there. Apparently I was to study the puppet theater at the County Theater for its cultural significance, and to determine if the performers could travel to the U.S. in a "cultural exchange." Sorensen said Ceausescu would like that because he was always trying to ingratiate himself with the West. I asked, "Ceausescu's going to approve this?" and Sorensen said, "He might. In any case, his underlings know his agenda."

Since there was a weekend, it had taken me until Tuesday to get approval. Wednesday morning, a week after arriving in Bucharest, Sorensen handed me a packet of documentation authorizing the trip by the Romanian government. "They weren't happy about you going by car," he explained. "They'd much rather you take TAROM or the train so they could make some money off of rich capitalists like us and keep an eye on you. Your driver has a specific route to follow, and you shall not deviate from it. You will be staying at the *Agentia de Turism* hotel in Pitesti. *Agentia de Turism* hotels aren't bad, but assume your room and every table in the restaurant is bugged. Assume all forms of communication are monitored. If you need to talk in private, use the car."

I nodded and took the thick packet. It was written in Romanian but I didn't bother to run a translation spell.

"One of the tricks of the DIE is to film foreign dignitaries in...shall we say 'compromising positions.' Don't let anyone else in your room."

I wondered if he meant what I thought he meant.

"Don't forget your passport," Sorensen continued. "If you get into trouble with the local authorities, that will give you immunity. Worst they'll do is kick you out of the country. So don't lose it. And for God's sake, don't give it to anyone."

"I won't." I wasn't too worried. Even if I lost the passport I was sure I could escape the authorities and the country, unless they knew I was an adept. "By the way, who's my driver?"

"Wynter," Sorensen said. "Only guy I could spare."

* * * *

The road to Pitesti was little more than cracked asphalt and concrete. We ran into what seemed to be an over-manned construction crew using shovels and wheelbarrows to move dirt around. Wynter had to snake the car—a decades-old brown Ford sedan the Embassy apparently owned—through the men who were sort of working.

"The Romanians have a saying," Wynter grumbled as we passed the work party. "'They pretend to pay us, we pretend to work.'"

I shrugged. It seemed very inefficient. Maybe the Ceausescu regime couldn't afford heavy equipment, but one man on a bulldozer could probably do the work that gang of fifty was attempting to do with shovels, and do it faster.

After passing the working men, we continued to slowly drive northwest. The land was flat and mostly farmland, it seemed. This time of year there was planting going on, and I was amazed to see it done by hand and horse-drawn plows. No wonder the children looked thin. Wynter was busy dodging holes in the pavement and didn't seem interested in talking, so I just watched the scenery go by.

Ours was the only car on the road but there was the occasional bus that looked as if they were one pothole from complete collapse and stuffed with humanity to the point the body was resting on the axles. I was glad I decided to go by car.

Pitesti revealed itself as a dark stain against the blue sky long before we got to the city. Wynter explained it was an industrial town and the air pollution was horrific. They built cars there, apparently. I had no idea what happened to them since I'd seen almost zero civilian cars. I had seen horses pulling wagons with car tires rather than wagon wheels, which seemed absurd.

As we got closer to Pitesti, the terrain became hilly and I could see mountains in the distance. I'd heard Transylvania was mountainous, but the mountains looked more like foothills compared to the Sierra Nevada or the Cascades.

I started to mask before we reached the outskirts of the city. I didn't want the necromancers feeling my presence, ever, if I could help it. I wondered about what they did to that berserker in Tromsø. I hoped that the reason they hadn't done that to Liesl or me was that they could only do it to lessers.

I was also somewhat thankful that I'd been kidnapped in Bonn. Had I been coming here thinking I was going to be looking for a ball bearing plant, I wouldn't have bothered to mask and the necromancers would have probably been on me the moment I hit town.

Pitesti, too, was dominated by large concrete apartment buildings. As you looked through the air, it seemed to be almost brown. The smell, sort of an oily mix of burning fuels and chemicals, was shocking at first but then you got used to it, until you smelled it on your clothes. There were propaganda signs, too, but their red color seemed dirty, as if the air was staining them.

It was near dark when we finally got to the *Agentia de Turism* hotel, which was near the center of the city. This was an old and almost picturesque part of town. Wynter had a map, but the streets in this vicinity were narrow and seemed to meander, and it took a while before we finally found the hotel. The street was growing dark and there were no streetlights. Passersby looked at us as if we'd shown up in a flying saucer. Like Bucharest, Pitesti was almost devoid of cars.

Wynter stopped the car on the street in front of the hotel. The road was narrow cobblestone and the buildings looked and felt old.

Inside the hotel was like stepping into another world. In some ways it was nicer than the Huntington or the Hilton in Bonn. The floor was marble, there was a chandelier hanging from the high lobby ceiling, and the check-in desk looked to be a dark expensive wood with a marble top. But everything seemed haphazard, as if it were put together by the men with the shovels and the wheelbarrows we'd passed on the way. There were large gaps in the marble where the slabs met, and I would have sworn the check-in desk was sloped slightly to the left.

Wynter checked us in; all I had to do was show my diplomatic passport. The desk clerk spoke passable English, but when Wynter asked what to do with the car, she became confused. She said repeatedly that he couldn't park it on the street, but refused to say where he could park it. Maybe we were the first to show up with our own car.

Frustrated, Wynter walked over to me. "I can't leave the car on the street. Someone will probably steal the tires, wheels, windshield wipers, or whatever they can. But there doesn't seem to be a different place to park it, either. Also, she said the *Militia* would probably tow it."

I shook my head. I assumed the *Militia* was the police. But unless I used meta and risked revealing myself to the necromancers, I was as helpless as he.

"And if something happens to that car, Sorensen will have my head!" Wynter exclaimed, with all the frustration I was sure he felt.

"Is there an American consulate?" I asked, thinking he could park the car there and take a taxi back.

He shook his head. "Only the embassy in Bucharest."

I thought a moment. "Do you have money?"

"Yes, of course."

"American money?"

"Yes, some."

I thought maybe some "hard currency" might work.

"Give it to me."

Wynter gave me an exasperated look and pulled out his wallet, then pulled greenbacks from it. I quickly counted it. It was about $200.

"That's the...." He hesitated. "That's our employer's money."

"Don't worry," I said. Apparently he didn't want to say "CIA" here.

I walked to the clerk, who was a younger woman with dark hair to her shoulders and angry dark eyes. She wore a blue uniform-looking dress that looked new but ten years out of style. It was cut almost the same as the uniform the stewardess wore on the TAROM flight.

"Excuse me?" I asked.

"Yes?" she asked, seeming exasperated.

"Is there an auto repair shop or gas station nearby?"

She looked at me as if she were debating answering. "Yes, my uncle Nae runs a gas station."

"Wonderful," I stated. "Would he keep our car safe for, say, one hundred American dollars?"

Her eyes grew wide and the anger in them seemed to evaporate. What I didn't realize was I'd just offered her uncle a fortune. "He'd be closed, now."

"Can you call him?"

"He doesn't have a phone."

I held up the money and her eyes grew very wide. "Can't you find a way?"

I'd learned when I was a petty thief in Seattle that money was a great motivator; almost as good as a persuasion spell. She had a relative who did have a phone, and they went and got the uncle at his apartment. The uncle met us at his garage, and I gave him $50 up front, promising the other $50 when we got the car back safely at the end of our visit. Then, because there were no taxies, we walked back to the hotel in the darkness. Apparently street lights were something the glorious Romanian Communist leadership didn't feel was worth the expense.

Wynter seemed unhappy with me, maybe because I'd solved a problem he thought was insurmountable, or maybe because I'd spent $100 of CIA money. I didn't care, and after we ate a pretty silent—we assumed the table was bugged—but decent meal in the restaurant, I returned to my room. Like the rest of the hotel, it was like someone had hurried to make it luxurious, but as quickly as possible. I noted the toilet paper was pinkish and felt like crepe paper that Americans use to decorate for birthday parties.

I had to think about how to find the necromancers. A group of adepts, especially powerful ones, would be easy to find if I wasn't masking. I would be able to feel them from quite a distance. I could stop masking, but then they'd probably find me, and I didn't want that. The image of the berserker exploding kept playing in my mind's eye. *If they could do that to an adept*, I kept thinking with my stomach twisting in knots. But if they could do that to me, why didn't they?

I wanted to put an alarm spell on the room's doors and windows, but again, couldn't. I slept fitfully in the lumpy bed.

Chapter Eight

Pitesti, Romania
April 25, 1968

The next morning I was awakened by Wynter pounding on my room door. You couldn't even leave a wakeup call at this "luxury" hotel because there were no phones in the rooms. Wynter said he had a travel alarm clock.

After getting ready, I met Wynter for breakfast. As we sat I asked, "Is there a museum in this city?"

He looked at the table as if to remind me it was probably bugged, and then looked at me. "I don't know; I've never been here. But we need to go to the Davila Theater today. They will have the puppets ready for you."

I looked at him, and then remembered our cover story. "Yes," I said, perhaps a little too forcefully. "But I would like to visit a museum, if there is one."

"I'll check at the front desk," Wynter said.

The food in the *Agentia de Turism* hotel was basic but fairly good. I wondered about the thin children I'd seen in Bucharest.

At the front desk we were informed that we needed to exchange $30 per day for the local currency, the lei, at the official government exchange rate. Wynter said this was tantamount to buying worthless paper for $30, and another way the regime got "hard currency." Since we only had about $100 left, that meant we either had only three days to stay, or we had to get more American money. Wynter was paying for the hotel rooms out of his cache of Romanian leis.

"Don't worry," I said. "We won't be here that long." Within three days I would have found the necromancers, or they would have found me. I couldn't mask all day for three days straight.

We were informed that there was a museum to the glorious Communist Revolution and the brilliant leadership of Nicolae Ceausescu. I didn't think that would meet my needs so we left to get the car.

We walked back to the gas station and Uncle Nae smiled and pointed to the unmolested vehicle. We got the keys from him and got in while he acted as if he wanted more money. Neither Wynter nor I spoke Romanian, so we just kept shaking our heads and saying "No" over and over. I was still masking, so I couldn't use a translation spell or a persuasion spell. I felt as if I was missing a leg.

In the daylight I could see what a dilapidated place the gas station was. It was dirty and there were two gas pumps that were not being used, probably because there were so few cars. The price of gas was displayed but in lei. I asked Wynter if he know how much it was in dollars. "About two dollars, I think."

"For a gallon of gas?" I exclaimed. Even I knew that gas in the U.S. was something like thirty cents a gallon.

"It's worse," he said. "That's per liter, and there's about four liters in a gallon."

That meant gas was eight dollars a gallon. No wonder no one had cars.

Wynter and I got in the car and the smell immediately hit us.

"What the hell is that?" I asked.

"Uncle Nae," Wynter growled. "Soap, shampoo, and deodorant are almost impossible for the regular citizen to purchase."

"I guess he really did sleep in the car," I mused, rolling down the window. Even the polluted air was better.

"Where do you want to go?" Wynter asked. "They are expecting us at the theater."

I shook my head. "And if we don't go?"

"It will blow our cover."

I sighed.

"Just show up, watch a puppet show, make some positive noises about talking to the ambassador about a good will tour, and then we can get on with whatever it is you need to do." Wynter stared at me and I gazed back.

"Okay," I said. "I assume you can find the theater."

"I have maps."

"Good." I sat back in the vinyl car seat and looked out the window. "Let's go."

Pitesti was a smaller, dirtier version of Bucharest. Again, there were no other cars on the road. I saw one parked in front of an apartment building with the wheels and the windshield wipers missing.

"Stripped?" I asked Wynter.

"No," he said shaking his head. "The owners remove anything that can be stolen and keep them, probably in their apartment."

I shook my head. *What a way to live*, I thought, remembering the rows of cars parked along the streets of San Francisco. I didn't see any children, but Wynter assured me that was because they were in school this time of day.

"We do have a tail," Wynter said, looking in the Ford's rear-view mirror.

"Oh?"

"Black Russian Zil has been following us since Uncle Nae's. They're trying to be subtle but there aren't any other cars on the road."

I turned to look. A big black sedan was a couple of blocks back. The styling looked early '50s American. "Who could they be?" I asked. I guessed "Zil" was a Russian car brand like "Ford."

"I'm sure they are *Securitate*. They always tail diplomats."

"What is the *Securitate*?" I asked. He'd said the driver that picked us up at the airport was *Securitate*, too.

"Romania's internal security forces," Wynter explained.

I decided in that case I didn't need to worry about them. The local paranoid security forces were not a concern.

The County Theater, named the Davila Theater for some local poet or something, looked as if it had been built a hundred or so years ago and, like everything else in this country, never maintained. It was in the historical and almost charming old part of the city. The front entrance was impressively ornate, or would have been if it had a coat of paint. We walked in to what I assumed was the lobby, although it was rather small and the red carpet was getting threadbare. The room was dominated by four full suits of armor against the far wall. Each one was carrying a menacing-looking medieval weapon such as a flail, long sword, or battle axe.

Wynter pointed to the flail, basically an iron ball about the size of a cantaloupe with iron spikes protruding from it. It was connected to a chain that led to a wooden handle. The handle was in the hand of one of the suits. "Wouldn't want to get hit with that!" he said jokingly.

I nodded my agreement, still pondering the incongruous display.

A small man in an ill-fitting gray suit scurried out of a side room, nervously brushing his fingers through his thick shock of white hair. "You must be Richard Jackson from the American Embassy," he said in accented English. It made him sound a lot like Peter Lorre in the *Maltese Falcon*. Even though he was dressed marginally well, I picked up a whiff of his body odor. I didn't know how I could live without the adequate personal hygiene that I learned from my master.

"Yes," I replied, taking the man's proffered hand and shaking it. He had a weak grip. It seemed he spent a moment looking into my eyes as if there were something wrong with them.

I released his hand and he introduced himself as "Doctor Hobai," the director of the theater.

I gestured at the armor. "That's quite an impressive collection."

The man smiled but it seemed an unhappy smile. "Yes, they are on loan from the *Germanisches Nationalmuseum* in the

Democratic Republic of Germany. One of the finest examples of Maximilian armour extant. Priceless artifacts, really. Comrade Ceausescu is very generous in ensuring the people of Romania have the finest cultural exchanges from around the world."

I glanced at the suits of armor. They seemed quite out of place in the small theater, but what did I know? Or maybe some bureaucratic snafu sent them here rather than a more appropriate place such as a museum.

"We are ready for you, Mr. Jackson," Hobai said, and indicated we should follow him. We walked past the armor and through a thick velvet curtain with a slit in the middle into the theater. There were rows and rows of empty seats and two aisles running down through them, making three sections of seats. On the small stage was what almost looked like a diorama. I realized this was the puppet stage.

We took a seat in the second row, middle section, and the show was started. The puppets were the type that were on strings. Puppeteers did both the voices and the puppets movements.

"We removed part of the puppet theater that normally hides the puppeteers so you could see their skill and dexterity," Hobai explained, seating himself between Wynter and me.

Unfortunately, the puppet show was all in Romanian so I had to guess what was going on, but it seemed to be a comedy. The villain was a fat, Germanic looking puppet (big blue eyes, blond hair) who chased the raven-haired heroine until the equally dark-haired hero stopped him.

I was wondering how long this was going to go on when I heard a woman scream and realized it was one of the puppeteers. She was pointing at the back of the theater. I turned around to see two suits of armor lumbering through the two doors at the back, ripping the velvet curtains with their extended weapons. The one to the right was brandishing the long sword and the one to the left held a battle axe that looked as if it could take off one's head.

I turned to Hobai, who was watching the suits of armor with his mouth agape as if he wanted to scream but couldn't. "Is there a back way out of here?"

He started jabbering in Romanian. I decided there was no need for me to mask any longer; the necromancers had obviously found me. I wrapped my fingers around my talisman, a feeling I had missed, and called up a translation spell.

"…back door behind the stage," he managed to say before he stared babbling incoherently.

Wynter, too, was just watching in amazement as the empty suits of armor, clanking with metal rubbing and bumping, lumbered down the aisles between the rows of seats.

"Wynter," I said, "back door, behind the stage. Let's go."

I half expected Wynter to pull out a gun and start shooting, but apparently he was unarmed or didn't think of it, because he bounded over the first row of seats and sprinted for the stage.

I followed; the suits of armor were not close enough to be any kind of threat, yet. Wynter jumped onto the stage, his shoes making a booming sound as they hit the wooden planks. I grabbed the edge and swung up next to the puppet stage. Most of the puppeteers were just staring agog at the armor, but a few wiser ones were running from the stage. I assumed they knew the way out so I followed. Wynter must have had the same idea as he was right in front of me.

The woman who had initially screamed did so again and jumped out of the way as a third suit of armor came in the back door, swinging its flail over its head. Wynter couldn't stop in time and the ball hit him right in the temple with a sick, moist crunching sound. Blood jetted in all directions from the impact, hitting me in the face and chest. Wynter made a sound of anguish that I hoped I never heard again as he was knocked against a wall, his skull caved in, and I didn't want to imagine what was gushing from the wound.

I ducked and shot an airbolt at the suit. That knocked it back a bit and dented the supposedly priceless metal, but it still kept coming. I turned and ran the opposite direction, wondering briefly where the fourth suit was. The two coming down the aisles had reached the stage and were coming up the stairs on either side, albeit slowly and with apparent difficulty, so I jumped off the platform in the middle and as quickly as I could, scurried over the rows of seats.

Hobai was sitting where Wynter and I had left him, still babbling. I ignored him and jumped over a few more rows of seats, then sprinted to the right-side aisle and toward the right-side door in the back.

I burst into the small lobby and ducked just as a battle axe was swung right at my head level. There was no doubt in my mind it would have decapitated me. I smacked my palms into the chest of the suit, trying to knock it over, as it brought the axe around for another swing. I grabbed its cold metal arm and stopped the axe in its arc. But the strength of the empty suit was amazing and I couldn't hold it long, I realized, even with a strength spell.

How do you stop an empty suit of armor? Nothing I knew about killing warriors was going to work. I couldn't take away its air; I assumed it didn't breathe. I couldn't touch it and kill it like every other lesser warrior, and I assumed fire would just make it hot. I could make it wet by pulling water out of the air but then what, wait a few years for it to rust? And I could hear the other three suits clanking back up the theater toward me. If I didn't escape, I was going to die, and probably as gruesomely and painfully as Wynter had.

I teleported a few feet to the right. The suit seemed surprised and swung its axe, but missed me completely. I sprinted toward the exit and pushed on the heavy wooden door but it was blocked. The armor was coming toward me. I shot an airbolt at it but it was only knocked back a bit and the metal dented. I assumed the individual pieces were held together with leather straps or maybe something more modern, and blowing the armor apart would take a lot of force: more force than I could muster.

The armor took a swing at me with the axe and I ducked but may have lost a few hairs off my crew cut as the blade sliced the air above my head.

I ran for the entrance to the theater. Through the torn curtain I could see two suits coming up the aisle in front of me and the fourth coming up the other aisle. They clanked as they walked. I gripped my talisman hard and shot the strongest airbolt I could at the nearest suit. It was knocked backwards into the suit behind it with a clang of crashing metal. That suit was, like a domino, knocked onto its back to the sound of more metal crashing. It didn't seem to be able to get up and right itself but, like a turtle, was stuck.

That airbolt had taken a lot out of me, but I knew the suit in the lobby was lurching toward me so I ran to the center of the seats just as it emerged through the portal. I stood there, breathing hard, as the suits seemed to not be able to follow me between the close spaces between the seats. The two stopped at the end of the row of seats and stood passively as if they were suddenly back to normal. The third suit, swinging its bloody flail, stayed at the other end of the row. The one I'd knocked down was still struggling to get up.

I stood there breathing, resting. If I jumped over the seats I could probably get to the front of the theater before the suits and escape out the back door. There had to be necromancers nearby—maybe they'd blocked the front door. Then I realized they could also block the back door. The front door had been physically blocked, not with a secure spell, which meant I could get out a window if I could find one, but theaters, even in Romania, tend to not have many if any at all.

Feeling more rested, I came up with a plan. I might be able to knock the suits of armor on their back if I physically pushed them over. But I couldn't get close to them because of their weapons' reach. Maybe a combination of meta and physical attack would work.

The lone suit to my right was standing there holding the flail with Wynter's blood dripping from it. I moved toward him. I wanted to run at him, but being between the rows of seats I didn't have room. As I got closer the suit started swinging the flail again. Just before I was in reach of the weapon, I shot an airbolt at the suit, which knocked it back and stopped it from swinging that spiked ball. I tackled it and knocked it down on its back with a crash of steel. I jumped off of it as it tried to swing the flail at me from the ground but missed. I imagined it could easily break a leg or an arm if it had connected.

I sprinted down the aisle toward the stage, knowing the other two suits were following me down the opposite aisle. Thankfully they moved plenty slow, and they couldn't seem to get past the one on its back. I jumped up on the stage and ran around the puppet theater to the backstage area. Wynter's body was still there, and the puddle of blood and viscera around him was the size of a dining room table. His eyes were looking at me accusingly as if I'd failed to keep him safe…at least that's how it seemed to me. I hit the back door, which was made of steel, with my shoulder and bounded out into sunlight. I didn't know where the necromancers were, but I decided to run away. I used the last of my meta energy to sprint away from the theater at speeds that would leave Olympic athletes behind.

Unfortunately, I became completely lost in a city I did not know at all.

I found a tree—the city seemed as bereft of vegetation as it was cars—and rested in its shade, only expending the energy needed to mask so the necromancers couldn't find me again.

I decided I needed a rug. I'd fly it to Bucharest, report to Sorensen and Brown, and get the hell out of Romania. The guilds could have a conclave and deal with this problem. They were too powerful for me to handle on my own, and I wasn't going to get killed trying to answer the CIA's question about them getting U.S. and NATO secrets.

I don't know how they found me. The airbolt seemed to come out of the blue and knocked me to the ground. As I tried to get up I was hit again. I glimpsed two people, a man and a woman, shooting airbolts at me before I lost consciousness.

* * * *

I was sort of amazed to be alive. I was not amazed to be, once again, handcuffed and tied to a chair. And my talisman was gone.

The room I was in had stone walls and smelled unpleasant. The door was wood and looked thick and old. There was one solitary incandescent light bulb illuminating the chamber. The electrical conduit ran across the stone ceiling and through a hole in the stone wall above the door's portal. It was obvious this was an old building that had had electricity added recently.

I was sore from where the airbolts hit me. Without a talisman, a healing spell was out of the question.

So, now what? I wondered. Apparently I'd been captured by the necromancers. Why they just didn't kill me I couldn't figure out. I did have one answer to a question: whoever sent that wooden Indian after me in San Francisco was a necromancer. Apparently it was some sort of power they had. Telekinesis or the ability to bring inanimate objects to life, I guessed.

The door swung open and a man walked in. He was wearing a gray suit much like the theater curator's, but this man was taller, younger, and angrier looking. He had dark hair and dark eyes and a prominent chin. Again I got a whiff of his personal scent. I could also feel his power as an adept.

He spent a moment looking at me. Since I hadn't been conscious very long I wondered if the room was bugged or there was a camera behind me I couldn't see.

"What did you tell the CIA?" the man asked without preamble. He was speaking passable English.

I looked at him. "I told them nothing because I know nothing."

"Then how did you know there are necromancers here in Pitesti?"

"The CIA told me," I stated matter-of-factly

"How did the CIA know?"

"I don't know. They wouldn't tell me. Said it would compromise 'sources.'" I squirmed in my chair; my hands were each handcuffed to an arm of the chair, my legs tied to the legs of the chair, and a rope went around my torso tightly. It was starting to get uncomfortable. That trick I pulled when tied to a chair in West Germany was probably not going to work here; I'd been tied up too well.

He glared at me, his black eyes seemingly burning with anger. "The only reason we haven't killed you is on the off chance you know something."

"And then you'll kill me?" I snarled.

He didn't answer. "Who told you that there were necromancers in Romania?"

I could think of no reason not to tell the truth; might put off my death a little longer. "A CIA officer named Thomas Karamessines. He's high up in the CIA. The DD/P." I'd forgotten exactly what that stood for.

The man looked at me again, as if trying to figure out if I was telling the truth.

"They lied to me," I said, trying not to sound whiny. "They told me to come here to investigate a ball bearing plant."

"What else do you know?" the man demanded.

"That you are a necromancer and there's at least one other, a woman, and you can move inanimate objects. Oh, and you've been after me since San Francisco."

I saw a quizzical expression cross his face.

"You tried to kill me there," I explained. "The wooden Indian."

"First time we tried to kill you was in Tromsø," he stated. "Our sources didn't get information to us that early."

"Your sources?" I asked without thinking.

He just glared at me some more. But I did now know that, yes, apparently the CIA had leaks, just like Rhoden stated back in Bonn.

"We were amazed you still came after it was obvious your mission was compromised," the man said, pulling out a package of cigarettes and lighting one.

I tried not to react but when the smell hit me, in combination to how helpless I felt, I nearly gagged. I didn't want to show this man any weakness and here he was unknowingly, I assumed, playing on one of my bigger vulnerabilities.

"Really?" I said. "I guess you don't know me too well, then."

He actually smiled. "We knew you'd be at the theater thanks to the bug in your table this morning."

"I thought the *Securitate* monitored those bugs?" Or the DIE, I didn't know and didn't really care.

He just smiled again. *Didn't mean the* Securitate *or DIE was working with the necromancers*, I decided. They could have used spells to get that information out of a *Securitate* or DIE agent. But if they were working with the *Securitate* and the DIE (since a DIE operative kidnapped me in Bonn) maybe the entire Ceausescu regime was working with the necromancers to some end. Maybe it was to get NATO secrets for the Warsaw Pact. Or maybe it was something more sinister.

All I knew was, if I survived and escaped (both of which seemed unlikely) I would high tail it back to the west side of the Iron Curtain, tell the CIA all I knew, and then contact Louis Brown so he could start the process of calling a Great Conclave and bringing the wrath of all the guilds down on this nest of necromancers. I hoped with what I'd already told Brown that if I disappeared he'd do that anyway.

The necromancer just looked at me impassively. "And what did you tell your guild?" he asked, as if reading my thoughts.

"Only what the CIA told me, that there may be a clan of necromancers here in Pitesti."

"And if you were to disappear?"

I suddenly realized I had a slim chance to survive this. "Then my guild's leader will assume that there is a clan here and will call a Great Conclave." I assumed I didn't have to finish that sequence for him. I was sure he knew what happened to Vlad the Impaler.

He looked slightly worried, and then without as much as a word turned and left the room, shutting the door behind him. He took the cigarette with him, but its stench still filled the room.

I took a deep breath. I was still alive—for now.

I felt bad about Wynter. Here he was just supposed to drive me to Pitesti and it got him killed. Maybe it would have been better if Sorensen had given me one of his hot-shot CIA agents. They might have had a better chance of surviving. But I didn't know the necromancers would attack us. Why I didn't realize after the attack in Tromsø that they were after me and probably knew my moves before I did, I didn't know. I guessed I wasn't very good at the spy business and it got Wynter killed. I hoped he didn't have a wife and kids.

Then I wondered what happened to his body. If the local authorities found it, they'd find his diplomatic passport and contact the embassy, I assumed. That would let Sorensen know something bad was up. Not that he could find me and rescue me, but maybe he'd get word back to Brown that I was missing and my driver was dead.

If the necromancers were smart, they would have taken the body or destroyed it somehow. And they seemed pretty smart to me—smarter than I, apparently.

I must have managed to fall asleep because I was awakened by someone pulling my head up by the hair.

"Ouch," I complained and not timidly.

The man let go of my hair and stepped back. It was the same man as before. "You need to write a letter to your guild and tell them you found nothing and are on your way back."

"And then you'll kill me?" I asked without sarcasm.

"No, we'll let you go."

I actually laughed. "No, you won't."

He gave me a look I couldn't mistake for friendly.

"You have no leverage over me," I stated simply. "You can't let me go, and you have nothing I want."

"There are more or less pleasant ways to die," he snarled.

"Yeah," I said, trying to call his bluff, "but you're still dead."

He turned on his heel, strode out of the small room, and slammed the door. The light went off shortly after that, making the only illumination what was coming under the door. I guess they were trying to intimidate me. I was glad to at least have darkness while I slept again.

* * * *

"If you have this room bugged, I really need to go to the bathroom," I said in both English and the ancient language. It wasn't part of an escape plan. Adepts have human frailties, too.

The same man walked in finally and looked at me as if I were a bug. "It's a moot point."

"What is?" By the look on his face I was starting to get scared.

"We have decided you are correct. There is no reason to keep you alive and we can't let you go. I'm sorry."

"Wait!" I said, trying to come up with something, anything to keep me alive. But he took a step back and with one hand in his pocket—I assumed on his talisman—and the other pointed at me, he took my air away. My pulse quickened as did my breathing as the air around me got thinner and thinner. I tried to pull it back but without a talisman, I was no match for his power. It was like I couldn't catch my breath, but every breath made it worse. I could feel my eyes going wide as I started to panic. Then my vision started going gray, then went black as my breathing got quicker and quicker and my heart was pounding.

Death is like a cold, wet, smothering miasma that envelops your body with frosty indifference, grays out your brain, blocks your throat, and seizes your heart, willing it to

stop
beating
beating
stop.

Chapter Nine

Pitesti, Romania
April 26, 1968

I felt warm soft kisses and soft breath on my face. "Wake up," I heard a woman's soft voice plead. "Please wake up."

I tried to open my eyes but the light made me shut them again instantly.

"Oh, yes, darling, wake up!" the voice exclaimed happily.

I tried to open my eyes again but they wouldn't focus. All I could see was a face surrounded by long dark hair.

"Ernestine?" I whispered, which took nearly a herculean effort.

"Yes, Peter, it's me," she said, still kissing and holding my head in her hands. My eyes slowly came into focus and I could see her face, and indeed it was her. I looked into her dark eyes.

"I thought I was dead," I said slowly; speaking still took effort.

She hesitated a second and got a very sad look in her eyes. "You were."

I studied her face but I saw no hint of humor. She was serious. I had been dead, or at least she thought I was.

As if to keep me from asking more questions, she kissed me again on the lips and I noticed a metallic tang to her breath. But the kiss lingered, and I enjoyed it thoroughly even in my weakened state.

153

Finally she stood straight, since she had been bending over to kiss me as I was seated. I then noticed I was untied, and apparently I had emptied my bladder at some point. Then I saw the blood on the floor along with the man who had been interrogating me, with his throat slashed.

Ernestine saw where I was looking and said softly, "I had to kill him in order to save you."

I didn't know if that meant she had to kill him to get to me, or kill him to bring me back to life, or maybe both. There wasn't enough blood on the floor, and I remembered the metallic flavor of her kisses. I almost gagged.

"What is going on?" I demanded and tried to stand, but found I could barely move.

"I know, Peter," Ernestine said softly, "you have lots of questions. But we need to get out of here."

"I can barely move."

She nodded and handed me my talisman. At its touch on the skin of my hand I felt its power flow through me, making me perhaps as strong as a weak toddler. But I managed to stand up slowly. Ernestine took my hand in hers and I felt her power as she pulled me out the door. We were in a stone-walled corridor. She pulled me to some stairs and we climbed them as fast as I could, my feet seeming to clomp on each tread. They seemed extra long, as if we were climbing more than one flight. About the time I thought I was going to have to sit down, we came into a room.

"What is this place?" I asked, looking at the sparse furniture, desks and chairs, and typewriters. It looked like a place of business, but was empty and strangely quiet.

"One of the local *Securitate* offices," she said. "I managed to scare all the lessers away with a fear spell, but they will be back soon and we need to be gone."

"And the necromancers?" I asked.

She showed no surprise at my use of that word. "There was only the one here at the time." I knew she meant the man she killed.

We walked out of the building into darkness. At that point I realized that the building seemed to have no windows. There was a car idling by the curb. I didn't recognize it, but from the smell of its exhaust I assumed it was burning oil. Ernestine got me in the passenger side and then climbed behind the wheel. She amazed me by knowing how to drive it. It oozed down the street with more noise then I imagined was possible.

"And this is one of the more expensive cars in Romania," she growled, "because it's made in East Germany."

After the exertion of climbing the stairs and walking to the car, I just sat back in the hard, bouncy seat and looked out the window. I gripped my talisman hard in my hand. I was glad it was a smooth, small pebble and had no sharp edges.

"How many necromancers are there?" I asked as she drove through the darkened streets. I was glad Romania hadn't invested in streetlights as the darkness made me feel better hidden.

"About ten I think," she said. "Maybe nine now. I'll answer all your questions later, darling."

"That include you?" I asked.

Again, the painful look crossed her visage. "I'll explain everything when we're safe."

I gave up and leaned back. I must have fallen asleep because suddenly she was pulling me from the car. We were inside a building, a garage of some sort. A large Romanian man in grease-stained overalls was walking over, speaking in a loud voice. I tried to start a translation spell but found I couldn't.

Ernestine talked to him and he helped her help me out of the car. They half led/half carried me to a room with a cot, which I lay down on and promptly fell asleep, despite trying to stay awake.

* * * *

When I opened my eyes again, daylight was streaming in the dirty window in the room, making crepuscular rays from the panes to the dusty floor.

The man in the greasy overalls was sitting there on a stool reading what looked to be a newspaper. He put down the paper and said something happily. I had no idea what. He stood up and walked out of the room.

I sat up on the bed. I felt much better. Ernestine came in and for the first time I noticed she was dressed plainly in out-of-style clothes, like a local woman would be.

"How are you feeling, darling?"

"Alive," I stated. Then I smelled dried urine on myself. "And in need of a shower and some clean clothes."

Ernestine looked unhappy. "You can take a shower in Vali's apartment over the garage, but I'm afraid there's no soap or shampoo; and we have no clothes for you. I'll have to see if we can steal some. That blood is how the necromancers hunted you down."

"Blood?" I asked.

She nodded. "I can smell it," she said with almost erotic need in her voice. "It's on your clothes and in your hair. Human blood. Once the necromancers got the scent of that they could follow you."

"Who's Vali?"

Ernestine moved her head toward the man in the overalls. "He's sort of my personal warrior. I pay him American dollars and he does whatever he can to help me. He used the money I gave him to bribe a local official to put him in charge of this garage, so we had someplace private to work and park his car. Unfortunately, he has no weapons and no weapon training so he's not much of a warrior. If you gave him a gun he'd be just as likely to shoot himself in the foot." She smiled at her own joke. "I picked him because he actually owns a car, even if it is a Trabant."

I opened my mouth to say something but she put her finger on my lips. "I know: you have hundreds of questions."

I nodded, enjoying the feel of her finger touching me.

"How do you feel?" she asked removing her finger.

"Almost alive," I said before I realized how appropriate that was.

She smiled. "Good. I'll see if I can get you some clothes."

"Listen," I interrupted, "I need to get to Bucharest to the U.S. Embassy, and I need to contact Louis Brown." Both the CIA and Brown needed to know that there were indeed necromancers in Pitesti.

She shook her head and for the first time looked anxious. "No, there's no time. We have to stop the necromancers here, now. We need to go to Poenari Castle as soon as you're able."

"Vlad's Castle? Why?"

"That's where the necromancers are operating."

"How do you know that?"

Now she looked sad. "It's all my fault."

"What is?"

I could see uncertainty slide across her visage as she looked at me with her dark eyes. "When I left Romania after the Communists took over, I left something behind I shouldn't have."

I looked at her intently. "That was 1945; twenty-three years ago. You were, what, two years old?"

She turned and pulled the room's one chair closer to my cot and sat in it. Apparently, this was going to be a long story. "You think I'm twenty-five?"

"About," I said, hoping I hadn't insulted her.

She smiled and I felt better. "I think I was born in 1450."

I looked at her, hoping she was going to laugh. She didn't.

"What do you mean you think you were born in 1450?"

"I know I was born around that time in a small village in Transylvania. It's still there, the village that is. But it may have been 1449 or 1451. I don't know; calendars were much less common in those days."

I kept expecting her to say, "Just kidding!" but she seemed completely serious.

She looked at me, her eyes wide. "Peter, don't you see, the *Book of Death* isn't about death, it's about life!"

I just kept studying her face, not knowing what she was trying to say.

"I joined the Transylvanian Guild when I was about seventeen. I was pretty, especially by the standards of those days.

You can't imagine how many deformed and invalid people there were back then, and we died so young. Forty-five was old age…living to fifty was miraculous." She looked at me as if to determine if I believed all of this. I kept my face passive so she continued. "Vlad was the leader of the guild and the Voivode of Wallachia. He was rich, powerful, and handsome by the standards of the age. When he took a liking to me, how could I resist? I slept in silk, had fine clothes, perfume—oh, you can't imagine how people stank back then—and plenty to eat. Vlad was my lover and my master. I apprenticed with him, and he taught me everything I know about necromancy."

"So you are a necromancer," I stated, having one of my fears confirmed.

She nodded, looking sad. "Yes," she whispered. "Until recently, the only one."

"And you're five hundred years old?" I asked, trying to keep the amazement from my voice.

"Yes, about."

"And you use necromancy to stay young?"

She nodded, looking as if she were about to cry. I wasn't sure why she was sad. Finally she said softly, "And to save you. You were dead; I brought you back to life. That takes strong meta."

Strong necromancy, I thought to myself. "You killed the man to get the power to save me?"

She nodded again, tears forming on her eyes, making them shiny.

"And back in my room in San Francisco, the funny smell?"

"I'd killed a small animal to get the power to listen in on your conversation with Anica without you knowing it."

I shook my head. "But you knew this wasn't about ball bearings?"

"No," she said softly. "That's why I sent the wooden Indian after you. I was hoping to scare you off, because I knew what you'd be facing here in Romania."

"If you thought that would scare me off, you don't know me very well."

She nodded. "I didn't, then."

"How did you know there were necromancers in Romania?"

She looked at me with those tear-filled brown eyes. I wanted to hold her and comfort her, but I knew I shouldn't. I couldn't trust her anymore, not unless she told me more.

"When Vlad started experimenting in necromancy, he kept a journal of the spells."

"Yes, the *Book of Death*."

She nodded again. "When the guilds killed him in 1476, they found one copy and destroyed it."

"There was more than one copy?" I asked. Kader's suspicions were correct, it seemed.

"Yes; I escaped with the other copy."

I took a deep breath and pondered the fact that this "girl" was over five hundred years old.

"But when the Soviets installed a Communist dictatorship after World War II," she continued, "I got out of the country and to the West as fast as I could. I should have taken the *Book of Death* with me, but I thought it was safely hidden."

"Where?"

"Poenari Castle. Even though it's a ruin it still has some secrets…or at least had secrets."

"Somebody found it?"

"Yes, rogue elements in the DIE and *Securitate*."

"Which is why I was being held in a *Securitate* facility."

"Yes."

"And do you know why the Cubans tried to kill Anica?"

She looked sharply at me. "No. Unless they mistook her for me…the necromancers know I'm a threat to them."

We were silent for a few moments. She looked miserable and I wasn't sure why. A single tear traced a wet line down her cheek. I fought the urge to take her into my arms and kiss her.

"Why do we need to go to Poenari Castle," I asked, instead. It seemed more important to ask than why she was crying.

"I don't know what exactly their plans are, but I think they are going to implement them soon, too soon for you to have time to get the guilds together to attack them."

I threw up my hands. "And how are you and I supposed to stop them?"

She started crying. "I don't know. But we have to try!"

Despite myself I leaned forward and took her into my arms and held her as she cried.

"And," she sobbed, "I've probably lost you."

"What do you mean?" I asked softly, realizing I missed the scent of her.

"I love you, Peter. But you think necromancy is an abomination."

She was right. I did. I just didn't know what I was going to do about it.

* * * *

Ernestine caught me in a vulnerable moment, our sweat-damp skin clinging as we cuddled in bed in Vali's apartment over the garage.

"Peter?" she whispered.

I grunted something sleepily.

"You can't tell anybody."

I opened my eyes, turned, and looked at her. "Tell anybody what?"

"What I am and who I am."

"That you're a five-hundred-year-old practicing necromancer?"

"Yes," she said with an undertone of pleading.

I just watched her dark eyes.

"If they know they'll kill me."

I still just looked into her lovely brown eyes. "I know."

"Then you can't tell anyone."

"I won't," I said. If she hadn't been a problem since Vlad was killed, I was sure she wouldn't be a problem now.

I lay down, pulled her warm, nude body near, and fell asleep.

The next morning I contacted Brown. He looked at me across thousands of miles. "Why did she go to Romania?"

"To find me, apparently, and help me."

"She has feelings for you?"

I nodded.

"And how does she know all this about the necromancers?"

I shrugged. "She says she has people here in Pitesti she remains in contact with, and they knew it." I hated lying to him even to protect her.

Brown seemed to be studying my face to see if I was telling the truth...or maybe that was just my guilty feelings.

"What are you going to do, Student?" he finally asked.

"I'm going to go with her to the castle, see what the situation is, then if we can't handle it, get out of there as fast as we can and come back to San Francisco."

"Should I work on convening a Great Conclave?" Brown said, more to himself.

"Wait two days, Teacher. If you don't hear from me by then, assume I'm dead and do so. If I'm alive, I'll contact you right away and let you know if you still need to convene one."

Brown nodded thoughtfully. "Why don't you come back now?"

"Ernestine says there's no time. We have to stop the necromancers now, and only she and I are here to do it."

Brown shook his head. "Good luck, Student. It's not going to be fun storming the castle."

"I know, Teacher." Sometimes Brown had a talent for understatement.

I ended the spell and stepped into the main garage where Vali was packing his little Trabant with gas, oil (apparently it purposely burned oil), food such that we could obtain, clothes (again, hard to come by; the set that Ernestine found for me was ill-fitting and scratchy), and water for human consumption. Apparently the car needed none. Vali tied two tires to the roof, but I wondered how he planned to get them on the rims.

Using a translation spell, I asked Vali how far of a trip it was.

"Long ways, seventy kilometers," he replied gruffly.

I looked at Ernestine.

"About forty-five miles," she clarified.

I was amazed at the preparation for a mere forty-five mile drive. Back in San Francisco I'd have a warrior drive me to Monterey so I could enjoy the scenery, and that was at least a hundred miles. He'd just put gas in the car, and we'd go.

"Do we need permission?" I asked.

"Hard to get permission to do illegal thing," Vali growled.

"We'll have to avoid the *Militia*," Ernestine added. "And if we don't, I'm sure we can convince them to let us go." She gave me a sweet smile.

I switched to English. "And what do we do when we get to Poenari Castle and there's a clan of necromancers waiting for us?"

"There's no more than ten," Ernestine said defensively. "And you managed to kill two in Norway."

"With the help of a very powerful Valkyrie," I added. The math didn't add up, and I didn't think Ernestine was powerful enough to take on eight or nine necromancers by herself, assuming I could handle one or two—which was a big assumption considering what happened at the theater.

"Do you know how they killed the warrior in Tromsø?" I asked.

Ernestine shook her head, which made her lovely long hair move in ways I liked. "How do you mean?"

"He just...exploded. But there was no flash, no bang of normal explosions."

Ernestine's face became pale. "You've seen how we can manipulate objects?"

"Like the suits of armor, right?"

"Yes," she said. "We can also teleport them. They probably teleported something inside his body...." Her voice trailed off. She didn't have to finish: two objects trying to occupy the same space would cause an explosion, destroying both objects.

"Can they do that to adepts?" I asked, trying to keep the fear out of my voice.

"No," she said. "For all the reasons they can't run spells on you."

I nodded. The spells to ward off other spells were easily maintained, and adepts learn to keep them up as easily as breathing or they don't survive long as adepts. Only if someone knows your real name can they overcome them.

"It's almost dark," Vali said interrupting us. "We go soon."

"Okay," I said in English but he seemed to understand it.

Maybe a five hundred-year-old necromancer and I could win the battle we were about to enter. I never sensed great power from Ernestine, but she could be masking.

The Trabant trundled down the dark street, noisily and producing clouds of blue smoke. I suspected Vali did something to make the lights dimmer, or maybe they were just that dim, because they hardly illuminated the path in front of us. I rode in the tiny back seat and tried to relax and build up my strength.

We were headed north, and not far out of Pitesti the road became a pot-hole-filled gravel mess that caused the little car to lurch and bounce. *So much for getting rest*, I grumbled. According to the speedometer we occasionally hit fifty. But I assumed that was in kilometers because there was no way we were doing fifty miles per hour in that car on that road.

It was the night after a new moon, so once we got away from the city, there was almost no illumination other than the dim headlights. We passed through another smaller town called Curtea de Arges. Vali seemed more nervous, and I wondered if he was worried about the local *Militia*.

North of Curtea de Arges the road managed to get worse. It was little more than a wide flat spot on the ground with multiple pot holes and random undulations. I decided Vali's spare tires were probably a good idea.

We passed through more small villages; most didn't have any lights visible, as if we were suddenly in the pre-electricity era. About five, the sky started lightening and I could see we were in a valley between high, tree-covered hills...or small mountains, depending on your perspective, I guess. They got higher and the valley got narrower as we went north. Most of the valley floor was dotted with farmsteads in various states of disrepair. Eventually the valley got so narrow there was just the river and the road that seemed to be carved into the basalt wall of the valley. It passed through numerous short tunnels.

About six Vali stopped the car at the side of the road. He pointed up a narrow valley that led off to the west. "Up there. I will go no farther."

"Wait for us here," Ernestine told him, putting her small hand on his meaty arm.

"How long?" he asked in his gruff voice.

"Until noon," she said. "Then you may leave."

I almost felt sorry for the guy, having to sit there for six hours, because I assumed we weren't going to come back.

Ernestine stepped out of the car, the door opening with a creak, and pulled the seatback forward so I could climb out the same door.

"What's the plan?" I asked, stretching my sore and stiff muscles with a groan.

"The castle is at the end of this valley, up a hill. They'll see us coming a long ways away. We just have to rush them."

I looked at her. It was almost as if she wanted to get killed. "Let's think about this a second," I said. "Would they expect invisibility?"

"Probably not," she said. "Why?"

"I could go invisible, check out the situation, and then we could make plans."

She shook her head. "I don't see how that would work."

I let out an exasperated breath. "If we simply walk up this valley they will probably attack us the moment they see us and…." I let my voice trail off. While she just stared at me I added, "Dying twice in three days isn't my idea of fun."

"Listen," she said. "I just need to kill one and then I'll be powerful enough to take them all on."

"But they're necromancers, too," I said, almost with a whine.

"But they'll have nothing to kill."

164

"Just us," I said grimly.

She gave me an exasperated look. "Are you a coward?"

"If not wanting to die stupidly makes me a coward, yes."

Her visage softened. "I'm sorry, Peter."

I just looked at her. "Then what do we do?"

"We need a fast way up this valley and into the castle," she said.

I smiled, and poked my head through the Trabant's window where Vali was sitting behind the steering wheel gleefully lighting the first cigarette I'd let him smoke in days. "Hey, Vali, got a blanket?"

"Yes, I do. Why?"

* * * *

Ernestine couldn't go invisible; that was an American Meta Association-known spell. But she could fly a carpet, or in this case, a blanket. We soared over the trees that were just beginning to show the buds of their leaves and up the valley toward Poenari Castle. Once we got high enough we could see it. It surprised me by being made apparently of red brick. I guess I thought all castles were gray. I suggested we come out of the east with the sun at our backs. I'd be casting a shadow on the blanket but I didn't think anyone would notice.

The first indication that they'd seen us was a very hot and very bright fireball shot toward us. It missed, badly. Ernestine didn't even have to dodge it. A couple more balls were fired at us but all missed. Only one even came close enough to feel the heat from it.

We flew unimpeded over the castle wall and into the courtyard. There were two necromancers there, and they immediately shot fire at Ernestine. She held both assaults off with ease. I could attack and stay invisible, so I took the air from the nearest necromancer, a man dressed in a uniform I didn't recognize. His flames died as the air left him. I saw him try to pull the air back, and he surprised me by succeeding, and starting to take the air away from me. I couldn't figure out how he knew where I was until I realized that, in my excitement, I'd forgotten to maintain the invisibility spell and was slowly becoming visible.

Ernestine threw the flames back at the other necromancer, who screamed and fell to the ground, dying. She then joined me in pulling the air from the one with the uniform. He crumpled to the dirt face down. I glanced at the man in the uniform, wondering who he was.

"Why don't they attack in force?" I asked, although I was glad I wasn't facing ten all at once, and now they were down to eight.

"Come on," Ernestine said, "They'll be coming!" She knelt down next to the body of the man she'd killed and pulled out a jeweled knife.

Fire rained down on us from the high parapets. I ducked against the wall and looked for a target. Ernestine seemed oblivious as her protection spell kept the flames off of her.

Three more necromancers burst from out of the ruins into the courtyard. I ducked just as one shot a lightning bolt at me. I heard it hit the wall and the bricks crack. I assumed it was strong enough to kill me. I shot fire at him but it didn't seem to have much effect.

Ernestine had slit the throat of the dead man and was drinking the blood that spilled out. She rose to her feet, and I swear, even with blood dripping from her chin, she'd never looked more beautiful. She screamed in the direction of the necromancers and they blew apart as if they were made of meringue. I could feel her power, and even I was a little afraid of her. She looked at me and gave me a grin that was a combination of desire and rage.

Five necromancers came at us; two from the direction the last three had come from, one from the sky on a broom, and two jumped down from the parapets, which ended the fire storm coming from the walls.

"Get down!" Ernestine called, and she put out her hands straight from her sides and started twirling. I wondered what the heck she was doing, but I dropped to the dirt just as a pretty rainbow emerged from her fingers. A rainbow didn't seem very offensive, but where the colors hit flesh the flesh was seared. The necromancers all fell to the ground holding their faces as if someone had thrown acid in them. I almost felt sorry for them.

"Take their air away," Ernestine cried and she started to do the same to the two closest to her.

It was over in a few minutes. All the necromancers were dead. I was winded and exhausted after the battle, but Ernestine just grinned almost crazily.

I shuffled to the man in the uniform and turned him over. There were dark blue tabs on his collar and blue piping on his epaulets. On his right breast was a gold-colored metal insignia shaped like a shield with a red star and a sword. It had Cyrillic writing: "КГБ СССР" and even I knew that "СССР" was the Russian version of "USSR." This guy was a Soviet officer. I tore the insignia off and pocketed it, surprised by how cheaply made it looked.

"We have to find the *Book of Death*," I said through my sucking in the cool mountain air.

"Yes," she agreed, nodding, then grabbed me and dragged me to the ground. For a moment I thought she was going to kill me until she kissed me hard and deep. I could taste blood and wanted to gag, but she was pulling off my clothes. A dirty courtyard surrounded by dead bodies is not my favorite venue for making love, but I wasn't sure she'd give me a choice.

* * * *

Vali looked surprised to see us. I handed him back his blanket, folded neatly and as clean as I could get it after it had laid in the dirty courtyard. I figured something like that was probably pretty precious in this economy. We'd barely made it back before the noon deadline. I wasn't too worried; we could use the blanket to fly back to Bucharest. I wanted the hell out of this country. There was only one problem.

"One of them must have escaped with it," I said, climbing into the tiny back seat of the Trabant.

"No, we killed them all," Ernestine stated with conviction as she sat in the front passenger seat. We were speaking the ancient language to ensure Vali couldn't understand us.

"You know for a fact there were only ten?" I asked. "How could you know that?"

I couldn't see her face but she moved her head as if she were thinking. "I don't. You're right. One could have escaped with it."

We'd searched the entire castle, including places Ernestine said hadn't been seen in five hundred years, and hadn't found the *Book of Death*, which meant somebody had it. It was like a virus: it would spread necromancy. We needed to find the necromancer, who'd escaped, but I believed killing most of them bought us time, and Ernestine agreed. I planned to get back to San Francisco as soon as possible and let Brown call a Great Conclave, and the guilds could hunt down the survivors.

* * * *

Vali drove us back to Pitesti. Since it was daylight we were stopped by a *Militia* vehicle. A few persuasion spells and we were allowed to continue. Neither Ernestine nor I had "papers," and my diplomatic passport must have been taken by the necromancers when they captured me.

At one point we did suffer a flat tire. Vali jacked up the car with a complicated jack that didn't look as if it could hold up a wagon, let alone a car. He took off the wheel and, using a crowbar, pried the tire off the rim. He was sweating despite the coolness of the weather as he got the new tire on the rim, but I wondered how he was going to seat it on the rim. He poured a little of the gasoline we'd brought with us into the tire, picked up the tire and wheel and shook them, then set it down and lit a match, dropping it on the tire. There was a frump of exploding gasoline and the tire seemed to almost jump off the ground. But the bead was seated on the rim. He pumped up the tire with a hand pump, put it back on the car, and we went on our way. We got back to the garage just in time to sleep. I decided I could contact Brown in the morning, as I was bushed. I snuggled up with a naked Ernestine in her bed in Vali's small apartment, and promptly fell asleep. Vali slept in the apartment's main room.

The next morning, after I called Brown to let him know the necromancer problem was mostly taken care of, Vali drove us to Bucharest. I got the feeling he'd never been there, as his eyes were wide from the time we hit the first huge apartment block. I had to direct him to the American embassy, but we were lucky and didn't run into any of the local *Militia*. Ernestine gave him a wad of American money, kissed him on the cheek, and said something softly to him in Romanian. I didn't bother to get up a translation spell.

The uniformed guard scowled at me when I asked to be let in. I was going to show him my diplomatic passport when I realized I didn't have it.

It took an amazingly strong persuasion spell to convince the guard we were Americans and needed in.

The receptionist in the lobby informed us that we'd need proof we were Americans before we could be issued new passports. We didn't have any proof, so I asked her if Phillip Sorensen was available. She looked surprised but picked up the phone on her desk, dialed a three-digit number, and spoke softly into it, swiveling in her chair so she was facing away from us.

Ernestine and I exchanged a look. I still marveled at how beautiful and powerful she was now that she wasn't masking. I was holding her hand in a silly adolescent gesture but I had trouble keeping from touching her. I wondered, briefly, if she were running some sort of spell on me. I had no idea how powerful she was.

The woman turned around. "Someone will be with you shortly. You can have a seat over there." She pointed to some uncomfortable looking wooden chairs set up along the wall.

We chose to stand, still holding hands. Ernestine got on her tippy toes and kissed me on the cheek, and the woman rolled her eyes.

A young man wearing the CIA uniform of black slacks, white shirt, and black narrow tie came out of the elevator, and the woman pointed us out to him.

"You're looking for Phillip Sorensen?" he asked me.

"Yes, where is he?"

"And who are you?" the young man asked impatiently.

"I'm Peter Branton and this is Ernestine…." I'd forgotten her last name.

"Vojir," she added for me.

"And if you talk to Mr. Sorensen and tell him I'm back he should be interested," I said.

"Are you Americans?" the young man asked.

"Yes," I said. "I've lost my passport and—"

"So have I," Ernestine said, interrupting me.

The man looked skeptical but he went to the woman. They talked in soft tones and she picked up the phone's handset and dialed a number, then handed the headset to the man. He spoke with someone for a few minutes, looking at us the whole time. I thought about using a spell to hear, but I wasn't that interested. The man eventually hung up the phone and came back over to us.

"Where's Wynter?" he demanded.

"Dead," I answered.

His eyes grew wide as he suddenly must have decided this was important. "Sorensen said I should take you to the CIA's station."

"Even better," I said, taking a step toward the elevator with Ernestine's fingers interlaced with mine.

"But not her," the man said, stopping me.

I debated what to do. Ernestine and I looked at each other, and I could see she wanted to come.

I fingered my talisman. "She needs to be there," I stated.

"She needs to be there," the man repeated.

"Sorensen will be glad she is," I stated.

"Yes," the man said, "Sorensen will be glad she is."

And that's how both Ernestine and I got into Sorensen's office.

Chapter Ten

Bucharest, Romania
April 29, 1968

"Why is she here?" Sorensen asked the young man, standing up as we came in.

"You'll want her here," I said quickly.

Sorensen glared at me but he sat and instructed the young man to leave and close the door behind him.

"Where's Wynter?" Sorensen demanded without preamble. "And where's my car?"

I was glad he was more worried about Wynter than the car. "Wynter's dead."

That statement seemed to almost physically knock him back in his chair. "How?" he asked softly.

"Killed by necromancers trying to get to me. It was almost an accident."

Sorensen sighed sadly. "I didn't think this mission would be dangerous. Hell, I didn't think it would result in anything."

"Was he married?" I asked.

Sorensen shook his head. "No, but he had a girlfriend back in the States." He spent a few moments staring into space as if he was thinking. "And the car?" he finally asked.

"The car is still in Pitesti, probably still at the County Theater, unless it's been stolen or stripped."

171

"How am I going to explain that to the ambassador?" Sorensen growled.

"The good news is," I stated, hoping to cheer him up, "that whatever the necromancers were planning to do, Miss Vojir thinks we stopped them."

"I assume this young lady is Miss Vojir." He glanced at her then took a longer look. Even he noticed how beautiful she was.

"Yes."

"And how would she know?"

"I have powers that Peter doesn't," Ernestine said with confidence. "I knew what their plans were, and they needed more than one or two to complete them."

"What were their plans?" Sorensen demanded.

Ernestine looked uncomfortable. "Obtain secrets from the West to use against you in an invasion of Western Europe that the Soviets are planning. They figure the U.S. is distracted in Vietnam, and now is the time to unify Germany and bring the rest of Europe under their domination."

Sorenson whistled softly. "But you've stopped them?"

"Temporarily, at least," I said. "At least one got away."

"How do you know?"

We told him about not being able to find the *Book of Death*.

"Oh, and I think there are Russians involved," I finished.

"Why?" Sorensen demanded.

I handed him the small metallic emblem. "There was a man in a uniform. He had that insignia on his chest."

Sorensen glanced at it and then his eyes got wide. "Damn. KGB."

"The Soviet spy agency?" I asked.

"Yes."

"Makes sense the KGB would be involved. This might go all the way to Brezhnev," Sorensen stated.

Even I knew Brezhnev was the Premiere of the Soviet Union.

"But we've bought time," I said. "The guilds will hunt down the survivors and kill them, no matter what it takes. I don't think the necromancers are a threat to the U.S. anymore."

Sorensen leaned back in his chair. "I have to report this to Langley right away."

"Of course, you do," I stated. "Ernestine and I just want to go back to the U.S. as quickly and as comfortably as possible."

"You still have your passport?" Sorensen asked.

I shook my head. "Sorry, when I was captured by the necromancers, they must have taken it."

Sorensen just looked sick. "You can't imagine what that passport is worth on the black market. At least the Romanian government doesn't have it, I hope," he said. "They love foreign passports to give to spies and terrorist groups."

* * * *

They put Ernestine and me up in the same small apartment they had let me stay in before. There was a small difficulty that we weren't married, but persuasion spells dealt with that. Lessers are such prudes.

The Armed Forces Network channel was full of news of a student protest at Columbia University in New York City. Apparently they were protesting the Vietnam War or the draft or something, occupying buildings, generally making asses of themselves.

We spent Tuesday being "de-briefed" separately and getting new passports. Neither the de-brief nor the passports were diplomatic. I told them everything I knew that wasn't a guild secret and told Ernestine to do the same. I spoke with Karamessines via the encrypted phone, which looked just like the one in Bonn. I told him that the necromancers posed no more threat to the U.S. or NATO and if there were any left, the guilds would deal with them. He seemed satisfied with that, but he was angry about Wynter's death and that I had failed to protect him, somehow. All I could do was apologize and reiterate that it was an accident. Sorensen said the officials in Pitesti had found no body, and someone had "vandalized" a set of priceless medieval armor. Sorensen grumbled that Wynter also had a diplomatic passport, and he hoped that losing two diplomatic passports wouldn't "come back and bite us on the butt."

Ernestine and I flew out on TAROM on Tuesday: Bucharest to Cologne, Cologne to London (on B.O.A.C), London to San Francisco (on TWA) with a stop in Bangor, Maine (of all places) for fuel. Karamessines kept his word. Except for the TAROM leg, it was first class the whole way for both of us.

We caught a taxi to the Huntington from the airport, and held hands in the back of the yellow Ford sedan. It was a wonderful spring day in central California and Ernestine watched the scenery in amazement, giggling and kissing me with delight. For a five hundred-year-old necromancer she could play the ingénue when required.

At the Huntington we climbed out of the cab, I paid the hack, and we walked through the small lobby to the elevator. I pushed in the twelve and the one button, and they both stayed in, taking us to the thirteenth floor, where they popped out with dual clicks. Ernestine and I took the moment of privacy for a chance to kiss long and hard, holding each other. We didn't know when we'd get that opportunity again. I was convinced I had fallen in love with her and her with me.

Brown and Vaughan were waiting for us in suite 1313 since I'd called from London to give them our itinerary. When Ernestine and I walked in holding hands, I wasn't positive but Brown seemed to give us a disapproving look. I led Ernestine to one of the chairs and I sat on the leather camelback couch. I didn't like being apart from her, but I decided we shouldn't display our affection for each other there.

"Teachers," I said as a way of opening the conversation.

"Students," Brown replied. "Tell us what happened in Romania."

Ernestine and I had already agreed on our story. I told Brown and Vaughan what happened, but left out my dying. I told them Ernestine killed the lone necromancer at the *Securitate* station in Pitesti, scared off the lessers, and rescued me. We then went and fought and killed the necromancers at Vlad's old castle.

Vaughan leaned forward. "The two of you killed ten necromancers?"

"Yes," I said. "They made a tactical error. They came at us in small groups instead of all at once."

"But we had to stop them," Ernestine interjected.

"Why? What where they planning?" Brown asked.

"To obtain secrets from NATO countries to help in an invasion of West Europe," Ernestine answered.

"They figured the U.S. is distracted in Vietnam," I added.

"How do you know all this?" Brown asked Ernestine. That was a question I hadn't thought to ask before. I felt stupid not having done so.

"The necromancer who was guarding Peter told me before I killed him."

"Why would he tell you? You couldn't put him under a truth spell."

Ernestine looked thoughtful for a moment. I guess at her age you can handle surprises. "He was bragging because he assumed he was going to kill me."

"And how did you, a young adept, kill him, a necromancer?" Brown pressed in.

"He was overconfident: I took his air away, and he passed out before he could pull it back."

"And why," Vaughan asked, "did you sneak off to Romania without telling Anica?"

"She's still recovering mentally if not physically from her gunshot wound. I didn't want to tell her there were necromancers in Romania, or she'd insist on going, too. And I was afraid if Peter encountered necromancers on his own, they'd kill him, and they nearly did. You see, I'm quite fond of Peter." This last she said softly, smiling at me.

I frowned. "And how did you know there were necromancers there?" I inquired. I remember I asked that question in Vali's garage and she'd ducked it.

She gave me a questioning look. I kept my face passive. This seemed to be a major hole in her story.

"I didn't know. I suspected because the Transylvanian Guild still practices some necromancy."

175

"That's true," Brown said. "Kader witnessed Anica do it in Norway during the fight with the Norse gods."

I nodded, remembering that conversation with Kader in Tromsø when he said the same thing. Was that only, what, three weeks ago? But I felt better. She'd made an assumption, one that turned out to be correct.

"Now what?" Vaughan asked.

"You think one escaped?" Brown asked.

"Yes," I said. "Ernestine said that they had a copy of the *Book of Death*—"

"The necromancer I killed told me," she interrupted.

I nodded and continued. "But we didn't find it at Poenari Castle so we're thinking at least one got away with it."

"Or they hid it somewhere else and we just didn't find it," Ernestine added.

Brown sat back in his chair and looked at Ernestine and then at me. "Is it worth calling a Great Conclave to deal with one or two necromancers?"

"In 1476 they did just to deal with Vlad," Vaughan stated. "And that was only one. We may have more than one now."

Brown nodded. "True. Problem is we don't know for sure if there are any or if these two killed them all." He looked again at Ernestine and me.

"I don't know," I said, raising my hands. This decision was Brown and Vaughan's.

"Let's talk to Anica," Vaughan said. "See what she thinks. She probably knows more about necromancers than any adept."

"Since she almost is one," Brown grumbled.

* * * *

Anica flew back to San Francisco from Spokane. I and a warrior picked her up at the airport in one of the guild's cars. It was a Lincoln, another huge slab-sided car like the Transylvanian Guild's Cadillac. I really thought cars had more style in the early sixties.

She walked out of the airport looking stylish and confident, a porter wheeling her luggage up. I tipped the porter after he put the luggage in the trunk of the car and Anica and I got in the back seat.

"May we talk?" she asked.

I shook my head and looked at the driver/warrior. He wasn't high enough in the Guild echelon to be trusted with too many secrets.

Anica nodded and watched the scenery though the large windows. I did the same even though I'd made this trip dozens of times. Brown sent me and a car to pick her up this time, rather than a taxi, to show he took this situation seriously. Our guild even paid for her plane ticket.

"How's Miss Vojir?" Anica asked finally. Her voice seemed strained, as if she were angry with Ernestine.

"She's fine," I stated. I didn't mention that Ernestine had said she wanted to join the AMA so she could stay with me.

We gave Anica a couple of hours to freshen up and rest. The meeting was in Suite 1313 at five in the evening. The sun was low, giving the city a golden light which was visible out the suite's windows. Ernestine was invited to this meeting. Anica greeted her perfunctorily. I started wondering if Anica were jealous of her or something.

After the preliminary greetings, Anica stated, "I now know why the Communists wanted me dead."

"Why?" Brown asked.

"I know how to stop necromancers. A counter-spell."

"But why Cubans?" Brown asked.

Vaughan interrupted. "It seems the Cubans, the Romanians, and the Russians were all involved with this," he stated. "All the commie intelligence services work together...even the Romanian DIE, apparently."

"But what I don't understand," Anica continued, "Is how they knew I can stop them." She turned her gaze to Ernestine.

I looked at Ernestine, who was looking at me.

"Did Ernestine know?" I asked slowly.

"Yes," Anica stated. "She was the only one who knew besides me. I was teaching her the spell."

All eyes were suddenly on Ernestine. I was amazed she didn't look shocked, unhappy, or defensive. She simply said, "Yes, I told them," is a soft, clear voice.

Then she jumped to the ceiling, clinging to it. That was a new spell I'd never seen. I shot fire at her as Brown and Vaughan did the same, filling the room with angry and bright orange light. It sloughed off of her body but charred the ceiling above her. After five hundred years of being a necromancer she'd apparently learned to spell with a protection spell up. She shot an airbolt through the flames that hit Anica square-on, knocking the woman back.

"Take her air!" Vaughan cried out and all three of us tried, my left hand clenching my talisman. The flames died but she shot lightning at Anica's prone body from her position on the ceiling, and then took the air from Brown, Vaughan, and me. The windows of the suite blew out as all the air was thrown away from us. That probably saved our lives as the air rushed in from outside.

Ernestine dropped to the floor, her eyes ablaze, and she sprinted for the broken windows and dove out. Brown, Vaughan and I rushed to the window to see her land in the street unharmed, thirteen stories below. She must have been masking somewhat whenever I was around her. She'd never given a hint of being this powerful.

"Damn!" Vaughan swore. We all knew it was useless to go after her, and whoever did would probably be dead.

I rushed to Anica but even from a distance I could see she was dead. There was no life in her body, and her neck was at an angle human vertebrae were not supposed to bend at.

I turned to Brown and Vaughan. I knew I'd screwed up. I knew I was in trouble, and I knew I'd probably be in on the fix. "I'm sorry," I said softly.

"You knew," Brown said as a statement.

"I knew she was a necromancer and a very powerful one, yes."

Brown shook his head, and there was no mistaking the look in his dark eyes. I couldn't have felt worse; I had disappointed him.

* * * *

The Great Conclave was scheduled for the summer solstice on Friday, June 21st, in Paris, France. I don't know why Paris was chosen. Maybe tradition.

Inter-guild messages flew back and forth by both modern and meta means as arrangements were made and guilds contacted. Some guilds still hated each other after various slights, such as helping Hitler during World War II. Vaughan wondered out loud to me if the Cuban Guild would show up, or if they'd be embarrassed by their working with Communists in an attempt to take over the world using zombie armies. We knew some guilds would only attend by far-seeing, such as those in the New Guinea and Amazonian jungles that hadn't had contact with modern man, yet.

A large, ornate and luxurious hotel called Le-Grande was chosen and basically rented out by the guilds. Lessers were turned away at the entrance by warriors who were well-armed and backed up by at least one adept at all times. Such a meeting of guilds hadn't happened for nearly five hundred years. Most participants flew in by commercial airliner. Some used more basic transportation. Liesl and Brunhild arrived from Valhalla on flying white horses. I saw Vaughan shudder when he saw a pterodactyl leashed to a lamppost.

"It's smaller," he said softly, as if trying to ensure the beast didn't hear him.

"Smaller than what?" I asked.

He just looked at me, his features pale.

From that and other incidents, the press got wind of the conclave. It managed to push the U.S. presidential election off the front pages for a day or two. The elections had been in upheaval since Senator Robert Kennedy, the presumptive Democrat nominee, was assassinated early in June.

We all met in the hotel's biggest ballroom. The chamber was gold with a huge chandelier hanging from the very ornate ceiling. I wasn't sure if all the gold was paint or if some of it was gilding. The meeting lasted all day and into the night. We all spoke the ancient language as the only common tongue. From our guild Brown, Vaughan, and I had come: me only because Brown insisted. Liesl and I exchanged a smile across the room, but I got the feeling hers wasn't sincere. Brown had tried to protect me, but word still got out that I had basically aided and protected a known necromancer.

The Germanic guilds kept to themselves, and the French guilds kept away from them. The Roundtable and the Welsh guilds were just coming off a small war, so they kept apart. The Cubans did show up but they hung out with the East Germans. The *Omi Uji* and the newly-formed Korean guilds also avoided each other. There were more dynamics, inter-guild politics, and conflicts that I didn't even bother to notice.

The first order of business was to elect a leader. Over a hundred squabbling guild leaders trying to decide who should lead them was impossible. I wondered how they did it five hundred years ago. Unfortunately, they didn't leave minutes of those meetings.

After three days and the hotel bills adding up—and that was another fight; how the bill should be divvied up—it was decided that twenty of the strongest guilds' strongest adepts would hunt down and kill Ernestine and any other necromancers they could find. How to find them was an open question. I was asked my opinion, and I simply stood and said, "I'd start in Transylvania."

Another half day was spent arguing which were the strongest guilds, and I swear some guilds were about to have it out on the streets of Paris to prove how strong they were. The whole thing made me ill. I went for a walk along the disjointed streets and promptly got lost. I wasn't worried; I could feel where the Le-Grande was by the presence of so many adepts.

That's when I found her.

"Hello Peter," she said, coming up behind me. I recognized her voice. I turned to see her dark eyes looking up at me. She looked like the girl I'd seen in Coeur d'Alene, Idaho three months ago, except she was dressed in a stylish multi-colored mini-dress with white boots to her knees. She looked like any young woman wandering Paris' streets. I resisted the urge to take her into my arms, but instead, after glancing around to see if there were any other adepts near, I dragged her into a coffeehouse that served very strong coffee in very small cups. The smell of the place was nearly intoxicating and I found myself craving coffee. I ignored that and took Ernestine as far into the shop as possible to be away from the street-facing windows, and sat at a small table with a white tablecloth. A waiter came over in a white smock. I used a persuasion spell to dismiss him and keep him away.

"Why are you here?" I asked.

"I saw on the news that the guilds were up to something in Paris, and I decided it must be a Great Conclave and it's probably about me." She smiled coyly if we were discussing going on a date.

"It is," I hissed. I was debating running back to the Le-Grande and telling them she was there.

She shrugged and looked at me. "If you want to tell them I'm here, well, they'll never find me."

It was true: Paris was a pretty big haystack to find this needle in, even in that dress. But it was smaller than Eastern Europe.

"Peter," she said softly. "I just want to tell you, don't go back to America. You'll be safer in Europe."

I frowned. "What do you mean?"

"I can't tell you."

"Why did you bring me back to life?" I blurted out.

"Oh, Peter, I'm in love with you." She looked at me with those eyes and I just wanted to fall into them.

I shook my head to both clear my thoughts and communicate my disagreement. "There's more to it than that."

Her face became hard and it was almost as if I could see all of her five hundred years of life etched in her features. "I knew if you disappeared in Pitesti the guilds would assume necromancers killed you, and then they'd have a Great Conclave and come after us. But if I could convince you they were no longer a threat...." She let her voice go soft.

"Then whatever it is you have planned, you could finish," I said.

She looked at me with blazing black eyes. "Yes."

"What about Anica?" I asked. "You had to know she would expose you as the only one who knew that she had a counter spell for necromancy."

"I was really hoping she wouldn't put two and two together, at least not until I could convince you to join me and help me in my plans."

"What do you have planned?"

She shook her head. "Sorry."

"And all those necromancers we killed at Poenari Castle?"

"Neophytes. I'd barely started their training, so I was willing to sacrifice them."

"And you just killed them?" I was shocked and amazed. This woman I thought I had feelings for was a cold-blooded killer.

"If you want to make an omelet, you must be willing to break a few eggs."

Why did that sound familiar? "What's in it for you?"

She sighed, looking unhappy. "Do you know how hard it is to mask your power constantly? Do you know what it's like to hide what you are from everyone, including your guild? I could run my guild, any guild. But, no, I'm hounded across the world knowing if the guilds found out what I was, they'd do whatever it took to kill me. But killing Vlad was easy compared to what it will take to kill me. I've had five hundred years to perfect my craft. It'll take dozens, if not hundreds, of adepts to kill me. Tell them that!"

"So what you're planning means you can be the powerful necromancer you truly are?"

"Yes!" she said emphatically. "The Soviets have given me a homeland to grow my guild, a guild that will soon rule all the guilds. In exchange, I've given them the means to win the Cold War, conquer the rest of Europe, and not have to worry about American nuclear weapons anymore."

"How?" I asked, not really expecting an answer.

She smiled.

"And Anica?"

"Yes, damn Cubans missing her…and choosing the day you were there to kill her was just bad luck."

"And the anti-necromancy counter spell?"

"It died with Anica."

I made a mental note to make sure that was true. I shook my head. "You think this is all worth it? All this death?"

"One death is a tragedy, a million a statistic," she said with grim determination. "I've seen millions of people die in my life, including some I loved dearly. I said I'd never love again until you came along. I was hoping to convince you to join me and we could live together forever. But I see now that was foolish of me." She gave a bitter laugh. "Five hundred years old and still able to have a schoolgirl crush."

She looked at me for a moment with her dark brown eyes. I just looked back, trying to see what I had loved there. She may have had her justifications, but that still didn't explain away her disregard for human life.

"Better go," she said standing and smoothing out imaginary wrinkles in her small dress. "Just don't go back to America, Peter. You'll be safer here. But don't come after me because then I'd have to kill you. And that would break my heart." She reached out and touched my cheek before turning and leaving.

I didn't say anything, just watched her walk away. She didn't seem to be in any particular hurry. I found myself blinking tears out of my eyes.

* * * *

The ballroom at Le-Grande was empty so the meeting must have broken up. I rushed to Brown's suite and pounded on the door. "I saw her!" I said bursting into the room. His warrior had opened the door upon recognizing me.

Brown looked up from the table in the middle of the main room where he was reading a book.

"Where?"

"Here, in Paris, not far from the hotel."

He reached over and picked up the room's phone and dialed a number. "She's in Paris," he said when someone answered. "He saw her." He hung up.

I imagined the adepts pouring out of the Le-Grande to scour the streets of Paris for her.

Brown pointed to a chair and I sat. "Did she tell you anything?"

"She said the Russians are helping her so she doesn't have to hide what she is anymore. And she's helping them win the Cold War and conquer the rest of Europe."

"How?"

"She refused to say. But she did say I shouldn't go back to America because it would be safer to stay in Europe."

"During a Soviet invasion, I doubt that," Vaughan said, coming out of one of the suite's bedrooms. He was wearing a robe since he apparently had been sleeping, judging from the mess his blond hair was in.

"Unless being in America would be more dangerous," I speculated.

"Nuclear war?" Brown asked.

"Yeah, but the Americans will launch a counter strike and the Soviet Union will suffer as badly as the U.S.," Vaughan said going to the kitchen and getting a glass of water. "Mutual assured destruction, they call it."

"I don't know what she has planned," I stated simply.

"What about the necromancers she killed?" Vaughan asked. "That's pretty cold-blooded."

"She said you can't make an omelet without breaking a few eggs," I stated.

"So did Lenin," Brown snarled.

I frowned at that. "She said something else."

"What's that?"

"'One death is a tragedy, a million a statistic.'"

"Stalin," Vaughan said sitting down. "Sounds like she's become a true believer in Communism."

"Yes," I whispered. "But what millions of deaths is she talking about?"

"You mean," Brown said, leaning forward and locking his brown eyes on mine, "her plans could cause a million deaths?"

"That's the feeling I got," I stated.

Brown shook his head. "We must find her and stop her."

"You'll have to kill her," I stated.

Brown nodded grimly. "So be it."

* * * *

I was not required to be one of the twenty adepts sent to kill Ernestine, for which I was grateful, because I didn't want any part of killing her. Oh, I knew what she was and that she'd killed in cold blood, but other than the wooden Indian, she'd never attacked me, and I believed her when she said that was just to try and scare me off.

One thing I didn't understand was why I was kidnapped by Romanian DIE operatives in Bonn if the DIE was working with the KGB on whatever it was Ernestine had planned. Ernestine said the necromancers were working with the DIE and the *Securitate,* but maybe she was lying. But one of the necromancers she killed was with the KGB.

I was sitting in an airplane seat going back to San Francisco when I shook my head, trying to makes sense of it all. The man sitting next to me was pointedly reading a magazine. I looked out the plane's window. We must have been over the Great Plains because the land was flat and patched with crops like some green, crazy quilt.

Brown and Vaughan hadn't demoted me, or even said a word to me about covering for Ernestine. She wasn't found in Paris and the group ordered to hunt her down had gone to Romania. I wondered how they were getting along with *Agentia de Turism.* Of course they probably weren't hiding the fact they were adepts, and were using persuasion spells to get whatever they needed or wanted.

I wished them luck. Ernestine would be hard to kill, and if she had more necromancers with her, she might be impossible to kill.

* * * *

The search party's first mistake was to break up to "cover more territory." They started disappearing, one by one, all over behind the Iron Curtain, except in Czechoslovakia. The Czech leadership was breaking with the Warsaw Pact, according to the news, and implementing reforms. The Soviet Union wasn't pleased about this, apparently.

Finally, the remaining eleven adepts reported they were going to Poenari Castle to look for clues, and they were going in force. They were never heard from again.

I went to Coeur d'Alene and met with Anica's second-in-command, who was now head of the Transylvanian guild. He was a middle-aged man with gray starting to streak his dark hair. He told me he'd escaped from Eastern Europe with the rest of the Guild and had, in fact, briefly met Francis Kader in London in 1950.

Together he and I went through Anica and the guild's papers. We found nothing on a necromancer counter-spell. I asked why Anica hadn't taught him but had been teaching Ernestine.

"I don't know," he said. "Perhaps it's a spell that has to be done by a woman."

I'd never heard of such a thing, but I supposed it was possible.

Brown was disappointed when I told him I didn't find anything in Idaho, but he seemed to appreciate that I had the idea and took the initiative.

I approached Vaughan late in July.

"I have an idea about how to kill Ernestine," I said. "I wanted to run it by you before going to Brown."

Vaughan was in his suite on the thirteenth floor. I made the mistake of showing up too early in the morning, and there was still a woman in his bed. I didn't know if she was an adept or not, but Vaughan closed the door to the bedroom and sat down at the table in the suite's main room, wearing a robe.

"What's that?"

"Thor," I stated simply. The Atlantian priest was still alive, still bound to Yggdrasil under a glacier in Iceland.

He stared at me as if to determine if I were serious.

"I see two problems," he said. "One, the Icelandic Guild would have to approve. And two, he was defeated by Loki when Loki had the Hammer of Thor, and Kader defeated Loki without the Hammer. Oh," he said quickly, "you'd need to get the Hammer of Thor from the Valkyrie and I don't see them giving that up except maybe to Thor. And even with the Hammer, I don't think he's going to be strong enough to defeat a five-hundred-year-old necromancer. I'm afraid no one is."

"So we just let her go?"

He shook his head. "No, we need to do whatever it takes to kill her. But first we have to find her."

"I have an idea about that, too," I stated.

"I'm all ears," he said with a grin, his blue eyes looking at me. I told him my plan and he said I should proceed with the first part, and if successful, take the idea to Brown.

August 2nd, a Friday, I went to the Purple Chrysanthemum. It'd been a little over four months since I had been there, and the place seemed even seedier. My contact wasn't there so I talked to the bartender. She used her tattooed arm to shove a drink at me. I'd never seen a tattoo on a woman before. Her long black hair—too black to be natural—hung straight to her mid back. Her eyes had thick black eyeliner, which made her look slightly like a raccoon to me.

"He ain't here," she said when I asked.

"When do you expect him?"

The word that came out of her mouth at that point, an Anglo-Saxon colloquialism for sexual intercourse, startled even me. "I don't know, he's in Costa Mesa," she said after.

"Where's Costa Mesa?" I had to talk loudly over the music.

"Near L.A."

"Why is he there?"

She rolled her eyes as if I'd said the stupidest thing possible and shoved a flyer at me. It was a round piece of paper, like a record; even had a hole in the middle for the spindle. It was advertising the "First Annual Newport Pop Music Festival" and listed something like twenty groups, most of whom I'd never heard of. I mean, who the heck were "Sonny and Cher"?

Seems I had a choice: go to Costa Mesa or wait for him to come back. Something about Ernestine's warning about not being in the U.S. was grating on me. For some reason I didn't think I had a lot of time to spare.

I took the flyer and left, happy to be out of the cacophonous racket that was called music, and then went back to the Huntington. Brown was in his suite reading. I smiled as I walked in. Rumor had it he was illiterate when he joined the guild during World War II.

"Teacher," I said.

"Student," he replied, putting down his book. I could see the name on the cover: *The Autobiography of Malcolm X*. I had no idea who that was. Brown just looked at me with those piercing dark eyes.

"I have a hunch about how to find Ernestine," I started.

He raised an eyebrow. "Oh?"

"It may not pan out. But I need to go to Los Angeles and maybe elsewhere after that."

"Europe?"

"Maybe. But I won't face her alone."

"That is probably wise."

"I need your permission to expend guild resources."

Brown looked at me. "It's not your fault...she fooled everyone."

I shook my head. "No, I knew what she was and I protected her."

"Because you love her."

"I thought I did. I let my feelings for her cloud my judgment."

Brown smiled for a moment then became serious. "How long do you need?"

"If nothing comes of it, a couple of weeks. Longer if I need to go to Europe again, but I don't know how long."

"Okay, report back to me regularly," he said.

"Thank you, Teacher."

He dismissed me with a wave of his hand and picked up the book again. He read a bit and shook his head. I got the feeling he wasn't enjoying the book.

Chapter Eleven

Costa Mesa, California
August 3, 1968

There were cars and young people everywhere. Some of the
women were in nothing more than short shorts and bikini tops.
And there were cops: cops standing around, cops in cars, cops on
motorcycles.

"You sure this is where you want to go, mac?" the taxi driver
asked, looking over his shoulder. I could hear music being played
loudly far off.

"If you don't want to go any farther, I'll walk," I offered. He'd
made a good fare bringing me here from the Los Angeles airport.

"This doesn't look like your type of crowd, mister," he said,
chuckling around an unlit cigarette. I'd used a persuasion spell to
keep him from smoking.

"It's not," I said grimly, and looking at the mass of humanity,
finding my contact seemed unlikely.

I just about jumped when someone knocked on the car
window next to me. I turned to see a cop peering through the glass.
He was wearing one of those black and white cop motorcycle
helmets and mirrored sunglasses.

"Sir, are you lost?" he asked when I rolled down the window.

I chuckled. "No, I'm looking for someone."

The cop shook his head. "There's something like a hundred
thousand people here. Good luck finding them."

191

"What is this?" the taxi driver asked.

"A rock concert," the cop replied.

"I think I can find him," I told the policeman.

Even wearing those sunglasses I could tell he was skeptical. "Okay, good luck."

I had to pay $5.50 at the entrance, and they stamped the back of my hand so I could get in the next day. I wondered if they really didn't expect me to wash my hands before then. Getting into the crowd I suddenly wasn't surprised by that. There was a stage with a striped canopy over it at the far end of an open field, and between it and the entrance was a writhing, dusty, smelly, smoky herd of humanity. The music wasn't loud enough for me to make out the words, but I'd heard rock music and that didn't seem to be a problem, to me. But the dust was billowing and oppressive, and I immediately felt filthy. I regretted wearing a nice suit, and my expensive shoes were getting filthy.

I stood still and tried to concentrate. He wasn't an adept, but I'd spoken with him enough times I should be able to at least get a general idea of where he was.

I found him shirtless and dancing with a Rubenesque girl, also shirtless, about half way through the mob. He looked at me, blinked, and then went back to dancing. The music wasn't even the type I would think one could dance to.

I tapped his bare shoulder. "We need to talk."

"Later, man!"

My fingers were wrapped around my talisman in my slacks pocket. I was regretting the suit coat as it was too hot to be wearing one. "Now," I said, with just enough persuasion to get his attention.

He looked at the topless girl, then at me, shook his head and walked toward the back of the crowd. Once we got far enough away the music was indistinct again, he glared at me, his arms crossed over his bare chest.

"I don't see you since March, and this is when you come to find me?"

"I'm in a hurry."

He shook his head. "What have you got for me?"

This was not how it was done, he was either on drugs or really mad, or both. "Nothing, I need your help."

"What, man?"

"In March you said the Cubans were importing drugs to the East Coast."

He looked around as if to make sure no one heard. "Yeah, what about it?"

"I need to talk to someone in the Cuban intelligence service."

"The DGI?"

"Yes."

"Why?"

I gave him a look he couldn't mistake.

"Okay," he said holding up his hands. "Maybe I can get you hooked up through some of my East Coast connections."

"How and when?"

"How? I call them. When, Monday."

"Tonight," I said. It was Saturday.

He studied my face for a moment. "Something's got you worried."

"Yes, but it's none of your business."

"Okay, I'll call tonight."

"Good, where are you staying?"

"I'm sleeping in my car. I'll have to find a pay phone."

I let out a long, frustrated breath. "Meet me in the morning," I stated, "At the front gate to this place, nine sharp."

"Damn, gates don't open until ten."

"Nine," I said.

I left, ignoring the stares my attire and short hair brought. It was longer than the crew cut I'd worn after getting burned by the wooden Indian, but was still shorter than any other male around except for the cops. Somebody snorted, "Narc!" but I ignored them.

I had a nice hotel room and enjoyed a nice long shower to get the dust off, but couldn't quite get the taste out of my mouth until I ate dinner.

At nine the next morning my contact looked much more lucid. He even had a shirt on. The girl he was dancing with waited a polite distance away while we talked. She, too, was more dressed.

"These East Coast dealers, they don't mess around," he said.

"I can handle myself."

"Yeah, they were all interested in meeting you when I told them you were a meta."

"Just give me a name and a place." I wanted out of there before the waves of humanity splashed up against the entrance.

He handed me a piece of paper. I didn't recognize the name but the place was Miami Beach, Florida. I thanked him and he said I owed him. I nodded and walked away. I caught a cab that was dropping off some kids and the driver took me to the airport.

* * * *

It took a strong persuasion spell to get a hotel room in Miami Beach. What I didn't realize was that the Republican National Convention was being held there that week. I was to meet a "lieutenant" in the local syndicate. There was a phone number to call on the paper I had been given in California, so when I got to my room, I called it.

"Hello?" a voice on the other end said. Was it my imagination or was it ominous sounding.

"This is Peter Branton. I was told to call this number."

There was some hesitation. Maybe he was talking to someone else in the room. "You know the Raleigh Hotel?"

"I can find it."

"The bar, six tonight."

"How will I—" They hung up.

I was in the bar at five-thirty. It was all modern with bright colors and uncomfortable chairs. A three-man combo played soft jazz in the corner. I sat so I could see the door. There were a few other people in the place, mostly couples quietly talking amongst themselves. The prices seemed to be keeping the conventioneers away.

A man walked in wearing an expensive suit that somehow didn't fit him right. Two other men followed, also in suits, also looking out of place. Then a girl came in, blonde, chewing gum, in a sequined mini-dress, her hair all piled on top of her head and too much makeup on. She sat at the bar, looking bored. The bartender gave her a martini without her asking. *She must be a regular*, I thought.

The first man sat down opposite of me at the table. "You Barton?"

"Branton," I corrected, then wondered why I did.

"You're the meta from California, right?" He said the name of the state as if it were something untoward.

"Yes," I nodded.

"You want to talk to someone from Havana?"

"Yes, the DGI."

He looked around as if he was scared someone heard that. He put his hands up and looked at me as if I were stupid. "What can you do for us?"

I glanced at the girl. "I could not turn her into a toad." I was trying to say, "I'm an adept, don't mess with me" in a lighthearted fashion.

He laughed. "Broads are a dime a dozen. What you going to do for my boss?"

I really hadn't considered this. I didn't think appeals to his patriotism would work. "What does your boss need?"

"For the feds to keep off his back during this whole Republican Convention thing."

"What do you mean?"

"I mean, they are cracking down on drugs, girls, gambling...gotta put on a good wholesome show for the GOP."

"I have no influence with the government."

"Yeah, but you have *powers*."

"Over people, yes, but governments, no."

He scowled at me. "I don't see how we can do business, then."

"There's got to be something," I said, trying to keep the whine out of my voice.

He just stared at me. "Either that, or it's money."

I blinked. Could it be that easy? "How much money?"

He shrugged. "Fifteen gees."

I assumed that meant $15,000 dollars. More than I expected, but not impossible. "Know any high-stakes poker games?"

* * * *

The Republicans nominated former Vice President Richard M. Nixon for their candidate for president. I knew this because I didn't have much to do in Miami Beach, except watch the convention coverage on television and wait. After paying the mobsters the money they wanted, they said "someone" would be in touch.

The three major networks had little but convention coverage. Even the black and white "public" station was mostly convention coverage. There was one independent channel but it showed mostly old movies that didn't interest me much. So I got to see the fight to make a governor named Romney be Nixon's vice president. He lost to someone named Spiro Agnew.

I did enjoy walking on the beach and exploring the art deco district. But nothing can ruin what looked to be a nice city like a thousand or so political conventioneers in big cowboy hats and bedecked with multiple huge buttons.

On Thursday—my fourth day in Miami Beach—my room's phone rang. I walked to the T.V. and turned it off and then answered the phone.

"Branton?" a male voice asked.

"Yes," I answered.

And they hung up. But then almost immediately there was a knock on my room's door.

I opened it. A young man in a business suit was standing there. He didn't look Cuban to me. "If you'd come with me, sir."

I grabbed my sport coat and followed him to the elevator, down to the lobby, and out the hotel's front door, where a white Chevrolet was waiting. White Chevys seemed to be pretty ubiquitous in Miami, I'd noticed. My escort never said a word but opened the back door of the car. I hesitated a moment, then decided I could probably handle most anything these folk could come up with unless they shot me with a dart gun.

196

The car was very simple inside with vinyl seats. It did have air conditioning, and the AM radio was playing Nixon's acceptance speech. The driver turned it off.

My escort got in the front and started to light a cigarette. I had my hand on my talisman so he stopped.

We drove east into Miami and the car stopped in front of a park. I was confused but my escort jumped out of the car and opened my door. "This way, please."

We walked into the park, which at this late hour, as the sun was getting low, was nearly empty. There was a man at a bench who appeared to be in his late fifties or early sixties. His gray suit seemed too big for him, and his rumpled hat was on his knees. Most people wouldn't give him a second look. He was reading a newspaper. The headline was about Nixon winning the Republican nomination the night before. My escort approached him; they spoke softly to each other in Spanish, and I didn't get a translation spell up in time. Then the escort stepped a discreet distance away. I sat on the bench.

"You're Peter Branton?" the man asked.

"Yes."

"I'm doing this as a favor for a friend."

"I appreciate that."

"Forgive me for insisting we meet here. Less chance of FBI bugs."

But, I thought, *anyone with a telephoto lens could take pictures*. I didn't bring it up. "That's fine." I hesitated a moment. "You're DGI?"

"Yes, I work in the *Dirección General de Inteligencia*."

"I need to ask about an assassination job the DGI did in Idaho in March."

"Idaho?" he asked.

"Yes."

"Where is this 'Idaho'?"

I didn't know if he was playing stupid or really didn't know. "The U.S. Pacific Northwest, east of Washington State."

"I know nothing about this."

"Who would?" I was about to hit him with a truth spell.

"Nobody I know. The DGI did not and would not run such an operation."

"One of the assassins told me he was with the DGI. And the CIA confirmed through fingerprints that he was with the DGI." I was simplifying the story for brevity's sake.

He looked at me as if questioning if I were serious. "My division of the DGI, we sell drugs from South America to the American mobsters, because it's a source of hard currency and helps undermine your capitalist imperial society. We do not do assassinations."

"Two of the assassins came out of Florida," I tried. "Did you have anyone reassigned who disappeared?"

I saw in his eyes that I'd hit on something. "In February, two of my operatives were ordered back to Cuba. I assumed they were assigned elsewhere. The DGI has many operations."

I wished I had Agent Shaw's color glossies of the dead men to show this man. "You said your division. The DGI must have other divisions."

He nodded.

"So who would know?"

He turned on the bench so he could look me in the eye. "I tell you this because I understand you are a meta."

"Yes," I confirmed, ignoring his use of the term "meta."

"So you could simply use a spell to get me to tell the truth."

"Yes, I'd prefer not to." Actually, I didn't care, but if he thought I was sympathetic he might tell me more.

He nodded. "And I would prefer you didn't. To authorize an assassination on American soil, that order would have to come from Raul Castro if not higher."

"Higher?" I didn't think there was anything higher.

"*El Jefe*," the man said, pulling on an imaginary beard. I knew he meant Fidel.

I let out a long breath. I'd hit a dead end. There was no way I'd be able to talk to Raul or Fidel Castro. And even if I did, they'd be protected by strong adepts. According to Vaughan, they were very strong adepts.

"Thank you for your time." I couldn't believe this meeting cost me $15,000. I felt like a sucker. I stood up, but the man grabbed my sleeve.

"There is one thing," he said. "Who was the target of the assassination?"

"An adept," I stated.

The man's eyes grew wide. "You need to talk to Major Pimenov."

"Who's that?"

"The KGB's specialist on dealing with the meta guilds."

"And where would I find him?"

"Dzerzhinsky Square, I would think."

"And where is that?" I asked with trepidation.

I said a bad word in the ancient language when he told me, confirming my fears.

* * * *

I got Helms' direct line phone number from Vaughan. Well, direct to his secretary, that is. I left a message with her stating I had information on necromancers and the KGB, and the phone number of my Miami Beach hotel.

Karamessines called me back a few hours later. He wouldn't talk on the phone because it wasn't "secure," but he did say he'd talk to me in person.

The next day I was in Langley, Virginia, walking across a marble CIA shield set in a terrazzo floor and past a display with black stars on it.

"Each star is a CIA agent killed in the line of duty," my escort explained.

"There's no names," I observed.

"Yes," the young man in a dark suit, white shirt, and narrow tie said. "Most of them are classified."

I wondered if there was or would be a star there for Wynter.

We took an elevator up to the third floor. This complex was huge, it seemed, with mostly white walls and non-descript (and often unlabeled) doors and highly-polished tile floors that made your footfalls echo.

But the elevator let us off on a floor with carpet, wood paneling, and doors with titles such as "Deputy Director for Plans." This was Karamessines' office.

He had a large antechamber with a woman sitting behind a large desk. She looked to be about fifty and would take no guff from anyone. My escort announced who I was and then said, "I need to get back to my office," and left, seemingly in a hurry to get away from her.

"Have a seat, please, Mr. Barton," the woman said pointing to an uncomfortable looking chair.

"Branton," I corrected.

"My apologies," she said perfunctorily, and went back to typing on a large typewriter.

About twenty minutes later the phone buzzed and she answered it. "Yes, sir." She hung up. "You may go in, now."

I smiled at her, getting nothing in return, and walked into the door in the far wall next to her desk.

Karamessines was sitting behind a larger wooden desk. The office was very plush and he had pictures on the wall. In one he was shaking hands with Nixon and in another he was posing with former president Joseph P. Kennedy, Jr. There were no pictures of the current president, Johnson.

I sat in one of the leather chairs before his desk and he gave me an unhappy look.

"I thought the necromancer threat was over," he said. "You told me so."

I found myself squirming. "I thought it was," I stated honestly. "And the threat to the U.S. was at least delayed a while."

"So what happened?"

"The young lady I was with turned out to be a necromancer, and she may be working with the Russians." No need to tell him what Ernestine told me, because then I'd have to admit I'd seen her.

"To what end?" Karamessines demanded, pushing up his horn-rimmed glasses.

"That's what I'd like to find out."

He looked at me intently. "How?"

"I have a lead, a Major Pimenov of the KGB."

Karamessines frowned. "Don't know that name, but only being a major I'm not surprised. I'm sure we have something on him. What do you need?"

"Full name, picture, where to find him."

"Probably Dzerzhinsky Square," Karamessines said with a smirk.

"What is that?" I asked emphatically. All the Cuban would say was it was in Moscow, Russia.

"KGB headquarters," Karamessines explained.

I frowned. "Not as if I can waltz into there."

"No," Karamessines agreed.

"Is there any way the CIA could arrange a meeting with Pimenov and me?"

Karamessines shook his large head. "No, he's too far down the food chain. The Russians will suspect something and deny it."

"Can you get me into Moscow?"

Karamessines shook his head again. "Until you can get me something more substantive, you're on your own." I had a feeling that was his decision, perhaps payback for my making him fly Ernestine and me home first class, or for losing the diplomatic passport in Romania, or both.

"Okay," I said softly. I thought about using a persuasion spell, but I didn't want to anger him further. I might need the CIA's help again. "How about any information you have on Major Pimenov?"

He nodded. "That's not a problem." He picked up the handset to one of the phones on his desk. That's when I noticed there were three.

* * * *

I was sitting in the back of a cramped taxi on a street not far from Red Square and facing Dzerzhinsky Square. I had to use money and persuasion spells to keep the driver from driving off...and smoking.

"They are probably watching us," he said nervously in Russian (I was using a translation spell).

I had a copy of a picture of Major Dmitry Ivanovich Pimenov of the Second Chief Directorate of the Committee for State Security. That is, the KGB. The picture had been taken with a telephoto lens, and Pimenov was standing with a group of KGB officers outside the building in front of me. The taxi driver called it the "Lubyanka Building" with his voice alloyed with fear. It was a bright, sunny day without a cloud in the sky, and the interior of the taxi was uncomfortably warm.

I used far seeing to watch every man that came out. Around six in the evening, I finally saw Pimenov, in uniform, walk out of the building and toward the subway line entrance. He kept his head down, perhaps against the glare of the sun. Maybe sunglasses were hard to come by in the worker's paradise.

"Follow him!" I ordered. I didn't want to lose him in the subway.

The taxi moved forward slowly as I watched Pimenov approach the stairs to the Metro.

Suddenly a small car with a flashing blue light on top pulled in front of us and its tires squealed as it stopped. Luckily, the taxi was still moving slowly or we'd probably have hit it. The taxi driver swore and put up his hands as a second car pulled behind us. Men were jumping out of the cars, waving pistols, and yelling in Russian.

I caught a glimpse of Pimenov turning around, looking confused, and then walking back toward the Lubyanka Building.

I was roughly pulled from the car by an armed man yelling Russian obscenities. The driver and I were put in separate vehicles and then all three police cars (as I assumed that's what they were) drove off, their high-pitched, two-tone sirens cutting through the air as their blue lights flashed garishly. I decided to wait and see what happened. Plus I had to explain that the taxi driver was innocent. I'd feel bad if I got him in trouble with the authorities. I'd misjudged Russian paranoia, apparently.

* * * *

On the third floor of the Lubyanka Building was an office. After talking to dozens of Russian officials I accomplished two things: I convinced them that the taxi driver was an innocent pawn whom I'd used my power on, and I'd managed to see this man, Yuri Andropov, Chairman of the KGB.

"Sit down, Mr. Branton," he said in Russian.

The office was dark with only a few lamps lighting it. Everything looked about twenty years out of style and date. There was something like seven black phones on his desk. If one rang, I had no idea how he knew which one to answer. Most of the light in the room was coming from a window overlooking Dzerzhinsky Square.

I sat, looking at the man's balding pate. He looked back at me through his glasses, which also seemed about twenty years out of style.

"I am a very busy man," Andropov said brusquely. "I know you are an American adept, and I know you were in Romania on a diplomatic passport from sixteen April to the thirtieth, at the behest of the Central Intelligence Agency."

He studied me as if to determine if that made an impression on me; it did.

"What is your interest in Major Pimenov?"

I leaned forward in my chair. I had no idea how to handle this. How far up in the KGB did Ernestine's plans go?

"I believe there is a threat to both our countries," I said simply. "Necromancers operating in Romania are part of it. I have reason to believe Major Pimenov may know how to find them."

Andropov nodded sagely. "He is in charge of our liaison to the adept guilds in the Soviet Union. But I know nothing of a threat to our country, at least not involving the adepts or 'necromancers' as you say."

"May I ask Major Pimenov?" I was wondering if I could use a persuasion spell. It would work, but what would be the repercussions? It is possible to kill or imprison an adept if you know what you are doing.

Andropov studied my face. "Yes, you may talk to Pimenov. Briefly."

"Thank you, sir," I said gratefully, and I meant it. Andropov picked up the handset on one of the phones.

I didn't know if the KGB headquarters was always so busy. There were men and the occasional woman running up and down the green-walled halls, their boots or shoes smacking the marble flooring. The tone of the place was that something was up. I didn't think it all had to do with me; I hoped it didn't have to do with Ernestine's plan to end the Cold War.

Pimenov was not happy about having to talk to me. He took me into a white-walled room that had a simple wooden desk and two wooden chairs. The floor was ugly green tile and the room was lit by one bare incandescent bulb. The door was solid steel.

"This room isn't bugged," he said in Russian as he closed the door with a solid sounding clang.

"Good," I said, sitting down.

He sat opposite me. "The woman you know as Ernestine I know as Gabriela. She came to me years ago with an idea."

"What idea?" I asked. I was still using a translation spell.

"How to end the Cold War. All she wanted in exchange was to be left in peace to form her own guild of necromancers."

This jibed with what she'd told me in Paris, so far.

"And how could she end the Cold War?" I asked.

"Destroy the United States."

I looked at his face to see if he were joking. He seemed perfectly serious. "How?"

"You know necromancers can manipulate objects, including teleportation?"

I nodded. "I have firsthand experience with that."

"The Soviet Union has enough nuclear weapons to destroy the United States. But the Americans will retaliate if we launch our missiles against them."

"Mutual assured destruction," I stated.

"Yes. But what if they had no warning? What if there were nuclear explosions that came from nowhere, destroying first their ability to respond, then taking out the leadership of the country? And maybe a few of the larger cities, making the United States no longer a threat."

"How?"

"Teleport the nuclear bombs over their targets. There will be no warning before they are detonated."

I was amazed he was telling me this, but I had questions. "What about the nuclear submarines and the bombers? I'm sure the U.S. will respond. There's multi-layers of command and control." I assumed there was, at least. That's how I would set it up.

"Every American nuclear missile submarine has a Soviet attack submarine following it. They will be sunk before they can launch. And if any bombers escape our attack, they will be stopped by our air defense forces. Even if one or two nuclear weapons manage to hit the motherland, the U.S. will no longer be a threat, and that will be worth it."

"Who in your government knows about this?"

"It goes all the way to Brezhnev. We have a little matter of Czechoslovakia to deal with, and then we will be ready. The biggest obstacle was the head of the Transylvanian guild, and now that she is dead, we can proceed."

"As soon as Czechoslovakia is dealt with?"

He nodded. "Yes, it actually works out quite well: we get our troops west, close to Western Europe, without drawing suspicion that we are going to invade."

I was surprised he was telling me all of this; it made me nervous. The more I knew, the less likely they would be to let me leave alive.

"Where's Ernestine—Gabriela?"

"She's in Transylvania training the necromancers that will teleport the weapons. One necromancer can teleport about ten, depending on how powerful they are, but we need to teleport hundreds all at one time."

S. Evan Townsend

I shuddered; hundreds of nuclear weapons detonating over the U.S. It would kill millions, and probably make large parts of the country uninhabitable.

"Wouldn't you have to gather them all in one place?" I asked. If I could find out where they were shipping nuclear warheads, maybe I could find Ernestine.

He shook his head. "The Strategic Rocket Forces and the KGB Ninth Directorate would never allow that. No, they will simply teleport them from their bunkers or missile-tips to their targets."

I was curious why Brezhnev couldn't order the Strategic Rocket Forces or whoever to do what was needed.

"Why are you telling me all of this?" It made no sense unless they were planning to kill me or imprison me.

"Gabriela told me to. She doesn't want you going back to the United States. Apparently she cares about you."

Any feelings I had for her were gone, knowing she planned to kill millions of people just so she could have a guild.

"So you're just going to let me go?"

"Gabriela is fine with us keeping you here until you are no longer a threat. But I think you are going to be tragically killed trying to escape."

He stopped masking and shot an airbolt at me. I tried to duck but it still hit my left arm, and I heard and felt the bone cracking as I was spun around and fell to the floor. Then my air started getting thin as he took it from me. I shot fire at his feet, which I don't think he expected because he jumped up and down with his black boots burning. I scrambled to my feet and shoved my left hand in my pocket, ignoring the pain this caused in my arm, and grabbed my talisman hard.

My air was getting thin again as he moved all of the air in the small room to his side. The problem was that meant he had more oxygen, and that makes fire burn hotter. My fireball looked weak until it hit that thicker air, where it blazed to life and hit him in the chest, knocking him against the room's door. His brown uniform was singed, and I felt the air return to my side of the room like a wave washing over me.

I shot lightning at his forehead that he was unable to avoid. He crumpled to the floor, and I used my last bit of energy to pull the air from him until I was sure he was no longer breathing. Then I sat in the chair and sucked in air as if I'd just run a mile. My arm was starting to hurt a lot, and between the shoulder and the elbow it bent in ways it shouldn't. If I healed it I'd pass out, and I didn't want to do that, yet.

Ernestine is back in Transylvania, I thought. Maybe I could find her and keep her in sight while alerting the guilds, and this time send a hundred adepts to kill her.

But my first problem was escaping this building.

Luckily, a glamor spell was low-power, and I'd seen enough KGB uniforms to emulate one. I didn't dare go back to my hotel that the INTOURIST bureau had assigned me. Instead, I found a taxi (which was tough, they were rare) and had it take me to the airport.

* * * *

Aeroflot made TAROM look luxurious and friendly. The stewardesses were rude, unattractive, and just plain mean. The plane was dirty, the seats were small, and the food inedible. I spent the flight from Moscow to Bucharest sleeping after healing my broken arm.

I was actually glad to step off the plane in Bucharest. I even had my *Agentia de Turism* visa and itinerary, obtained in the Moscow airport with the usual combination of money and persuasion spells. My only lead to Ernestine was Vali in Pitesti. My *Agentia de Turism* visa was only for Bucharest, but I didn't worry much about that. I had to ditch my *Agentia de Turism* escort, dress like a local, and walk a lot. There was no disguising my green eyes, which for some reason a lot of the locals refused to look into. The bus ride to Pitesti was long and miserable. It was the middle of August and the heat was beyond oppressive.

In Pitesti I had no transportation and had to walk, which a lot of the residents seemed to do, also. There were some buses that ran on erratic schedules, according to a young woman I asked. I had a vague idea where Vali's garage was located. Pitesti is not a small town but the area that is not huge apartment blocks or ancient cobblestone streets was thankfully much smaller. I asked passersby, and eventually one actually knew where it was.

I opened the door and stepped inside. The Trabant was parked there, inside, and I heard Vali call out from the rear. I brought up a translation spell: "Vali, it's me, Peter."

Vali walked out from the back of the garage. "Who are you?" he demanded and picked up a large wrench that would make a good cudgel.

"It's me, Peter," I said, making sure my hands were visible. "Ernestine's friend."

"I don't know any Ernestine and I don't know you."

I studied his face and saw no deception there. "Where were you born, Vali?"

"Right here in Pitesti, why?"

"What's your birthday?"

He opened his mouth as if to answer, then looked confused for a moment. He dug in his overalls and pulled out his identification papers. "March 28, 1926," he read.

I shook my head. Ernestine had messed with his mind, making him forget her, me, and apparently his birthday, which is a typical side effect.

"Do you mind?" I said, suddenly weary, and I sat in a wooden chair that was incongruously in the garage.

"Who are you?" Vali demanded again, holding the wrench in a threatening manner.

I sighed, reached in my pocket, and tossed a ten dollar bill on the floor. "Leave me alone," I whined. My last lead to Ernestine was gone, and I didn't want to think about what would happen if she completed her plans.

Vali picked up the bill and his attitude changed completely. "Can I help you?"

I just looked at him. "No, I don't think so."

"I have a question for you, then," he said. "What is your name?"

I frowned. "Peter Branton, why?"

He looked surprised. "I have something for you."

I sat up, curious despite myself.

"For me?"

He nodded, looking confused. "I found it in my car after I took a drive. I get it."

I watched as Vali walked into the back of the garage, leaving me alone with the Trabant. He returned a few minutes later with a standard envelope you might buy in a stationary store. Written on the outside was "Peter Branton." I opened it and pulled out the note inside. It was in English:

* * * *

August 16, 1968

Peter,

If you're reading this you've escaped from the KGB. I've gone home. Please don't follow me, and please stay out of America. I've erased Vali's memory so he can't help you find me, either.

Ernestine

P.S.: I love you

* * * *

I'd missed her by two days.

Home, I thought. She told me once she was born in a small village in Transylvania and it was still there. Problem was, there were probably thousands of small villages there. She knew the chances I could find her were slim.

"The *Militia* almost confiscated it," Vali said for some reason.

"*Militia*?" I asked.

He nodded, having long since set down the wrench and pocketed the money. "They stopped me on the outskirts of town. Had to bribe them with some of this that I had." He pulled out the ten-spot and then quickly re-pocketed it. "Don't know where I got it."

"Where were you coming from?"

"I don't remember."

I wondered if there was a chance. "May I see your papers?"

He looked confused but handed them over. I leafed through them. They were much like a passport, with stamps representing places Vali had permission to go. The most recent stamp was a *Militia* stamp for Pitesti. But the one before that was the same day in some place called Hunedoara.

"Where's Hunedoara?" I asked.

"Transylvania," Vali said. "Why?"

I smiled. "I need you to drive me there."

"I don't know where it is," Vali stated.

I rolled my eyes. Ernestine had done a number on his brain.

Chapter Twelve

Pitesti, Romania
August 18, 1968

Apparently in Romania, maps are hard to come by. Don't know if that's because the central planners of the economy don't think they are important, or if it's a security measure. I suspected the latter. I remembered Wynter had maps the CIA provided him, with the added advantage of being in English. I had Vali drive me to the County Theater. The car was gone, which after almost four months didn't surprise me. We tried the local library, but since it was Sunday it was closed. I sat in Vali's car, looking at the obviously old building and the wooden doors. "Have any wire, Vali?" I asked. He found some in the trunk, perfectly thin and stiff for my needs. The lock on the door appeared as ancient as the building, and I could have picked it in about a minute. But someone had installed a modern looking but poorly built second lock with Cyrillic writing on it; apparently it was made in Russia. It took me a good twenty minutes to pick it while Vali kept lookout for the *Militia*.

Inside I didn't turn on the lights, but there was plenty of illumination coming through the windows.

"What are we looking for?" Vali whispered.

"Atlases, maps of Romania," I whispered back, not sure why.

We found three maps of Romania, but none were very detailed and the proportions seemed wrong, as if they were purposely distorted. None showed where Hunedoara was.

I was frustrated. We walked out of the library just as the sun was setting, and Vali lit a cigarette. That's when the men set upon us, waving machine guns and pistols and yelling loudly. I put up my hands. I could have teleported away, but that would have left poor Vali to face these guns alone. This getting captured was getting old.

* * * *

A big black car pulled up—one of those that Wynter had identified as a Russian car called "Zil"—and looked new yet also looked twenty years out of style. A man stepped out wearing a suit. All the uniformed men came to attention and saluted, either with their right hand or by clasping their weapon across their chest. The man was short, thin, and had old-fashioned horn-rimmed glasses. His hair was dark and pulled back from his receding hairline. He did have a rather prominent nose. If you'd seen him on the street you wouldn't have given him a second look.

He talked briefly with the man who, up until then, appeared to be in charge. The man pointed at me, saluted, and stepped back. The little man walked up to me and smiled. I was in handcuffs and against the library wall. Two men were holding me so I couldn't teleport. Vali had been whisked away in a car.

"I'm sorry I missed you last time you were in my country, Mr. Branton," he said in English with just a trace of an accent.

"I'm sorry, who are you?" I asked.

The man gave me an almost coy grin. "I am Ion Parasca, and I am the head of the *Departamentul de Informatii Externe*."

I didn't say anything so he continued talking. "The *Militia Economica* has been keeping an eye on your comrade here ever since the revolutionary captain on his street said he was throwing around American dollars."

I assumed that was some sort of economic police, an interesting thing for a country to have. I still stayed silent.

Parasca looked at me. "We need to talk, Mr. Branton. I believe we have interests in common and should work together."

"Let Vali go," I said. I realized I didn't know his last name.

Parasca nodded and smiled. "Of course. We will interrogate him briefly and release him."

"He doesn't know anything," I stated. "The necromancer cleared his memory."

That got Parasca's attention. "Pity. But again, don't worry, I will personally order his release."

Normally I'd be about as likely to believe a Communist government official as to flap my arms and fly. But something about the way this man talked and looked me in the eye made me believe him.

"If you'll come with me, please?" he said and he spoke to one of the men holding me. They let me go and one undid the handcuffs. We walked to the car and got into the back seat, and it sped away from the group of men.

"How much do you know?" I asked.

Parasca shook his head and smiled. "There are rogue elements in the DIE and the KGB working with a female necromancer. To what end, we don't know, yet."

"Rogue?" I asked. "I was told this goes all the way to Soviet Premiere Brezhnev."

Parasca look surprised. "And who told you that?"

"A KGB officer named Pimenov."

"Major Dmitry Pimenov?" he asked

"Yes," I said emphatically.

Parasca was quiet for a moment. "I hope he was lying to you."

"Andropov didn't seem to know anything about it," I stated. "At least that was my impression."

"The chairman of the KGB?"

"Yes," I confirmed.

"That's good news, I think."

I had to think a minute. "So this isn't an authorized operation of the KGB and the DIE."

"No," he said. "I know my DIE has nothing to do with this, and I don't believe the KGB does either. That is, unless the Soviets are lying to us…which is possible, but they pretend to be as confused as we are, including Andropov."

"What about the DGI?"

"The Cubans? What about it?"

"Elements seemed to be involved, too. My sources say the Castros would have had to approve it."

"Damn," Parasca spat. "The rot goes deeper into the roots than I imagined."

He sat quietly for a moment, then his mood lightened and he chuckled. "You picked an interesting night to return to Romania, Mr. Branton."

"What do you mean?"

He just looked at me with that same coy grin.

We rode in silence for a few minutes. I had no idea where they were taking me—I assumed to a *Securitate* station. "How did you know we were at the library?"

"DGTO microphones picked you up talking about Hunedoara and looking for maps. It was unusual to hear activity in the library when it is closed, so this got our attention right away."

Oh, great, I thought, *another acronym*. Why did governments insist on using so many of them? I wondered. "DGTO"? I asked.

"*Directia Generala de Technica Operativa*," he explained, which explained nothing. "We know your friend Vali was in Hunedoara, so we suspect the necromancer is there, too."

"As do I," I said. "And there's probably more than one of them."

He gave me a look that indicated he was surprised I knew that. "Yes," he finally said softly.

It was dark when the car pulled into an airport, past a high chain link fence with circular barbed wire around the top and electric lights everywhere. There were many guards, all holding that same weapon it seemed all soldiers and guards in Romania and Russia used. The long, curved box underneath to hold the bullets was distinctive.

The car pulled up next to a helicopter. It was roundish and had a long tail with the rotor at the end. The four top rotors drooped over the body so low I wondered why they didn't hit the boom tail when the engine was started. It sat on four tires: two on each side at the end of triangular booms, and two together under the nose, sort of like a tractor. This one was painted in blotchy brown colors like camouflage, and had a row of round windows down the body.

"Please forgive the Spartan nature of our transportation. It was all I could arrange on short notice."

"Where are we going?" I asked.

"Ceausescu wants to meet you."

I looked at him intently to see if he was serious. Apparently he was.

As we stepped out of the car, Parasca leaned in and talked to the driver, who nodded and sped away. Parasca chuckled. "The local governor will be glad to have his Zil back."

I followed him through the door on the side of the aircraft.

The inside of the helicopter was indeed very austere. There were about thirty metal seats, four abreast with a center aisle, all facing forward. The rows were close together and there was no padding on the seats. There were also no seatbelts.

Parasca sat down in the front row so I did the same, across the aisle from him. *Almost as bad as Aeroflot*, I mused. When the helicopter started its engines (they started one at a time, that's how I knew there were two), the noise became almost unbearable. As the aircraft climbed into the sky, my ears started hurting. Parasca pointed at his face, made an exaggerated yawn, moved his lower jaw back and forth, and then indicated I should do the same. I followed suit and the pain went away, but the noise got louder. It was too loud to talk, so I was left with my own thoughts. Maybe the Romanians were going to help me; this seemed like an elaborate ruse to simply kill or imprison me. Of course, I didn't know what help the Romanians could offer. I wasn't sure Ernestine couldn't defeat a full army. When Hitler attacked the Valkyrie in order to steal the Hammer of Thor, he sent tens of thousands of men and barely defeated a few dozen Valkyrie. Ernestine was more powerful than probably all of them combined. *It might take a nuclear weapon to kill her*, I thought bitterly, and I didn't think Romania had any.

The helicopter landed after about an hour. Parasca and I got off, and I enjoyed the relative silence.

I recognized the Bucharest airport, even at night. A black car pulled up, almost identical to the one in Pitesti. Getting inside, it seemed to be a bit more luxurious and cleaner.

"My car," Parasca said proudly. He dropped me off at an *Agentia de Turism* hotel and said he'd be back at six. I looked at my watch: almost midnight. I decided I'd better sleep quickly. The room had been chosen and paid for already, so I fell into the bed, ignoring its lumps, and promptly fell asleep.

* * * *

Parasca was punctual. His black car was in front of the hotel just before six. I was dressed in the best clean suit I had. I'd been traveling for two weeks and was running out of clothes, and *Agentia de Turism* hotels didn't offer cleaning services.

We sped through the empty streets of the city, Parasca smiling quietly as we traveled. I wasn't sure why he was smiling, but he just seemed to be a genuinely content man. Maybe he knew something I didn't; or maybe he was high up enough in the Romanian government to not suffer the deprivations the general population did.

"I need to ask you something," I said.

"Yes?" he replied without any trepidation.

"Was it a rogue agent who kidnapped me in Bonn, or did you order that?"

His composure seemed to waver for just a moment. "I ordered that. We knew the CIA was sending an adept to Romania. We had to find out why."

"And the order to 'liquidate' me?"

He didn't look at me. "Standard procedure. Better for you to disappear than to tell the CIA what you'd told our intelligence services. Nothing personal."

Pretty personal to me, I thought. "And how did you know about me in the first place?"

He was silent for a moment, and then said, "I think it's going to be a lovely day, today."

We pulled up in front of a huge building, where there were more armed guards with those ubiquitous weapons. They saluted Parasca, even though he was wearing a business suit, as we walked up stairs to the front door, where another guard opened it for us. A few steps inside, our feet echoing on the marble tile, a small elderly man greeted Parasca.

"How is he today, Professor?" Parasca asked. I'd had the translation spell going since the car.

"The Czechoslovakia situation has the Comrade agitated, boss," the man replied. "I'll say a prayer for you."

Parasca patted the older man on the arm and smiled. "Thank you, Professor."

I was surprised by the talk of prayer. I thought all Communists were atheists: at least that's what the label said.

We continued walking down the hall and came to a large red door with vinyl upholstery on it, perhaps as a sound deadener or maybe they thought it looked classy. It was all the rage in the West twenty years ago.

We walked into an antechamber and Parasca pointed me to a chair. I could hear loud talking but it was indistinct. I used a spell to hear it better.

"...a spontaneous rally of the people to protest the Soviet invasion," a male voice said.

"When, Comrade?" another voice replied.

"Tomorrow. I will condemn the invasion. You will ensure the plaza is full."

"Yes, Comrade Ceausescu. May I be excused?"

"Of course," the man who must have been Ceausescu barked.

The door opened and a middle-aged man in a business suit scurried out, closing the door behind him. He was carrying a sheaf of papers.

"What is wrong, Comrade Buscan?" Parasca asked jovially.

Buscan gave a harried scowl at Parasca. "He wants a spontaneous rally tomorrow to protest the invasion."

"A lot of work to prepare for a spontaneous rally," Parasca said, patting the man on the shoulder.

"Yes; now if you'll excuse me, Comrade General."

"Yes, yes," Parasca said, and the man hurried out the door to the hall.

"There was an invasion?" I asked. Pimerov had talked about the Soviet Union invading Czechoslovakia.

Parasca studied me for a moment, and then must have decided it wouldn't hurt to tell me. "The Warsaw Pact, with the exception of Romania, is invading Czechoslovakia tonight."

I felt my eyes go wide. Pimerov said this was one step in their plans to eliminate the United States and invade Western Europe. We were running out of time.

The door to the office opened and I saw Ceausescu for the first time. He looked older than in his propaganda pictures. His angular face was etched with wrinkles, and his hair had a natural curliness to it the propagandists had failed to capture. It was also a lighter color, probably as it was starting to turn gray.

"Come in," Ceausescu growled, leaving the door open as he walked back into the room. Parasca walked in and I followed. The room reminded me of Yuri Andropov's office in that it was plush and luxurious, just twenty years out of date. The windows were covered with heavy red velvet drapes that were closed. On one wall there was a long shelf laden with what appeared to be heavy tomes. The author's name on all of them was Nicolae Ceausescu. The office was large enough to contain a massive desk and a conference table. There were no chairs before the desk, but there were some around the table.

Parasca waited until I entered the room and then shut the door. He stood before Ceausescu's desk, so I did the same.

"This the meta?" Ceausescu asked without preamble.

"We prefer 'adept,'" I said in Romanian.

Ceausescu glared at me. "Do you know what's happening in my country? I tolerated you and all the other metas here the last time so they could clean out this infestation of vampires. But apparently you have all failed."

"We use the term 'necromancers,'" I said, giving nothing. I wasn't going to let this man intimidate me.

Ceausescu looked as if he were going to spit. "Can you kill the leader?"

"The woman?" I asked, meaning Ernestine.

"Yes, the woman!" Ceausescu nearly screamed.

"No," I said, "not without a lot of help."

Ceausescu grumbled then asked, "What do you need?"

"About fifty powerful adepts, and maybe a small army."

Ceausescu looked as if he were about to order me shot. Parasca looked embarrassed...for whom, I didn't know.

At that moment a woman barged in unannounced. This surprised me, and I wondered who could get away with doing that. I turned to see a dark-haired, small woman who needed to lose about thirty pounds. Her face was hard and angry-looking, but it wouldn't have been attractive even if she were smiling. She was dressed almost stylishly, and her clothes looked expensive.

"I want this man shot!" she demanded, pointing at Parasca.

"Elena, why now?" Ceausescu almost pleaded.

"You know perfectly well why. He travels to Beirut and does not bring back one of the items I asked for."

"Madam Ceausescu," Parasca said, without a hint of contrition. "Urgent matters for the security of Romania took precedence. I had to rush back home to meet with this meta." He indicated me.

"Pah," the woman spat. "What are you men conspiring about now?"

I just stayed silent. Apparently this was Ceausescu's wife and I had no idea how much power, if any, she wielded with her husband.

Ceausescu smiled at her as if he truly loved this shrew. I couldn't imagine. "There is a grave threat to our security and this man—" he pointed at me "—is here to help us."

She looked me over as if I were a bug or some medical specimen. "He looks like an American."

I was about to confirm that when Parasca said, "Madam Ceausescu, this man is an adept."

The woman then glared at me for a moment, seemed to be studying my eyes, and then excused herself, almost rushing from the room. Parasca gave me a smile that Ceausescu didn't see and closed the door again.

"You cannot learn her abilities?" Ceausescu asked, again talking loudly and going on as if his wife hadn't just fled the room.

I shook my head. "Not without the *Book of Death,* and I assume she guards that with her life." I'd have to kill her to get it, but I couldn't kill her without first getting it.

Ceausescu stared at me as if in amazement. "You don't have a copy of the *Book of Death?*"

"No, there's only one copy and the necromancer has it, I assume. Or has it hidden."

Ceausescu and Parasca exchanged a look. "I assumed all guilds had a copy," Ceausescu stated.

"No," I said. "Up until recently, we thought all copies had been destroyed five hundred years ago."

Parasca chuckled. "Not all copies."

"No, the necromancer escaped with one," I said.

Ceausescu glared at me. "Listen, members of my DIE, my *Securitate*, and maybe my *Militia* are conspiring with rogue elements of the KGB to do something with the necromancer. I'm not even sure what, but we need them stopped."

"I know their plans," I stated.

Ceausescu stood and leaned over his desk. "What are they?"

I told the two Romanians what Major Pimenov of the KGB told me about using necromancers to teleport nukes over U.S. targets.

"Where is this Pimenov?" Ceausescu demanded.

"Dead," I said. "I killed him in Moscow."

Again, Ceausescu and Parasca exchanged a look I didn't understand.

"But wasn't he a necromancer?" Ceausescu asked.

"If he was, he was a weak one," I stated. "Perhaps just begun his training."

Ceausescu hesitated as if he were thinking, then he picked up one of the phones on his desk. "Bring it in."

I wondered what "it" was. A few minutes later, the door opened and a man walked in carrying a thick book. "No," I whispered with disbelief when I saw it. The man gently laid it down on the desk and then stepped back behind Parasca and me. I involuntarily took a step forward. The covering was leather, strange crinkly leather that was a dark brown, either with age or stain. I opened the book and the pages were made of the same material. Burned into the pages were symbols. It took me a second to recognize them.

"Do you have a mirror?" I asked.

Ceausescu opened a drawer and pulled out a hand mirror. I smiled; apparently he was vain. I held the mirror so it reflected the writing on the leather pages. It was the ancient language, and first thing it said was "Book of Death: Vlad III Dracul." And there was a date: 1475. Just a year before he was killed.

"Where did you get this?" I whispered.

"We have been trying to decipher it for twenty years," Ceausescu stated.

"It's not code," I said, "It's a different language."

"Yes, but we still could not translate it."

I nodded. "Yes, it's designed that way. You have to be an adept to read it."

"Why?"

"The language itself is a spell," I said. "It's very complicated, and frankly none of your business."

"Is this the *Book of Death*?" Ceausescu asked softly.

"Yes. How did you get it?"

"It was among the items we found in the royal palace after Michael the First voluntarily abdicated."

I snorted. I doubted very much there was anything voluntary about it.

Ceausescu ignored it. "Turn to the last page."

I did. Here the writing was not mirrored and was in what I suspected was Latin. Another quick translation spell and I read: "Keep this safe, for if the necromancers return, you shall need it." There was another date: 1699, more than two hundred years after Vlad's death.

"1699?" I asked myself.

"Do you not know what happened in 1699?" Ceausescu demanded.

I was still looking at the book and just said, "No."

"The Hapsburgs finally expelled the Ottomans from Transylvania," Parasca said, as if it were common knowledge.

"Do you know our history, Mr. Branton?" Ceausescu asked angrily.

"Not well," I said looking up from the Latin text. "I know you cooperated with the Germans up until the end of World War II, when you switched sides. Then shortly after the war you went Communist."

Ceausescu appeared to be deciding whether to get angry or not. He must have decided not to because he sat back down in his chair. "I meant prior to that?"

"I must admit, no, I don't."

Ceausescu shook his head. "That book has been passed down by monarchs and leaders of Romania, Transylvania, the Hapsburg Empire, and even the Ottoman Empire, for four hundred years as protection against the return of a necromancer."

"But you couldn't read it," I stated.

"But you can!" Ceausescu exclaimed.

I nodded. "One thing," I said. "Ernes—the necromancer has five hundred years of perfecting her abilities. I would be a neophyte. And I don't have time to learn a lot if the Warsaw Pact is invading Czechoslovakia tonight."

"Why?" Ceausescu demanded.

"Because according to Pimenov, that's a prelude to invading Western Europe after the United States is destroyed."

"He must have been lying," Ceausescu said sharply. "Unless this does go all the way to the top," he added almost as a whisper.

"Would they leave us out?" Parasca asked, surprised.

He and Ceausescu looked at each other in silence for a long moment.

"Brezhnev!" Ceausescu finally yelled. "I knew we shouldn't trust him."

"So now you think it does go all the way to Brezhnev?" I asked.

"It must," Parasca said, as if he didn't want to admit it.

"And they have undermined my own security and intelligence forces!" Ceausescu nearly screamed. "I'll double, no triple, the DGTO!"

"If we want to stop this," I said, interrupting Ceausescu's anger, "we need to hurry." I wasn't sure why a Communist leader would want to stop Communism from winning the cold war. Maybe Ceausescu was just upset he was left out, or maybe it was the "hard currency" he got for Western Europe. I didn't know.

"We must stop this madness!" Ceausescu exclaimed.

"They'll be at least a week in Czechoslovakia," Parasca said calmly. "Probably longer."

"I hope," I said. "A week is not a long time to learn five hundred years of necromancy."

* * * *

I convinced Ceausescu that my time would be better spent studying the *Book of Death*. I also asked for a bigger mirror. He set me up in a small office in the government building that held his office (and many others that I didn't pay attention to). The first thing I did was try to see if the necromancy counter-spell was there. It wasn't. I started to read the book, taking notes in the ancient language but not mirrored. It was late that day when I realized what I was doing: I was studying necromancy. But to defeat Ernestine I had to be as powerful as Ernestine. I knew I should contact Brown and tell him I'd found her—the *Securitate* agents that were still loyal to Ceausescu assured him and me they knew where she was, and it was indeed Hunedoara in

Transylvania—and I was going to go after her. But I didn't want to tell him I was going to become a necromancer to do so. Maybe he'd understand, or maybe he'd order me to wait until twenty adepts could come and fight her. I wasn't convinced that would be enough to defeat her, nor would it be in time.

I had, according to Ceausescu and Parasca, a week or more. That wasn't enough time to learn the whole book. I was looking for that one devastating attack that I could use on Ernestine and other necromancers.

A small man in an ill-fitting business suit interrupted me. He looked to be about a hundred years old and shriveled up like a dried prune.

"What do you want?" I asked.

"Comrade Ceausescu said I am to assist you in any way possible."

I looked at him. It took me a moment to think of things I needed. "Bring me some lunch. And find out what time it is in San Francisco. And I need more paper."

"Yes…is that all?"

"For now." I assumed at some point I'd need something to kill. I hadn't seen any dogs or cats in Romania. I suspected a starving populous wasn't going to share their food with animals that didn't do work, such as horses.

The little man returned with a white-smocked chef carrying a full lunch of meat, soup, breads, cheeses, and fruit. I assumed Ceausescu was eating better than I, which was better than the average Romanian citizen.

"Oh, and sir?" the man said.

"Yes?"

"It's approximately 4:15 in the morning in San Francisco."

I nodded. That gave me an excuse to wait two hours before contacting Brown. I hoped by then to have found the devastating attack I could use to justify to him why I was using necromancy.

At four-thirty in the afternoon I closed the door to the small room and sat in the chair. The *Book of Death* was in front of me, open to the last page I had read. I thought I had found an attack to use on Ernestine. I was surprised she'd never used it or any other necromancers up until then. Perhaps different copies of the books held different spells.

I made contact with Brown, once again while he was eating breakfast. The first thing I did was tell him what KGB Major Pimenov told me about Ernestine's plans to end the cold war with selected nuclear strikes on the U.S. using her ability to teleport objects.

Very little seemed to get Brown excited. This news had him angry and scared, judging by the look on his face and that for the first time ever I heard him use a bad word in the ancient language.

"We must stop her!" he exclaimed.

"Yes, I know. And there's now hope we can."

"What?" he demanded.

"Teacher," I said, "Apparently there were at least three copies of the *Book of Death*."

"Three?" he asked. "How do you know this?"

I wasn't trying to be dramatic but I said, "One was destroyed in 1476, Ernestine apparently still has one, and—" I tilted the book up so he could see it "—I now have one."

"Where did you get that?" he exclaimed.

I explained about the Latin inscription and how it had apparently been handed down by governments for the past five hundred years.

Brown actually looked surprised. "Vaughan would say that was remarkable that government could manage to not lose it in five hundred years."

"Yes," I said. Now came the tricky part. "With this book I think I can take on Ernestine and stop her."

"With necromancy?" Brown whispered.

"Yes," I stated.

Brown seemed to be studying my face over thousands of miles. "Do you think you should?"

"I don't know, Teacher. It's necromancy, and I've always been told it's an abomination."

Brown hesitated while studying my face, it seemed. "Do you know the story of Custer's Last Stand?"

I frowned. I wasn't sure where he was going with this. "Yes, of course, most Americans do." Custer's troops were massacred by Indians who apparently out-numbered them and ambushed them at a place called Little Bighorn. I understood that was somewhere in eastern Montana.

"What a lot of people don't know is that Custer wanted to move quickly," Brown continued, "thinking that would give him tactical advantage."

I just listened, not sure where this was going.

"So he left behind two Gatling guns that were big and heavy and might slow him down. Do you know what a Gatling gun is, Student?"

"Yes," I said, "early machine gun." It was a big hand-cranked weapon mounted on a wheeled frame that had to be pulled by a horse.

"Exactly. And if Custer had had his two Gatling guns, the battle of Little Bighorn might have turned out quite differently."

Brown looked at me expectantly.

"So," I finally said, "I shouldn't leave any weapons behind?"

"Yes," Brown said softly.

"But doesn't that make me as bad as Ernestine?"

"When the U.S. and its allies invaded Europe to defeat Nazi Germany, they used many of the same weapons the Germans did. But does that make them as bad as the Nazis?"

"Of course not," I stated.

"Yes; it's not the weapon that's evil; it's what's done with it."

"So you have no problem with me using necromancy?"

Brown seemed to hesitate for a moment. "In this situation, no."

I nodded. Keeping up this connection for this long conversation was wearing on me.

"But," Brown added, "I expect that and any other copies of the *Book of Death* will be destroyed."

"Gladly," I stated.

We spent some time discussing whether I needed help, and I said I definitely did. Brown said he'd see if he could get me some, but he made no promises about how much. We broke the connection and I leaned back in my chair, an uncomfortable wooden thing. I would have loved to have taken a nap right then, but I still needed to study.

* * * *

There were five of us standing around a table with a map of Hunedoara. It was a small city across the Carpathian Mountains in historic Transylvania, in a valley between two sets of hills or low mountains. The city was long north to south, and narrow east to west. There were also aerial photographs that were taken ten years ago, but I assumed little had changed since then. Ceausescu and Parasca were to my left with a general of the Romanian Land Forces. To my right was Liesl, the Valkyrie. When Brown asked for help, she was the only one who showed up in Bucharest, dropping out of the sky on a large white horse. She also had the Hammer of Thor with her which, other than when the Nazis stole it during World War II, hadn't left Valhalla for over a thousand years. I told her about the *Book of Death,* and she agreed I should use its power to stop Ernestine.

"There are two ways to approach this," the general was saying. "Overwhelming force or stealth and surprise."

"I don't think you have overwhelming force, General," I said politely. I didn't want to anger him. It was his helicopters that would be taking us to Hunedoara.

He glared at me with his dark eyes. "Our comrades in the *Securitate* assure us the adepts are barricaded in the ruins of *Castelul Huniazilor*. They make no secret about it."

"Yes," I said. "And they'll spot you from miles away, and I wouldn't assume that they couldn't do whatever they wanted to do to your forces, General."

"Plus," Liesl pointed to one of the photographs of the castle, "it looks like the only way into the castle is across this bridge. That bottle neck will let them devastate any force. It must be done by stealth and surprise."

"Or a distraction," I said. "Have the general run his tanks up to the bridge, and while the necromancers are dealing with them we fly in the back way." I could use a carpet and Liesl her horse.

I was having trouble believing I was making plans with a Communist government to attack a cabal of necromancers in order to save the United States from nuclear devastation. Just to think that a couple of months ago I had been unhappy about working with the CIA. When I asked if we should let the U.S. government know about this threat, Ceausescu went into a rage. "We will not let anyone know that we cannot keep security within our borders!" he screamed at me. So I contacted Brown to contact Karamessines at the CIA. So far, no word back from the United States.

"My forces are not pawns for you to sacrifice," the general growled.

"Your forces can't handle some necromancers, General?" Liesl said in a voice that communicated disappointment, yet the possibility of redemption and layers of sex.

The general stammered and looked confused. "Yes, of course. I'll run two tank divisions up that bridge if need be."

Liesl gave him a smile that made *me* want to run tank divisions up that bridge.

"How soon?" I asked. It had been three days since the Warsaw Pact invaded Czechoslovakia.

"It will take a week to get my forces to Hunedoara," the general said.

I looked at Parasca and he whispered to Ceausescu. The leader of Romania said, "You have four days."

"Yes, Comrade Ceausescu," the general said with a firmness I didn't think he believed.

"So we attack on the twenty-seventh?" I asked.

"Dawn, on the twenty-eighth," the general said.

"How many tanks in a tank division?" I asked, looking at him.

"Three hundred and twenty T-55 main battle tanks," he answered proudly.

I blinked. "Seems to me that many tanks in that small of an area would just be getting in each other's way."

"I think perhaps a battalion would be sufficient," Parasca said softly.

"How many is that?" I asked.

"Thirty-one," the general grumbled. "Plus support vehicles." He pointed to a wider valley to the east of Hunedoara. "I'll want to set up one company of artillery here for fire support."

"What's artillery?" I asked.

"Big guns," the general said, giving me a derisive glare.

"Like howitzers?" I asked, having somewhere in my past having heard that term.

"Yes, exactly," the general stated. He pointed on the map to a hillside overlooking Hunedoara. "We'll set up the OP near here."

I had no idea what he was talking about, so I just nodded. "Sounds good. We just need you to distract the necromancers while Liesl and I fly over the wall."

"Just you two?" the general demanded.

"Unless more adepts show up," I grumbled. I never thought cowardliness was so prevalent in the guilds, but I guessed after the first twenty "strongest" adepts disappeared hunting for the necromancers, no one else wanted to sacrifice their life.

"Are we ready?" Ceausescu asked, as if daring anyone to say "No."

"Yes," the general stated.

"Yes," I concurred.

It felt good to have a plan. Now we just had to manage to survive it.

Chapter Thirteen

Bucharest, Romania
August 25, 1968

I had two days to rest and study the *Book of Death*. A small Japanese woman calling herself Akio showed up, claiming to be a member of the *Muraji Uji*, the upstart guild that was gaining power in Japan at the expense of the *Omi Uji*. She had long black hair to her waist and her talisman seemed to be a ring she wore. I smiled and thanked her for coming, thinking I was probably going to get her killed, despite the power I felt she had. Gudlang, the head of the Icelandic guild also came in on a broom—since 1950 the Icelandic Guild had been using flying for the first time in their history. Her blond hair, slightly curled, was nearly as long as Akio's. The two standing together made quite a contrast. Liesl smiled at me. "It seems the females are braver than the males," she said.

"I guess," I grumbled. We may be four powerful adepts, but our odds against a clan of necromancers were slim, even if I did have one powerful necromancer spell perfected.

The day before we were going to leave for Hunedoara on Romanian military helicopters, a lesser showed up at my *Agentia de Turism* hotel room door.

"Who are you?" I asked as the man stepped into my room uninvited. He had a black duffle bag slung over his shoulder.

"I'm CIA," he stated. "Dan Helsing. I've been NOC in Romania for two years now. Karamessines ordered me to help you in any way I can. He wouldn't tell me why."

"You have weapons?" I asked.

He grinned, which I took for a "yes," and patted the duffle bag.

* * * *

The helicopter was a nicer version of the one I'd flown in from Pitesti to Bucharest. It had square windows, and the interior was like a first-class section of an airliner. There must have been more sound-dampening, because even with the engines running we could talk at almost normal levels. Gudlang, Akio, myself, Helsing, and Parasca were the only occupants. Liesl was travelling on her horse after Parasca gave her an accurate map. The general was getting his troops ready to invade Hunedoara, and Ceausescu was staying behind in Bucharest.

I sat next to Parasca.

"Why is Ceausescu helping us?" I asked as softly as the engine noise allowed.

The head of the DIE studied my face for a moment. "Why wouldn't he?"

"Getting rid of the U.S. and taking over Western Europe has got to be good for Communists," I said. It seemed obvious.

"Maybe good for the Soviet Union," Parasca stated, "but I doubt even that, which is why I suspect this plot is by rogue agents, and does not go to the top."

"Why? Why wouldn't it be good for Romania or Russia?"

"Without the West, we'd be on our own. We steal so much technology, so much money, so much wealth from the West to prop up our countries. If the West disappeared, our countries would be plunged into first poverty, and then chaos."

I looked at him. He was perfectly serious, and as the head of the Romanian spy organization, he should know.

"What was with Mrs. Ceausescu's running away from me?" I asked, not having a chance to do so before now.

Parasca smiled bitterly. "She really is a peasant. She believes, like a lot of Romanians, that blue or green-eyed people can put the 'evil eye' on a person. Add to that you're an adept, and she was frightened away."

I frowned. Apparently that was why so many Romanians didn't want to look me in my green eyes.

Parasca and I were sitting in the front row of the seats. He looked over his shoulder. "Are you going to be able to defeat the necromancers with just four adepts and a CIA agent?"

I shrugged. "I have to try." Helsing was cleaning his weapons. He had a submachine gun in his duffle bag and a pistol under his suit jacket. I hoped he carried plenty of ammunition. If the necromancers had warriors of their own he might be in for one hell of a fight. Otherwise, I was hoping he'd distract a necromancer or two long enough for us adepts to kill them.

I seemed to be hoping a lot.

* * * *

The helicopter landed at the Romanian Land Forces' temporary headquarters ten kilometers east of Hunedoara, just outside a small village called Orasul Nou. The tents and vehicles were lined up in a farmer's field next to a river. We had no idea how far the necromancers would be watching for threats and we hoped ten kilometers, or just over six miles, was far enough away. The *Militia* was stopping any civilians from leaving or entering the city. That in and of itself might arouse suspicions, but I thought the necromancers might not be paying much attention to the civilian population...at least I hoped.

The RLF had split its tank brigade in two: fifteen tanks north of the city, fifteen south with the "command tank." Since the castle was on the south side of town, the northern forces would be entering town first, under the cover of darkness. The southern tanks would come up timed to reach their guns' range on the castle just as the sun was coming up. Both the north and south contingents would open fire at the same time, shelling the castle and hoping that distracted the necromancers enough for the four adepts and Helsing to get inside. With luck, maybe a few necromancers would be killed by the shelling, too. Helsing was given a large radio that was at least a foot long, a foot deep, and three quarters of a foot wide. He was to call in when we were in the castle and the shelling should stop, lest it kill us. He grumbled something about "Sov equipment" but listened politely as a Romanian sergeant taught him how to use it. I got the feeling he already knew. It had leather straps and a cover that was held with metal clips, and he carried it over his shoulders like a backpack.

"Thing weighs almost fifty pounds," he grumbled to me in English when the sergeant went away. "Based on a German World War II design, if you can believe that!"

I shook my head. That made the design at least twenty years old, like everything else seemed to be in this country. No wonder the Commies needed the West.

For some strange reason, dawn in this part of the world was at almost nine in the morning —it didn't get dark until nearly eleven the night before. Everything was coordinated to happen at 8:48 a.m. We synchronized watches and prepared to "move out" as Helsing called it. The military provided Akio and me with rugs. Gudlang was using her broom, and Liesl insisted on taking her horse. Helsing was to ride on my rug, which would be a new experience for me, and for him, too, I assumed. He was dressed in a military uniform with no markings. "Sanitized?" I asked, and he seemed shocked I knew that term. He had a black, boxy sub machinegun slung over his shoulder, and a belt around his waist with ammunition pouches and a holster holding his pistol.

First time I saw some of the CIA agent's bravado fail was when we took to the skies, him riding behind me and me having to adjust for his weight and the weight of the radio. We flew over the mountains between the valleys. The moon had set before midnight, so it was a dark night as we landed on the outskirts of Hunedoara. We would have looked odd to anyone who spotted us: three people riding rugs, one a broom, and one a flying horse. We were hoping the necromancers were sleeping and wouldn't feel our presence from approximately two miles away where we were waiting; also, that the necromancers wouldn't notice the thirty tanks rumbling into town from the north and the south; and further, that the artillery barrage that was planned would kill enough of them that the four of us and Helsing could deal with the rest. Again, it seemed we were hoping a lot but not knowing much. Helsing had grumbled to me earlier that day that this better be worth it, because it blew his cover and now he'd have to work a desk job at Langley. I didn't tell him I didn't expect him, or any of us, to survive.

We waited in darkness. Liesl's horse amazed me by waiting patiently without making an extraneous sound. As the sky was starting to lighten in the east, I suddenly felt weak. I nearly fell to my knees and thought I might vomit. I was scared I was getting hit with a rune and looked at the other adepts. They, too, looked ill. Helsing was looking at all of us with questioning eyes.

"Do you feel that?" Liesl asked.

"Yes," Akio hissed. "What is it?"

"I don't know," I said. For some reason it seemed to hit me harder. "Are we under attack?"

We all gripped our talismans, and Helsing uselessly held his submachine gun. But nothing happened. After about fifteen minutes it passed, and I felt fine, just a residual headache reminded me of it.

As it got lighter we could see our target. It was an ancient castle, pretty much in ruins from neglect, but still with high walls, towers, and parapets. It was built on a hill that looked artificial due to its squared-off shoulders. I tried to pick out an entrance such as a large window or hole, but seeing none decided I'd have to go over the wall.

"Red sky," Guldlang said with foreboding, looking east.

I didn't know why she did. Akio gave me a determined gaze and I smiled back. I was going to hate myself for getting these women killed.

As my watch clicked over to 8:48 there was a boom from the east and we heard whistles overhead. Then there were explosions against the walls of the castle. The general's artillery had fired. At the same time, the tanks started shooting at the castle.

"Those are HE rounds," Helsing said. "Should make quick work of those stone walls. Communist militaries won't cross the street without artillery support."

I just nodded, thinking this information was not very useful. Even from here I could see blocks of stone the size of small cars being flung from the explosions. "Let's go," I stated grimly.

More artillery rounds rained down on Hunyad Castle. Helsing once again got on the carpet with me. Akio got on on her own, and Gudlang's broom was hovering a few feet off the ground as she got on it. Lastly, Liesl mounted her steed. She patted its long neck affectionately and it let out a soft snort.

I'd suggested we not bunch together so as to give the necromancers more targets to worry about. Helsing seemed to approve of my tactics. I flew right at the castle, Gudlang went south, Akio went north, and Liesl went as fast as she could on her horse, which she said was pretty fast, to approach it from the west. I would get into the castle, and then Helsing would radio that we were in and the bombardment would stop unless we asked for more.

"Not really interested in calling in artillery on my own position," Helsing had said the evening before.

"We'll do whatever it takes to kill the necromancers," I had replied.

As we approached the castle, its stone walls growing taller each moment, the bombardment seemed to stop. We could still hear the distant thunder sound of the guns firing, but the shells weren't hitting the castle.

"Damn!" Helsing yelled as a tank exploded. It was followed by more tanks going up in flames, their hamburger-bun shaped turrets often being blown off.

"Land!" Helsing cried. "I've got to stop them!"

I dropped the carpet to the ground in a field not far from the castle. I felt like a sitting duck, but Helsing started pulling the cover from the radio and flipping switches almost maniacally. He put the handset to his ear and mouth and yelled "Stop firing, you're hitting yourself!" He was speaking Romanian.

I decided I knew what was happening. The necromancers were redirecting the shells away from the castle and at the tanks. The tank's shots, too, were being thrown back at them. Most of the tanks were destroyed, burning and in pieces in short order, and the rest were trying to retreat. I wondered how many men were now dead.

The artillery stopped and Helsing pulled the radio back over his shoulder. "Either I or the OP got them to stop," he breathed. "Let's go."

Back on the carpet, I headed for the castle again, expecting an attack at any moment. Helsing hung on to my waist. I could see Akio and Gudlang, but not Liesl. I hoped that was just because the castle was blocking my view.

Fireballs spat out of the parapet toward us and I dodged them, not wanting to be knocked off the carpet for a probably fatal fall to the ground. They seemed extra hot and I could feel the radiant heat from even those that passed by far away. I hoped they dissipated before hitting anything and lighting it on fire.

As I crossed the stone wall, the fire balls stopped. I heard and felt Helsing firing his machine gun. I landed on the parapet and two necromancers were glaring at me. A third was lying in a puddle of blood. They apparently hadn't expected us to use guns. I found myself thinking that blood was going to waste.

Both necromancers attacked at once, pulling away mine and Helsing's air. I gripped my talisman hard and pointed. It would have been a stronger spell if I had some blood, but it worked well enough. The stones around the necromancers' feet started burning. I pointed at stones on the high wall and brought them flaming down on top of them as liquid rock. Their screams of agony were mercifully short. As they died my air returned. I rushed over to the one Helsing had shot and with a small knife Parasca had provided, I slit his throat. Blood sprayed over my hand and I put my mouth to the wound. There wasn't a lot but there was enough. I stood, feeling more powerful than I ever had. It was like an amazing drug. Now I knew the temptation of necromancy. This was going to be hard to resist.

Helsing took one look at me and said "Damn! You're a vampire?"

"I am now, I guess." I had to let that sink in.

"Come on," I eventually barked. "I'm amazed we're still alive." We ran down the parapet to stairs that led into the castle. I could hear fighting going on elsewhere, and hoped the women were having luck even without necromancy skills. I came up behind Gudlang just as she passed out. The three necromancers she was trying to fight tried to take my air away, but I pulled theirs away, making sure Gudlang had plenty. The burning stones then finished them off. The stones could burn and melt in near vacuum, I discovered.

Gudlang blinked and sat up. "They are too powerful!" she said, fear causing her voice to shake.

"And so am I!" I stated, trying to keep bravado from my voice.

Gunfire interrupted me. I turned and Helsing was spraying gunshots into a group of about five necromancers running toward us from the bowels of the castle. It was doing no good: they could move and keep up a protection spell. Helsing stop firing when bullets began ricocheting back at us.

"Gudlang, take their air!" I called out as I aimed my finger at the rocks at their feet. We needed to get through their protection spell as quickly as possible.

One shot fire at Gudlang and she ducked, but the flames touched her long blonde hair briefly. They stopped firing fire balls as the stone floor below them went molten. They screamed as the heat reached their feet and tried to run away, but the lower part of their legs were on fire. They stopped shimmering and Helsing fired again, killing them mercifully before the flames could consume them.

"You people play hardball," Helsing said, breathing hard.

"You okay?" I asked Gudling. It seemed half her hair was burned off.

"It'll grow back," she stated strongly.

I could feel my power diminishing with all this spelling. I needed more blood, but the charred bodies around us wouldn't work.

Just then Liesl burst into the room riding her horse and shooting airbolts into the corridor from which she emerged. "There's five after me!" she called out, seeing us.

Gudling and I shot flames into the corridor and I found myself wondering how many necromancers Ernestine had managed to recruit and train. Four burst into the room. Helsing opened up with his gun, the pounding sound echoing off the stone walls. One went down, again surprised by the lesser weapon. The rest put up protection, but with three of us, including me, pulling on their air, they soon passed out.

"Keep one alive!" I yelled, and we let one have air. As he started to sit up I physically attacked him, slicing his throat open with my knife. I was surprised by the popping sound it made. Blood spurt from the wound over my hands. I put my mouth to the gash and consumed, feeling the power build in my body as Gudlang and Liesl looked on in disgust. I didn't care anymore; the power was too intoxicating.

"Has anyone seen Akio?" Helsing asked as I stood, feeling warm blood drip from my chin.

No one had.

"How about Ernestine?" I asked. I noticed all the necromancers so far had been men.

No one had.

We walked into the corridor Liesl had come out of. It was dimly lit by sunlight coming through cracks in the wall. There was a dead man there that apparently Liesl had managed to kill.

"We need to interrogate one," Helsing said, frustrated, as he reloaded his weapon. "I'm down to my last magazine for this baby."

"What else do you have?" I asked.

He pulled out the pistol. "I have three mags for this." When I didn't say anything he clarified, "Twenty-four rounds."

We found Akio's body next to a dead necromancer. I said a bad word in the ancient language. Liesl and Gudlang just looked sad. I wondered if it was a mistake to split up like we had.

The deeper we went into the castle the darker and danker it became. Two necromancers tried to surprise us from behind. Gudlang and Liesl were angry and killed one pretty quickly. The second one died when I dropped molten rock on him.

Without warning the narrow corridor widened into an open space. I wondered if this was a great hall or a throne room. The ceiling was high and vaulted. Pillars spaced at regular intervals seemed to hold it up. At one end was Ernestine and five necromancers standing beside her. They just watched us as if they weren't worried about us at all.

"Hello, Peter," Ernestine called out. I tried to ignore how beautiful she was. "I see you've discovered the power of blood."

I unconsciously wiped my chin, not sure if there were still bodily fluids there.

"It's over, Ernestine," I said. "I am at least as powerful as you."

She laughed a harsh, bitter sound that seemed to have five hundred years of disappointment and betrayal wrapped up in it. "You're more right than you know."

I studied her face, trying to figure out what she meant.

"It's over, Peter. At midnight Washington D.C. time we attacked," she continued. "All U.S. nuclear forces, its command facilities, its bomber bases, and most of its major cities are nuclear wastelands. The Soviet Navy is just mopping up their missile submarines. It's over, Peter. There is nothing left to fight for. Please don't make me kill you."

Helsing spat. "That's seven our time. More than two hours ago!"

That was what I had felt, the weakness that had washed over me. The deaths of millions of people in America had reverberated through me even this far away. The other adepts felt it too, but since I was from America, I felt it worse.

"In time, you'll see this is for the best, Peter," Ernestine was saying. "We can forge a new guild, a new world, where necromancy is welcome."

I smiled and walked toward her, my hands out. "You're right, Ernestine."

"I love you, Peter."

"I love you, Ernestine," I said getting closer. It was the truth, the painful, awful truth. "There is nothing to fight over."

"Yes," she exclaimed as I got within almost touching distance. I knew I was alone; Gudlang, Liesl, and Helsing had stayed back.

"Except revenge," I growled, and melted the rocks at her feet.

She jumped even as I melted the rocks over her head and the lava rained down on her. A necromancer to my left fell over as I heard Helsing's gun fire. The air around us was getting thin, and I assumed Gudlang and Liesl were pulling it away. I stepped back to miss the falling lava and the growing puddle of it on the floor.

Ernestine jumped to the wall and clung to it as a spider would. Her necromancers were dying as she scurried away. I couldn't pursue her because I'd blocked the way with molten rock.

"Son of a gun," Helsing said with a grin as I walked back to the group. "I was about to shoot you: thought you had gone over to the other side."

"Never," I growled.

"Now what?" Gudlang asked.

"We have to find her and stop her, and find her copy of the *Book of Death*," Liesl said angrily. Her horse seemed to snort its agreement.

I nodded.

We found another exit and tried to head the same way as Ernestine, but the castle seemed to be a maze of corridors, rooms, and stairs. We all tried to feel for her but either she was masking or it was another necromancer trick. I didn't want to split us up again so we moved together through the ancient building. I could feel its age, and it seemed to press down on me.

"Have we killed all the necromancers except Ernestine?" Helsing asked.

"I think so," I said softly, as if I didn't want to break the centuries-old silence.

We came to a wooden door with light glaring through the cracks in the old wood. I pushed it open and we were in the castle's inner courtyard, I guessed. It was a large open space, open to the sky, with muddy ground and a few tufts of yellow grass, and more groups of weeds.

That's then the first grenade attack hit. One appeared in the middle of our group and fell with a plop into the mud.

"Grenade!" Helsing yelled, scooped it up, and threw it across the courtyard where it exploded with a bang that was incredibly loud for something the size of a baseball.

"She's teleporting grenades at us!" I cried out. I imagined she'd pull the pin and teleport them, which meant she knew where we were.

"How do we protect against that?" Liesl asked, her voice showing fear for the first time. She gripped the Hammer of Thor harder. Her horse shook its head.

"Keep your eyes open," Helsing said. "If you see one, you have about four seconds to throw it away."

I slowly counted to four. It didn't seem like a lot of time.

"How does she know where we are?" Gudlang asked.

"Far seeing," I stated.

"Without us knowing it?"

"Yes," I stated. Same thing she did in San Francisco in my suite while Brown, Vaughan, Anica and I met. Now they were all dead, except for me.

"But," I realized. "She needs blood."

"Where would she get it?" Helsing asked.

"Animals, people, it doesn't matter."

"The dungeon," Liesl said. "She must have animals or people in there."

I shuddered, thinking about her killing a person in cold blood just to get the power.

"Where would that be?" Gudlang asked.

"Down," Helsing stated.

We found stairs going down and slowly descended them. Liesl had to leave her horse at the top as the corridor was too small for it. I worried about a grenade attack in this small space. I was right. One appeared in front of us, dropped to the stone steps and started bouncing down the stairs. "Protection spell!" I yelled and all three of the adepts started to shimmer. I tried to stand between Helsing and the grenade when it went off.

It worked although all our ears rang from the explosion. Helsing got a bit of shrapnel in his leg but he said it was superficial. I could smell the blood and it was almost sexual, the power it had over me.

We came to a metal door. This wasn't ancient technology but a modern steel door. And it was locked.

"Can you open this?" Helsing asked.

"I can try to pick it," I said. "But I doubt it." It was a good-quality lock.

"Teleport," Gudlang stated.

"Yes, but that leaves Helsing behind," I stated. He'd been remarkably useful, I realized.

"What I wouldn't give for some C-4," Helsing said for no apparent reason.

"Can't you shoot the lock out?" Liesl asked.

"Don't believe everything you see in the movies," Helsing stated.

"Are we even sure she's in there?"

"She's in there," Gudlang stated with conviction.

"Damn," I said. "I need to get used to my own powers."

I melted the lock.

We burst into the room and the smell of blood and death permeated the chamber, immediately making me feel ill and exhilarated at the same time. I could see dead small animals everywhere. Ernestine was killing one, a small horse, as we entered. Interrupted, the horse jumped and knocked her down. I remembered reading in the *Book of Death* that horses were second only to humans for the power they gave. Even a small horse was bigger and stronger than a small woman.

Ernestine was on the floor, picking herself up when all three of us attacked. Helsing seemed to want to get as many bullets flying at her as possible, Gudlang and Liesl took her air away, and I started melting the rock ceiling over her.

She looked at me sadly as she got to her feet. "Too bad I ran out of grenades," she said, hard to hear in the diminishing air. She pointed at Helsing and he simply vanished, his weapon clattering to the stones where he had stood. Gudlang's eyes went wide as the rainbow from Ernestine's fingertips slammed into her, burning her skin. Liesl shot fire at Ernestine but it simply seemed to wash off of her, as did the lava falling on her. Liesl died when the rainbow enveloped her and seared her skin almost to the bone, her screams evaporating like her flesh.

But Ernestine didn't attack me. I melted the stones at her feet and she walked off the liquid rock as if walking on solid pavement.

"Please, Peter," she said. "I don't want to kill you."

I had no doubt she could at that point.

"Join me." She gazed into my eyes, hers so dark, so beautiful, so full of deadly power.

I shook my head. "Now that I know what you are capable of?"

She frowned. "So I've lost you, too?"

"Too?" I wondered but didn't say anything.

"Soviet tanks are going to enter West Germany soon," she said. "They'll deal with Ceausescu later, I'm sure."

I shook my head.

"I'll kill you if I have to, Peter."

"Then you have to," I stated simply.

She reached out to touch my cheek and I jerked my head away.

She almost looked as if she were going to cry. "Good bye, Peter," she said.

I gripped my talisman hard, getting ready to fight her. She disappeared, the air clapping in to fill the space she left.

I said a bad word in the ancient language. I turned and saw Liesl's burned body, still holding the undamaged Hammer of Thor. I scooped up the world's most powerful talisman and ran up the stairs to the courtyard. I couldn't see Ernestine but I could feel her. She was moving quickly away from the castle, heading north. Liesl's horse was there, looking sad. I jumped on its back and seeming as if it knew what I needed, it sprang into the air. I grabbed its mane for dear life as it ascended. It snorted unhappily but continued ascending. But, now I could see Ernestine, a dot against the brightening sky, fleeing on a carpet, perhaps mine or Akio's. I gave chase on the horse.

The faster you go on a carpet, the faster you deplete your strength. Go twice as fast and you burn through your strength four times more quickly. I had no idea why: I was just taught that as dogma. I had no idea how long or far a Valkyrie horse could fly, but I had to catch Ernestine.

Ernestine must have heard or felt me coming because she sped up.

"Faster!" I said to the horse. Nothing happened, so I tried the ancient language and the horse did, indeed, speed up.

This could go on for hours, I thought, *and we could be somewhere over Norway or Finland or whatever was directly north of here.* As I got closer she shot a few fire balls at me, but her efforts seemed half-hearted. Maybe she just wanted to scare me off, or maybe she was getting tired.

As we were passing over a forest she dipped below the top of the trees. I followed and suddenly she was right in front of me. Her airbolt smacked me in the chest and knocked me off the back of the horse to the forest floor. I don't know how I didn't pass out or lose my grip on the Hammer.

I felt heat as I started to sit up. The forest was on fire; Ernestine was lighting trees up around me with fire balls. I shot fire at her, amazed at how powerful it was.

Suddenly the horse flew out from the forest and knocked her off her carpet. The carpet fluttered to the ground and caught fire. For the first time I saw fear in her eyes. We'd probably die there if we didn't get out of that growing conflagration. There was a long stick on the ground that was not on fire. Ernestine picked it up, mounted it like a broom, and flew up and away.

The horse dropped onto the forest floor next to me and seemed to whinny impatiently. The heat was getting unbearable. I jumped on its back and we chased Ernestine again. She seemed surprised to see me and simply stopped by a river. The horse came down near her.

"Peter!" she cried, "I don't want to kill you!"

"You're going to have to!" I growled and ran at her. I think this surprised her as she cowered for a moment. I hit her with the Hammer, and this knocked her to the grassy ground next to the river. She shot fire at me but I had the protection spell up in time. Then I hit her again with the Hammer. The horse circled around her, and when she tried to scramble away it blocked her escape. Kader said one hit took away his power for days. But that hit was from Loki. I was hoping my hits were at least reducing her meta power.

"Peter, please stop!" she cried, and for a moment I realized what I was doing. But I had to do it. She was far too dangerous to let live. I hit her again.

I stepped back and took her air away. The horse scurried away from her. She was too feeble to stop me. The look on her face, the pleading written on her visage, broke my heart. The river peacefully gurgled by. It really was a beautiful place to die. That was more consideration than she'd given millions of Americans—than she gave Akio, Gudlang, Liesl, and Helsing.

I cradled her body in my arms, stroked her hair, and cried.

Epilogue

Hunedoara, Romania
August 28, 1968

Ernestine's copy of the *Book of Death* was found in the castle dungeon. If there were any more necromancers, we didn't find them. The Romanian general was almost in tears as he surveyed his destroyed tank regiment.

Parasca said a thermite grenade would destroy the book. When I questioned that he said it could melt an engine block, so I let what was left of the RFL's troops burn it in a field. I observed from a distance to make sure it was gone. They wouldn't let me look directly at it until a bright, white, actinic light stopped flashing. Then I watched it burn. I threw the ashes in the river that ran along in front of the castle.

Parasca reported that Soviet and East German tanks were rolling into West Berlin and West Germany. The American forces stationed there were hopelessly outnumbered. American forces in Vietnam were still fighting but without resupply from America, it wasn't known how long they could. And North Korean forces were invading South Korea, and the American forces there were retreating.

Spotty news out of America indicated that most major cities had been destroyed. The survivors were facing starvation, disease, and radiation sickness. People on or near farms seemed to be the best off. The worst were those in smaller cities that hadn't been hit with a nuclear weapon but were running out of food.

Parasca said a few Soviet cities had been hit, too, apparently by American bombs that were missed. He shook his head sadly and whispered, "The needless destruction of life."

We flew back to Bucharest on the same nicer helicopter that seemed suddenly empty. I was going to have to let Brunhild and the leadership of the Icelandic and Japanese guilds know what happened, and return the Hammer to the Valkyrie. And I needed to tell someone in what was left of the CIA that Helsing died bravely for his country. Langley was probably a radioactive crater but maybe someone somewhere could put up a memorial for him.

I wasn't sure what I was going to do after that. Life in a Soviet-dominated world didn't seem very appealing, even for an adept.

I was about to order the Romanian copy of the *Book of Death* destroyed when I decided to give it one last look. I didn't know why. What secrets it could possible hold that could change this situation I didn't know.

Until I came to the last spell in the book. I hadn't had time to even glance at it before.

I had Parasca bring me a horse. It was a broken down old nag but it would do. In the street in Bucharest I put a spell on it to put it in a near state of sleep, and I slit its throat. As the blood washed over me and into my mouth, I invoked the spell. It was a very powerful spell.

* * * *

The first thing that hit me was the odor. Everything smelled. The air reeked of death and human and animal waste. The man smelled and his clothes under his armor stank. I wondered if I was imagining the bugs crawling on his skin. I doubt he'd bathed in a year. I was holding a spear and wearing heavy, uncomfortable armor. I knew what Vlad had told the man to do, and I was letting him do it. It had taken me what seemed ages to find this person, this mind to inhabit. Years might have passed back in Bucharest, where I suspected my body lay in the street next to a dead horse, Parasca watching over it.

I walked through the tunnel of the entrance to Poenari Castle. The big wooden door in front of me opened as men on each side pushed it open. I walked to where the stones ended. In front of me were two mounted people. One was a woman, looking so much like Liesl it broke my heart. She was on a white horse and had a pendent on a necklace that I could tell was her talisman. The other was a blond man with hair almost to the saddle of his black horse. The woman was looking impatient, and the man was looking sick. I could see why: behind and beside them were hundreds of impaled human bodies. I tried not to react since my first reaction was to vomit.

I had to speak loudly but I spoke in the ancient language. It was about all the meta power I could muster. I decided to stick to the basics. "Hail, Brunhild. There is a young woman with Vlad. She, too, is a necromancer. Do not let her escape." Yes, it felt like killing Ernestine twice. "And there's more than one copy of Vlad's document that he calls the *Book of Death*."

Brunhild was staring at me. "Who are you?" she demanded in the ancient language. But her pronunciation was just a bit off from what I was used to.

"I am an adept from the future," I said. "If you fail at this, if the woman escapes with a copy of the *Book of Death*, in five hundred years there will be a horrible conflagration that will kill millions of innocent people."

She looked as if she were trying to believe me. The man, the Icelander I remembered, was looking at her and then at me, both in amazement.

"What do you call yourself, adept one?" Brunhild asked.

"Peter Branton," I stated. "I come from the land across the ocean." I had no idea what they called America at this time. The European Guilds knew about it and were in contact with some of the adepts there even though it was about twenty years before Columbus sailed.

"How are you here?" she cried.

"A powerful spell allows me to occupy this man's body and mind." It wasn't really time travel. It simply allowed me to occupy any person in the past that I chose. The possibilities of mucking with the past were endless. I may have been the first person to use the spell. Or if someone had changed the past, how would we know?

The man on the black horse looked almost frightened.

"Stop the girl, destroy all copies of the *Book of Death*," I cried out. I felt myself slipping away. It sort of felt like dying again as I felt nothingness surround me.

"We shall," Brunhild called out. My world went black.

* * * *

"You must be Mr. Branton," the blonde Valkyrie stated simply. "I'm Liesl."

I blinked and looked at her. "*The* Liesl?"

She laughed—a happy cheerful sound that was almost musical. "I suppose I am," she said. "Shall we go; I have a car waiting."

I just nodded and followed her out of the building and into the cold. There was a square shaped sedan waiting by the curb. A large man was standing next to it. I didn't see any chainmail but I presumed he was a berserker, one of the Valkyrie guild's warriors.

Liesl slid into the back seat and I followed. It was roomier inside than I expected. The berserker got in the front and drove the car into the street. It seemed the airport was not, as typical in America, a long way from the town, but nearly right in it.

"You'll be meeting with Mr. Kader at our house here in Tromsø," Liesl was saying as I looked out the window.

The buildings all seemed to have steep roofs, to let snow slide off, I presumed. "Oh?" I asked.

"And we've arranged for a hotel for you to stay in. You can probably leave tomorrow."

"No hurry," I said. I was hoping to see Valhalla. That hope was diminishing.

Liesl simply gave me a lovely smile. I looked at her, amazed. She was startlingly beautiful. Rumor had it that Vaughan had fallen in love with her. I could see why.

The house was smaller than I expected, and in a dense neighborhood in the city. Most houses were right next to each other, but this one seemed to have a buffer zone around it. It looked old but that may have just been the style.

Liesl opened her door and I did the same.

"He's waiting for you," she said.

"Are you coming in?" I asked.

She shook her head. "This is your guild's business. We'll wait out here."

I hoped she meant in the car. It was dang cold and the coat I had brought which was suitable for "cold" weather in San Francisco seemed like thin gauze here in Tromsø. I glanced at my watch, which I'd set to Stockholm time, which I assumed was the same time as here. It was getting close to noon.

"Thank you," I said. I walked through the snow to the house and pushed the heavy wooden door open.

Kader was sitting at a table made of rough-hewn lumber. A fire was filling the room with wavering light and tepid heat. There were some chairs but the room was otherwise sparsely furnished.

The old adept stood and smiled. His hair was almost completely gray and he had crow's feet around his eyes. He was wearing a gray suit that seemed too big for him. He extended a thin hand in greeting and I shook it.

"Greetings, Teacher," I said reverently.

"Hello, Student," he replied. "Did you have an enjoyable journey?"

"Yes," I stated. "Airlines in America could learn hospitality from SAS."

He smiled. "Yes. And how do you like Norway?"

I chuckled. "Colder than I expected."

"Sit down, please," he said with a smile, doing the same. "Lunch will be arriving soon. I don't know about you but when I travel I get hungry."

251

I sat and smiled. "Thank you, Teacher."

He dismissed it with a wave of his hand.

"You're probably wondering why I wanted to see you," he stated.

"I am," I said. He wouldn't even tell Vaughan or Brown but simply said it was urgent that he meet with me.

"There's not a lot to do in Valhalla," he said. "Don't get me wrong, it's beautiful and I love it there. But there's not even phone service."

"Yes," I said, wondering where this was going.

"Brunhild has let me read her guild's documents."

I nodded, not knowing what to say. She must really trust him. Even I hadn't seen all of our guild's documents.

"You know about Vlad the Third Dracul?"

"Of course," I replied, surprised by the subject. "He was dabbling in necromancy and the guilds decided he had to stop." Even five hundred years ago it was remarkable for the guilds to agree on anything, that's how serious necromancy was. "He was killed; details are murky."

Kader nodded knowingly. "He was killed by a Valkyrie and a member of the Icelandic guild."

"I didn't know that."

"Very few do. But it's in the Valkyrie's archives. Actually, that's not quite accurate. He was killed by his own soldiers after an attack by the Valkyrie and the Icelander weakened him sufficiently."

That was interesting, I thought. That detail, lost to history most guilds thought, was in the Valkyries' archives. But I didn't see how that pertained to me

Kader hesitated and looked at me seriously. "According to the Valkyries' archives, you were there."

I looked at him to see if he was joking. He looked perfectly serious.

"What do you mean, I was there?"

"The archives say that an adept from the future named Peter Branton warned them to kill Vlad's consort who, too, was a necromancer, and that there was more than one copy of Vlad's document called the *Book of Death*. So they did, killing the consort and destroying two copies of the *Book*."

I was still trying to take all of this in. "Must be a coincidence or something."

"He said he was from five hundred years in the future."

And it had been nearly five hundred years since Vlad had been killed.

"But there's no way to travel into the past!" I cried. "Something is wrong here."

Kader sat back in his chair. "No, there isn't. But apparently you will, or did, find a way."

I shook my head.

"According to the archives," Kader stated. "You said that in five hundred years there'd be a great conflagration that would kill millions if they didn't succeed."

"That sounds like nuclear war," I said almost as a whisper.

"Perhaps," Kader whispered.

"So in 1976 there will be a nuclear war?" I asked.

"No," Kader stated. "I think you, or this Peter Branton, stopped it by making sure they killed the consort and destroyed both copies of the *Book of Death*."

"I hope there were only two copies," I said with a chuckle.

"Probably," Kader stated. "Or they would have destroyed them, too."

I shook my head. "This is too much to take in."

"I know, Student," Kader said softly. "But I thought you should know."

"When did you read this?"

"Just last week. I got you here as soon as I could."

I nodded. The last week I was in Idaho meeting with Anica of the Transylvanian Guild. Not much happened except we needed to find a way to keep her guild from going extinct. She had a warrior serving us meatball soup because she had no apprentice.

"I don't understand," I stated. "Either I did something or will do something that will change the past or the future."

"Perhaps," he said. "We may never really know. If you changed the past, we're living in the results of that, good or bad."

"I guess so," I stated. I wondered what the world would have been like if I hadn't changed it. I guess we'll never know.

Book of Death

Available Now

About the Author

S. Evan Townsend is a writer living in central Washington State. After spending four years in the U.S. Army in the Military Intelligence branch, he returned to civilian life and college to earn a B.S. in Forest Resources from the University of Washington. In his spare time he enjoys reading, driving (sometimes on a racetrack), meeting people, and talking with friends. He is in a 12-step program for Starbucks addiction. Evan lives with his wife and two teenage sons and has a son attending the University of Washington in biology. He enjoys science fiction, fantasy, history, politics, cars, and travel.

www.ingramcontent.com/pod-product-compliance
Lightning Source LLC
Chambersburg PA
CBHW021957170626
46808CB00001B/189